MURDER IN FLORENCE

T. A. WILLIAMS

Boldwood

First published in Great Britain in 2023 by Boldwood Books Ltd.

Copyright © T. A. Williams, 2023

Cover Design by CC Book Design

Cover Photography: Shutterstock

Every effort has been made to obtain the necessary permissions with reference to copyright material, both illustrative and quoted. We apologise for any omissions in this respect and will be pleased to make the appropriate acknowledgements in any future edition.

A CIP catalogue record for this book is available from the British Library.

Paperback ISBN 978-1-80483-238-7

Large Print ISBN 978-1-80483-237-0

Hardback ISBN 978-1-80483-239-4

Ebook ISBN 978-1-80483-236-3

Kindle ISBN 978-1-80483-235-6

Audio CD ISBN 978-1-80483-244-8

MP3 CD ISBN 978-1-80483-242-4

Digital audio download ISBN 978-1-80483-243-1

Boldwood Books Ltd
23 Bowerdean Street
London SW6 3TN
www.boldwoodbooks.com

To Mariangela and Christina as always with love

PROLOGUE
MONDAY NIGHT

One of the first things I quickly learned about being a private investigator is that it isn't all beautiful heiresses, diamond necklaces and bottles of bourbon. In my limited experience in the first three months of my new career here in Florence as Dan Armstrong, Private Investigator, beautiful heiresses had been sadly lacking, and a motley selection of unfaithful spouses, pilfering home helps, nasty neighbours and missing persons had predominated. My most exciting case so far had been a senior member of the Florentine city council caught in flagrante with a councillor from the opposition party behind an immaculately pruned and particularly dense bush in the Boboli Gardens. That had been back in August when the sun had been shining – so brightly in fact that I feared that the couple in question might have ended up with uncomfortable sunburn.

Today had certainly not been sunburn weather. There's rain and there's Tuscan rain. When it rains over here, it rarely wastes time with drizzle or light showers; it just goes for it. It suddenly becomes easy to see just how the river Arno was able to flood so much of Florence back in 1966 and destroy so many priceless

works of art. Tonight the city wasn't going to be flooded but my
dog and I were drenched. I pulled up the collar of my raincoat and
glanced down at Oscar. Even he – the dog who lives for splashing
about in water – was looking bedraggled. He and I had been
wandering through the side streets of the suburbs of Florence for
several hours now. This was an unprepossessing area packed with
nineteen-sixties apartment blocks in varying states of disrepair
and, on a night like this, totally lacking in any charm whatsoever.

We had been circling one particular block containing a far
from glamorous two-star hotel and we had been getting wetter and
wetter. Ostensibly just a man walking his dog, I'd been keeping an
eye on a silver BMW belonging to Osvaldo Dante, a wealthy
industrialist and owner of OD Textiles, a factory in the neigh-
bouring town of Prato. He had parked the car outside the rear
entrance by the bins, and if it hadn't been for the rain keeping the
bad boys indoors, I would have been seriously worried for him
that he might return to find the car on bricks and his wheels miss-
ing. It was that kind of place.

As I had quickly worked out since starting my new venture as a
private investigator, Florence doesn't just consist of the World
Heritage *centro storico* with its buildings of breath-taking antiquity
and beauty. Like all cities, it has its less salubrious underbelly, and
that was where Oscar and I now found ourselves and, like I say, it
was seriously wet – and for somebody used to English weather, I
know what I'm talking about when it comes to rain. It was
miserable.

However, I felt sure the inclement weather didn't bother
Signor Dante in the slightest. The reason he'd chosen to come
here was to be with the glamorous Giuseppina Napolitano, his
secretary and alleged mistress. The person making the allegations
– and paying me to be here splashing about looking for proof –
was Signora Antonia Dante, his wife. This formidable lady had

marched into my office a couple of days earlier, dolled up to the nines and dripping with gold jewellery, to tell me she'd finally had enough of her husband's philandering and wanted me to provide evidence of his infidelity. I had done a bit of digging and as a result had photographed him arriving at the hotel tonight with none other than Ms Napolitano. From the way he had been groping his secretary as they'd hurried into the hotel, I seriously doubted that this could be considered a work meeting.

So far I had managed to get photos of their arrival together and a partial shot of the alluring Giuseppina standing entwined with her boss by the window of their room on the second floor. Alas, she had lowered the blinds shortly afterwards so Oscar and I had been hanging about in the hope of a passionate departure scene I could photograph with my very expensive – and heavy – new camera that I was desperately trying to keep dry. This thing had a telephoto lens that could not only pick out the face of a man standing a hundred metres away but could probably also identify the brand of cigarette he was smoking, although on a night like tonight, the cigarette would soon have been extinguished by the rain.

After doing another circuit of the building, my soggy Labrador and I returned to my ageing VW minibus and opened the tailgate. Oscar needed no encouraging to jump in. Unfortunately, if unsurprisingly, he then set about shaking himself violently, transforming the inside of the boot area into a swamp. And I wasn't much better. As I slid into the driving seat, I could feel the water running off my raincoat and soaking into the seat covers. My hair was drenched, and the water had run past my collar and down my back as far as my pants. Not for the first time, I envied the sleuths of the black and white crime noir movies their broad-brimmed hats. I'm sure Philip Marlowe never had water soaking his underpants. I reached for my all-important bag and felt around inside it;

not for a Colt 45, a shot of bourbon or a cigar, but for a Thermos of coffee and a packet of biscuits. I lobbed a biscuit back to Oscar and poured myself a welcome cup of coffee. I was sipping it, my eyes skipping between the window of their room and the back door of the hotel, when my phone started ringing. It was Virgilio.

Since making the big decision to move from London to Italy and settle here in Tuscany, I had struck up a close friendship with Inspector Virgilio Pisano of the Florence Murder Squad. He was in so many ways what I used to be. Until my fifty-fifth birthday last year, I had been a detective chief inspector in the Metropolitan Police in central London. Although he knew I was retired, Virgilio called me in from time to time to help out with investigations here when English speakers were involved. I glanced at the time and saw that it was just after 10 p.m. It came as no surprise to find that he was still in the office.

'*Ciao*, Dan. *Come stai?*'

Although his English was good, we always spoke Italian together and I answered in Italian.

'*Ciao*, Virgilio, I'm fine. What about you? Still working?'

'I'm just on my way home. I thought I'd give you a call to tell you I've sent a bit of business your way.'

'That's good of you. What kind of business? Not another extra-marital affair? Haven't you Florentines got anything else to do with your time?'

'You've seen the quality of the TV here; what else is there to do?' He hastened to qualify his statement. 'Not that I have the time or energy even to contemplate infidelity.'

He and his wife, Lina, had been together for almost thirty years and it was one of the happiest marriages I knew. I envied him that. Mine hadn't survived the test of time or, more precisely, the constraints of my job.

'Well, what've you got for me this time?' He had been sending me clients on and off over the past few months, ever since I had taken his advice and set myself up as a private investigator.

'Does the name Selena Gardner ring a bell?'

'Selena Gardner – you mean the film star?'

'The very same. She's here in Florence making a movie for a few weeks.'

This was big. Selena Gardner was one of the top five, maybe top two or three, movie stars in the world, her face – and body – known to millions of people around the globe. Even I had heard of her succession of three – or was it four? – short-lived marriages and divorces. The streets of Hollywood were allegedly strewn with the men she had cast off and the scandal sheets would have been half as thick without her.

'So how come a humble detective inspector is involved with movie royalty?'

'I'd better explain. They've been getting death threats. I've never met Selena Gardner, but I've had a couple of visits from one of the producers of the film.' I could hear a note of something in his voice and I struggled to identify it: amusement maybe? 'She came to ask the police to provide protection for Miss Gardner and the rest of the crew, but she couldn't tell me who they're afraid of, who in particular is being threatened, why they're being threatened, or where and when these threats are supposed to be carried out.'

'What form do these threats take? Poison pen letters, social media trolling, abusive phone calls, burning bags of dog poo on the doorstep?'

'Threatening notes, but they're always delivered attached to an arrow.'

'An arrow?' This was a new one on me. 'You mean somebody fires arrows at them with a bow like in the westerns? Why on earth?'

'Not so much westerns as medieval dramas. The movie they're making is set in Renaissance times, five or six hundred years ago or so. Maybe the guy making the threats wants to stay in character.'

'But surely somebody wandering around the centre of a city full of tourists carrying a bow would be easy to spot.'

'Not necessarily. Our ballistics people say these aren't really arrows, but crossbow bolts. Apparently some crossbows can be folded up into something the size of a violin case or even smaller.'

'And have your people managed to get any clues from the notes or the arrows?'

'Nothing at all. No prints and they're standard aluminium crossbow bolts, readily available on the Internet. Owning a crossbow isn't illegal in Italy so no registration required. We've run the usual checks and we've drawn a blank, so unless the film company can let us have something more concrete, there's not a lot more we can do. I explained that we can't investigate something that hasn't happened, and we don't have the manpower to provide a bodyguard service, but I told her I know somebody who does.'

'And that would be me?'

'That's you, my friend, and you can expect a visit tomorrow morning from a most unusual lady called Rachel Hindenburg, like the famous airship that exploded into flames. She's appropriately named. You'll enjoy meeting her.'

Just at that moment the hotel door opened, and Signor Dante appeared with the lovely Giuseppina draped all over him. I blurted a quick apology to Virgilio and grabbed my camera. I wasted a few seconds starting the car and switching on the wipers to clear the screen, but the pair of lovebirds were making a meal of it, and I had ample time to shoot off a dozen shots, some in such close-up detail that I could tell the colour of her lipstick all over his face.

Finally, they made a run through the rain to his car and drove off. I replaced the camera securely in the bag and glanced in the mirror. Oscar's nose was resting on the top of the back seat, and he gave me a quizzical look. I hastened to reassure him.

'That's it, dog, we're going home to get something to eat.'

He licked his lips. I knew how he felt. Neither of us had eaten this evening. That was another discovery I had made recently: missing meals also came with the turf for people in my new trade.

1

TUESDAY MORNING

The producer from the film company was scheduled to arrive at nine-thirty next morning so I got into the office early in order to finish writing up the events of last night before emailing an interim copy of the report so far to Signora Dante. I indicated at the end of the email that I would send her the complete report along with the full series of compromising photos that afternoon after one final lunchtime photo session at a restaurant where her husband often entertained his lady friend. With that, she should have all the ammunition she needed to file for divorce on the grounds of infidelity.

As I waited for my visit from the film producer, I stood and looked out of the window. My office was situated on the first floor of a historic building within Florence's famous *centro storico*, roughly halfway between the main Santa Maria Novella station and the duomo. I stared down into the courtyard below with its weathered statue of Venus and its medieval fountain. Yesterday's rainstorm had passed, and the sun was once more shining from a cloudless sky, making this a very pleasant autumn day. I loved this place: not just Florence, but my new office. It was so redolent of history with its high ceilings, the magnificent fresco on the wall, and the ancient terracotta tiles beneath my feet.

Since taking on the lease, I had made friends with Nando, who lived on the ground floor and acted as doorkeeper, manager, cleaner and arbiter for the different apartments that occupied the fifteenth-century *palazzo*. As well as all that, he looked after the interests of the wealthy old aristocratic family who owned the place. He had pointed out all manner of little treasures to me over the past few months, like stained-glass windows, iron rings set in the walls for tethering horses, and grooves gouged in the flagstones by the wheels of carriages in centuries gone by. It felt amazing to feel so close to the history of one of the most iconic cities in the world.

Even the little picture-framing workshop on the opposite side of the courtyard had been in existence for centuries and the interior was an Aladdin's cave of ancient tools and apparatus probably designed in the Middle Ages. White-haired Signor Rufina who worked there single-handed looked as though he'd served his apprenticeship under Michelangelo. Yes, this part of Florence was very different from Osvaldo Dante's concrete love nest.

The doorbell rang and Oscar opened one eye. He wasn't a natural guard dog, and he didn't bother getting up from his bed by the window. I went over to open the door and found myself confronted by an unexpected vision. Standing before me on the fifteenth-century landing was a woman wearing fifteenth-century clothes, complete with a long sweeping robe and a hairstyle that vaguely reminded me of Princess Leia from *Star Wars*. The look was rendered even more startling by the very twenty-first-century bright-blue-framed glasses she was wearing, and the little lime-green backpack slung over her shoulder.

'Dan Armstrong?' Her accent was soft American, maybe West Coast?

Recovering my aplomb, I nodded and held out my hand. 'Good morning, yes, I'm Dan Armstrong. Would you be Ms Hindenburg by any chance?'

To my surprise she laughed. 'I certainly would be Rachel Hindenburg. How very English you sound.'

'That's probably because I *am* English.' I stepped back and waved her in. 'Do come in and make yourself comfortable. Don't mind Oscar; he's very friendly, probably too friendly.'

She shook my hand. 'Hi, Dan, and *buongiorno* to you, Oscar. Are you a good doggie?' Ms Hindenburg swept in and made a beeline for the Labrador, who had worked out by now that our visitor was female, and he had always liked the ladies. I was not surprised to see him jump to his feet, shake himself gently, and pad across to meet her halfway, tail wagging. She crouched down to make a fuss of him for a few moments before straightening up and coming to the point. 'Dan, we need your help.'

I indicated she should take a seat and she came over to the desk where I had been sitting. Whether it was the long dress or some problem with her footwear, she managed to trip just as she reached the desk and fell forward. She only stopped herself from ending up on the floor by throwing herself across the desk, scattering papers everywhere and almost toppling my computer onto the floor. Her head ended up barely a foot or two from my crotch, and I couldn't miss the bright beetroot-red flush that spread across her face. It was a pretty face beneath the blushes, and she had intelligent eyes – what I could see of them beyond the thick plastic frames of her glasses. She was probably only thirty or so and I was surprised. I had always imagined movie producers as being overweight, cigar-smoking sexagenarians with gravelly voices.

'I'm so sorry. My dress must have caught on something.' She pushed herself back onto her feet and slumped down onto a chair.

'Anyway, like I said, my name's Rachel and I'm the AP for *Lust For Power*.'

'Sorry, AP?' The acronym was unfamiliar to me.

'Assistant producer. I report to Mr Lyons, that's Gabriel Lyons, the producer.' She rearranged the neckline of her dress and retrieved the heavy gold necklace that had lodged down her front in the fall. She tugged it out and reattached it with a few words of explanation. 'Don't worry, it's all fake.' She tapped the bejewelled gold chain with her fingers, and I could hear that it, like her glasses, was plastic. 'The clip's always giving way.'

I allowed her a moment or two to sort herself out before giving her a gentle prompt. 'You were saying that you need my help?'

'Yes, that's why I'm here. You see, we've started getting threatening notes.'

'Yes, Inspector Pisano called me last night and told me. When you say "we", do you mean some people in particular or the production company in general?'

'It's hard to say. The company in general, I suppose, and the threats don't come by mail. I don't know if you've heard from the police, but they come attached to arrows.' She looked up and caught my eye. 'I know, weird, right? Three of the arrows were found in random places around the lot, but yesterday morning we found that one had been fired at the door of Miss Gardner's trailer hard enough to punch a hole right through it. And if that wasn't bad enough, this morning Mr Lyons, the producer, found one sticking into the side of his trailer. All of the arrows had notes attached to them, rolled around the shaft and fixed with sticky tape.'

'Do you think Miss Gardner and the producer are being specifically targeted?'

'Like I say, we just don't know. That's what's so worrying. It all seems so random.'

'And what do the notes say?'

'They all say the same.' She shrugged off the little backpack and extracted a stiff folder. She handed it across to me and I saw that it contained small sheets of coarse cream-coloured paper, all bearing the same wording, written in immaculate calligraphy.

Stop filming or start dying.

No signature. I had seen a lot of ransom notes and anonymous threats in my time at Scotland Yard and most had been type-written or even old school, made of words cut and pasted from newspapers. Finding threatening notes written by hand was unusual, and written in such formal lettering even more unusual, but then notes delivered by arrow weren't exactly commonplace. Whoever was responsible for this wasn't your run-of-the-mill villain.

'How long have you been filming here?'

'Filming? Just under a week, although we've had people here for almost a month scouting for locations and getting set up.'

'And how much longer will you be staying?'

'We're reckoning on just over a week and a half more filming. The movie's actually a modern-day thriller set in LA and the bits over here are for cutaways – you know, when the director wants to emphasise the similarities between characters or events in the twenty-first century and things that happened during the Renaissance. The location shooting here in Florence is more a series of cameos really, so it shouldn't take too long. At the end of next week, the producer, director and the cast will go back to the States while a skeleton crew will stay on to wrap things up here.'

'Any idea who might be behind these threats?'

'No idea at all.'

'And the police have seen all of these arrows?'

'All except the one that arrived this morning, but it's exactly the same as the others. The police did a fingerprint check on the others but found nothing, so I imagine this one's the same. They told us there isn't a single print anywhere. Partly that's because they think the perpetrator wore gloves, but also because the notes are written on such coarse paper and fingerprints don't show up on it for some reason.'

'And what about on the arrows themselves?'

'Same again.' She reached into her bag once more and pulled out a transparent plastic bag. Inside it I could see there was an arrow. As she handed it to me I glanced across at her.

'Has anybody handled this?'

'I'm afraid so, everybody from security at the trailer park to Mr Lyons, so I'm sure you can do what you want with it. Like I say, the police checked the others and said they'd all been wiped clean.'

I opened the bag and drew out a slim arrow just under a foot long with rather fancy deep blue flights with bright mustard-yellow squiggles on them. I don't have a lot of experience of bows and arrows, but I've seen *Robin Hood* and I could immediately see that this was a good deal shorter than your average arrow. It was made of aluminium, as Virgilio had said, and the tip was shiny polished steel with a sharp point. No doubt one of these could do a lot of damage, particularly at close range. Over in the UK we had long been begging the government to make these subject to the same checks and restrictions as firearms, but to no avail as yet. In the wrong hands, this could well be a deadly weapon. I replaced the arrow in the bag and looked across at the AP.

'All right if I hang onto this?' She nodded and I tapped the folder containing the notes. 'And are these all the notes you've received so far? When exactly did they all arrive?'

'The police still have one of the notes, but these are all the others. They first started arriving four days ago. The first was found lying by the entrance to the trailer park, the second was over by Scott Norris's trailer, and the third stuck in the ground. Then there was the one found in Miss Gardner's door yesterday morning and then the one shot at Mr Lyons's trailer last night.'

'Did the trailers have the occupants' names on them?'

'Not for the top people, for security reasons.'

I realised that if these last two arrows had been destined for the star of the show and the producer, this implied inside knowledge. 'Where are all these trailers?'

She went on to tell me that the Florence city authorities had allocated the company a private car park for their trucks and trailers just to the north of the *centro storico* on the other side of the *viali*, the inner ring road that circled the old part of town. In answer to my query, she confirmed that they had two full-time security guards as well as some local help working for the production company, but that none of them had seen or heard anything.

'If you have your own people, why do you need me?'

'Jim and Chuck have both come with us from the States. They're good guys but they're more for crowd control, keeping fans away and so on, than for a proper investigation. And Mr Lyons insists that we need to get to the bottom of what's going on.'

'Well, if you want me to investigate, I'll be happy to help out but I'll need access to the set and to all the cast and crew, from the director to the cleaners and bag-carriers.'

She caught my eye and grinned. 'You mean "from the *producer* to the cleaners and bag-carriers", don't you? Mr Lyons is the big boss.'

'I'm afraid I don't know much about the movie business. What's the difference between the producer and the director? I thought the director was the one who called the shots... like Tarantino or Spielberg.'

She gave me another little smile. 'The director has creative control – up to a point – but the producer's the person in overall charge and Mr Lyons is a very hands-on producer. He hired the director, and directors can be fired.' Her smile broadened. 'Did you know that the original director of *Jaws* was fired because he kept on referring to the shark as "the whale" and it drove the producer crazy? It does happen. The producer hires all the actors and crew, and, above all, the producer raises the money. Without the producer, the movie wouldn't happen. Think about it; at the Academy Awards, when a film wins the best movie category, it's the producer, not the director, who goes up to collect the Oscar.'

'We live and learn. Thanks for that. I'll have to read the names of the producers more carefully in future when they roll the credits.'

'Of course, often the big-name directors have a personal stake in the movie and so they become producers or associate producers themselves. It's a bit confusing but as far as *Lust for Power*'s concerned, Mr Lyons calls the shots.'

'Right, thanks for the heads-up. I'd better remember that. So if Mr Lyons is the producer, who's the director?'

'Emiliano Donizetti.' Seeing the expression on my face, she provided some explanation. 'Not heard of him? I'm not surprised, he's a relative newcomer to directing.'

'Italian?'

'Italo-American.' She actually lowered her voice although we were the only people in the room. 'He used to be Miss Gardner's boyfriend. They broke up a month or two ago, and the atmosphere on set can be tense at times.' She caught my eye. 'And when I say tense, I mean toxic.'

I started to read between the lines. 'I see, so might I be right in thinking that it could have been a matter of "love me, love my dog" for Selena Gardner, or in this case "employ me but only if you hire my boyfriend as director"? Something like that? And then, once he was sure he'd got the job, he dumped her?'

She nodded nervously. 'Yes, I reckon that's about the size of it from what I've heard, but for God's sake don't tell anybody I said that.' The little smile crept back onto her face. 'I'd be fired so fast you wouldn't see me for dust. For what it's worth, when you were talking about bag-carriers earlier, you were pretty close to the mark. In spite of my grand title, I'm not much more than a gopher – you know, I go for this, I go for that, and I do everything from answering the mail to bringing Mr Lyons his coffee.'

I decided that I rather liked Rachel Hindenburg. I've never been fond of people who are too full of themselves, and I appreciated her almost Anglo-Saxon self-deprecation. I laid out my terms and she agreed without a murmur, even to my request for my dog to accompany me. Oscar himself, clearly keen to reinforce the request for his presence, had stationed himself alongside her, his head resting on her thigh and his eyes staring lovingly up at her. Like I say, he likes the ladies. And why not?

She looked down at him affectionately and stroked his ears. 'Sure, but just keep him away from Mr Lyons and keep him off the set. If he wanders out in front of the cameras and spoils the scene, Emmy will go crazy.'

'Emmy being Emiliano, the director? Sounds like an award; let's hope that his name's a good omen for the success of the film. Come to think of it, having a dog called Oscar around might be a good omen, too. By the way, what's the movie about? How come you're filming here in Florence?'

'It's a dual-timeline movie; like I said, it's mostly in twenty-first-century LA, but with a series of cutaways to Renaissance Florence. Have you heard of the Medici family?'

Now it was my turn to smile. 'Heard of them? I studied them

for a couple of years. I'm a writer as well as a PI, and my first book was set at the time of the Medici. They were legendary.'

'Terrific, you'll have to sit down and talk to Anna; she's our historical consultant. She works at the university of Florence, and she knows everything about the Renaissance. She even designed the dress that I'm wearing.'

'And a very nice dress it is.' I gave her another smile. 'I've been meaning to ask about that: do you usually go around dressed like this?'

She gave a resigned nod. 'While I'm over here, yes, at least when I'm working. It's the idea of our PR guru, Donny Lopez. Everybody has to stay in costume, even off-set, so that we get people talking. In fairness to Donny, he's prepared to put his money where his mouth is, and he wears the same outfit as the rest of the guys. It seems to be working and it's already aroused a good bit of media attention.' She looked up from the dog and rolled her eyes. 'I don't know how they managed back in the Middle Ages. The trouble with this dress is that the material's so thick, it weighs a ton. At least we're in October now and it's not too warm but imagine wearing this kind of thing in the height of the summer.'

'If it helps, I believe they didn't wear underwear back then.'

She raised her eyebrows and smiled. 'On the subject of clothes, would you mind terribly if we find you a Renaissance costume to wear while you're with us? Donny says we need all the publicity we can generate and, apart from anything else, it'll make you less conspicuous on set. Besides, we need extras for some scenes, so you might find your face in a movie.'

'It's not my face I'm worried about. Five or six hundred years ago men were wearing tights. I'm not sure the twenty-first century is ready to see my legs in tights.' In particular, any of my former colleagues at Scotland Yard, who would probably do themselves a mischief laughing.

'You'll be fine. After all, everybody else will be in costume. There'll be no need to feel self-conscious.'

Some hopes. Still, if that was what the job demanded – and it promised to be a welcome supplement to my bank balance – I gritted my teeth and said yes. At the AP's request, I scribbled down my chest, waist and leg measurements and she promised to get Wardrobe to look something out for me. I wasn't looking forward to it.

We arranged that I would come over to the trailer park a bit later that morning to interview as many of the admin staff as possible while the majority of the actors and crew were occupied shooting inside the Palazzo Vecchio. After a brief hiatus while I would zip off to take the last few photos of Signor Dante and his lady friend, I would return to meet up with the rest of the crew, the director, producer and actors in the afternoon or after filming had finished for the day.

Finally, we both stood up and I gave her my card with my contact details. As she took it from me, she asked me a personal question. 'Can I ask how come an Englishman's working as a PI here in Italy?'

It was a fair question, so I gave her the slightly longer than usual answer. 'I retired from my job as a detective chief inspector in the Metropolitan police in London last year. My wife divorced me, so I came over here and stayed on, and I don't regret it for a moment. Tuscany's in my blood now.'

She nodded in agreement. 'It's gorgeous, isn't it? Florence has so many wonderful historic buildings, it's hard to know quite where to start. Our location managers have managed to find a number of super picturesque places for the movie and, as long as the sun keeps shining like it is today, the results should be great.' She pulled up a long brocade sleeve and glanced at a very twenty-first-century watch. 'I have to go. Mr Lyons will be shouting for me any minute now.'

She turned towards the door and managed to do that tripping-over thing yet again. This time I was on hand to catch her elbow and steady her while Oscar looked on with an expression of canine amusement on his face. She was blushing again.

'Sorry, that's just me. You can probably guess my nickname. Ever since school, people have called me Dizzy, shortened from Disaster, after the Hindenburg airship disaster. I'm afraid I've always had a talent for tripping up, bumping into things, knocking stuff over.' She shook my hand. 'You might as well call me that too. That's what everybody on set calls me.'

'Okay, Dizzy it is. Goodbye for now, see you later.'

She grabbed a hefty handful of her long skirt and set off down the stone stairway. I listened to the sound of her heels, waiting for the crash, but she must have managed it without disaster striking.

2

TUESDAY MID-MORNING

The trailer park was crammed with motorhomes and caravans, and somebody had erected a screen of two-metre-high wire fence panels all the way around it. When I turned up at the entrance, I was stopped by one of the biggest men I'd ever seen. The word 'Security' was emblazoned across his powerful chest in large white letters that stood out against the black background of his T-shirt. Presumably the costume department hadn't been able to find him a medieval outfit his size, although it might have been because there probably hadn't been too many characters around Florence during the Renaissance period with dreadlocks. It came as no surprise to see that he was wearing dark glasses. I've often wondered why American security guards, federal agents and police officers conduct so much of their business behind dark glasses. As a look it's intimidating, but from a practical point of view – literally – it must make reading tricky. As I approached, the guard held up a forearm the size of the leg of Tuscan cured ham I kept in my larder.

'Can I help you, sir?' He spoke in English, making no attempt to speak Italian. He sounded cordial enough, but it would have taken a brave would-be intruder to try to push past him.

'I'm here to see Rachel Hindenburg. My name's Armstrong, Dan Armstrong.'

He checked his clipboard and nodded. 'She's in the trailer over by those trees. It says "Production" on the door. You have a good day now, sir.'

I thanked him and made my way across to Dizzy's trailer, passing half a dozen assorted people on the way; the women all in long dresses and the men dressed in garish red and yellow striped pantaloons, tunics and red tights. I took one look at them and swallowed hard. Part of a PI's job is to blend in with the surroundings, but the idea of wandering around looking like something out of a fairly camp version of *Robin Hood* didn't appeal in the slightest. When I got to the long static trailer, I tapped on the door. It opened a moment later and Dizzy beckoned for me and the dog to go in. She gave me an apologetic smile and nodded towards the phone at her ear. I grabbed Oscar's collar to stop him from climbing all over her and went inside. I couldn't help overhearing her end of the conversation and I was impressed at how business-like she sounded; a far cry from the clumsy girl who had almost fallen over twice in my office.

'Tomorrow morning at the train station. I'll send a car for you. What train are you taking? The 08.10 from Rome, gets in at 09.47? No problem... See you tomorrow.'

She set the phone down on a table and came over to greet me and my Labrador. As she stroked Oscar, she apologised. 'Sorry about that, Dan. A journalist from one of the celebrity magazines.'

'Sounds promising. Presumably your PR guy will handle that sort of meeting.'

'Donny or his PA, Loredana. I just make the arrangements and then they get on with it. It's pretty much what I do all the time.

Like I told you, I'm a gopher and a fixer. I make things happen for other people. Now, as far as your investigation's concerned, how do you want to play it?'

'I'd quite like to sit down for five minutes with whoever's around here now and ask them a few questions. I presume from what you said that most of the cast and crew are over at the Palazzo Vecchio filming. If you can find me somewhere I can see each of them in turn that would be great.'

'You can see them in here if you like. Mr Lyons won't be back for a few hours. Give me five minutes and I'll check who's about and prepare a schedule. Five minutes each, right?'

'Perfect, thanks. Hopefully I'll be able to see all the people who're here this morning before lunch. Like I told you, I'll have to go off on another job for an hour or so at twelve-thirty, but I'll be back around two to carry on.'

She left me to my own devices while she went off to make the arrangements. I let my eyes range around the surprisingly large interior, which had been set up like a boardroom with a single long table surrounded by half a dozen chairs all facing a huge monitor at the far end flanked by a bank of electronic equipment. A smart steel and glass desk – presumably belonging to the producer – stood at the other end with a separate smaller table alongside it that was obviously Dizzy's workstation. The producer's desk was bare but Dizzy's was piled high with paper around and on top of a laptop. I wandered over and flicked casually through invoices, receipts, a variety of legal-looking documents on City of Florence headed paper and a clipboard with a long To Do list on which I spotted my name. Later entries ranged from *Hair – Miss G* at five to *Rushes* at 6 p.m. Rushes, if I remembered rightly, referred to scrutiny of the footage shot that day. Presumably the powers-that-be would sit around this table and take a long hard look at what had been achieved. Dizzy's voice outside the door interrupted my snooping.

'Dan, this is Big Jim. I wonder if you can guess why we call him that. You already met him at the gate.'

The caravan swayed on its blocks as the massive figure of the security guard climbed in. The doorway was a good six inches narrower than his shoulders, so he had to slip in sideways. I asked him to sit down and I eyed the chair anxiously as he lowered himself onto it. Although it creaked ominously, it held up, but I shot off my series of questions as quickly as I could, just in case. I told him I was trying to discover what he knew about the arrows and the threatening notes.

The upshot of my questioning was that he knew very little, apart from the fact that whoever had fired arrows at Selena Gardner and the producer's trailers must have either got into the lot by climbing over the security fence or been a good shot to hit them at over fifty yards. I made a mental note to check the range of a crossbow bolt. Big Jim also pointed out that it must have been dark when the arrows were fired and that would have made it even more unlikely that a perpetrator outside the perimeter fence could have been specifically targeting the two trailers that had been hit. Both events had taken place overnight when the compound should have been empty, except for a small team of locally sourced security guards from a well-known company in the city. The police had questioned each of them closely but nobody had seen a thing.

Big Jim told me that the crew were distributed around Florence in a selection of hotels ranging from basic to luxury, depending on where you stood in the pecking order. He gave me a wry smile and indicated that his was one of the more basic hotels. Finally I asked him if he had any ideas as to who might be behind the threats and he came up with an observation that gave me food for thought.

'It's no business of mine, but Chuck and I've both noticed that there's lot of tension between Mr Lyons and Emmy, as well as between Emmy and Miss Gardner. We even wondered if maybe Emmy might be behind what's going on; you know, just to piss one or the other off.' An expression of apprehension crossed his face. 'But don't you go telling people I said that.'

I noted that although the producer was referred to as 'Mr Lyons', the director went by his first name, Emmy. 'Your secret's safe with me, I promise. And what about the other actors... Scott Norris, for instance? None of them disgruntled about anything?'

'No more than usual.' He glanced over his massive shoulder to check that the trailer door was closed. 'You know actors: highly strung at the best of times.'

I didn't know actors terribly well and it looked as though this was going to be a voyage of discovery. After a few more questions, I thanked him and asked who had been guarding the gate while he was talking to me – his fellow security guard, Chuck, maybe?

Jim shook his head. 'No, Chuck's at the palace where they're shooting this afternoon. I've got a local boy, Max, helping out. Dizzy said to send him along next for you to talk to him.'

Before talking to the local security guard, I went for a quick prowl around the trailer lot with Oscar, paying particular attention to the wire fencing protecting the perimeter. This was made up of two-metre-tall panels, which constituted a fairly formidable, but far from insurmountable, barrier to anybody seeking to get in. I couldn't see any security cameras so I made a mental note to ask Dizzy to organise some so that anybody attempting to get in or lurking about outside could be recorded and identified. Beyond the wire fence were the rear gardens of the surrounding apartment blocks. I checked the windows all around, but I felt sure they were too far away for the attacker to have used one of them. He or she must have got close up to the wire, if not inside it. In all, I counted eight trailers and a handful of vans and trucks. Gaps between them indicated where other vehicles would probably be parked when they returned from today's filming.

After five minutes or so I returned to the trailer to meet Max, the locally recruited security guard. Max turned out to be Massimo Fornace, a history student at Florence university who moonlighted for the local security company responsible for this site. I queried if he had been on duty when the arrows had been fired, but he shook his head and told me the night team came on duty at 8 p.m. and he went off every night at that time. I asked him the same question about whether he had any idea who might be behind the threats, and he initially shook his head but then threw out a suggestion that mirrored what Jim had just said.

'I don't think Emiliano Donizetti, the director's, too happy. Every time I see him, he's looking angry about something. He's snapped at me a few times over nothing.' He lowered his voice, even though we were speaking Italian. 'He and Miss Gardner seem to spend a lot of time shouting at each other. My English isn't great, so I can't tell you what's being said, but every time I go past her trailer I can tell if he's with her from the arguments going on inside.'

This tied in with what Dizzy and Big Jim had told me, and it didn't sound as though the set of *Lust for Power* was such a happy place. After Max had left, I interviewed the next four names on the schedule that Dizzy had very efficiently prepared for me and by the time I reached number five, I was getting a bit more used to seeing people dressed in Renaissance costume, although I was still dreading joining their number.

Loredana Belluno, the assistant to the PR man, was a very beautiful woman and in her long gown she looked like an actress herself. She told me she was a newcomer to the company, and it sounded as though she would like nothing better than to be taken on permanently. Predictably, she couldn't tell me much about the other members of the company, but she did give her boss, Donny Lopez, a glowing review. From the way she referred to him and the sparkle in her eyes, I even wondered if there might be something going on between them. Alas, like the previous interviews, I learnt nothing new from her either and it only started to get interesting when I reached the last two names on the list.

The first of these was the writer, Martin Taylor, and he was a Brit like me. He was about my height, a bit younger than me – maybe in his late forties or early fifties – and quite a good-looking guy with dark hair and broad shoulders. He arrived with a face like thunder. I wondered whether this was just because he had been squeezed into a red and yellow costume that looked as if it was a bit too small for him or if something had happened. The explanation took a bit of time to extract from him, but I finally managed to get him to reveal all, and it came as quite a surprise.

'You have to understand that in this business the writer is the lowest of the low. Our names appear way down on the credits although, without us, the film could never have happened in the first place. Over the past months I've got used to my lines being changed, new characters foisted on me, and even major plot changes, but half an hour ago I got a text from Emmy telling me to write a completely new scene to be filmed tomorrow in the hills outside Florence. A text! He didn't even have the decency to tell me in person.'

I gave him a sympathetic smile. 'Not exactly giving you a lot of time, is he? What happens in the scene? Is it vital to the plot?'

'Definitely. The movie's about a modern-day criminal family in LA, but there are parallels with the Medici. That's why we're here, shooting a number of cameos where the modern characters are transported back five hundred years or so. You probably know the Medici spent centuries as rulers of Tuscany.' I nodded and he continued. 'This sequence is about a fictitious encounter between Lorenzo de' Medici – the man called "Lorenzo the Magnificent" – and a would-be assassin. It was originally planned as an interior scene but now Emmy wants me to rewrite it so that the assassination attempt tomorrow happens as an exterior scene outside Florence in the countryside. How the hell am I expected to do that?' His expression remained deeply frustrated.

'I can see that would be a problem. Have you written scripts for lots of movies?'

'Screenplays, yes, quite a few. This is the first time I've gone for something with a historical element, though, and I'm beginning to regret it.'

'Why's that?'

'To be honest, I'm not that interested in history, and I certainly don't know much about Italian history.'

Then why, I wondered, had he chosen to try his hand at writing something historical? Although, from the sound of it, it had been a successful new venture as it had resulted in him being chosen to write a big Hollywood movie screenplay.

'How long have you been shooting the movie?'

'We started shooting back in the States just over six weeks ago, but I've been involved in pre-production for four months now.'

'And during that time there haven't been any death threats?'

'Nothing at all.' He glanced at his watch. 'Anyway, if we can get this little interview over as quickly as possible, I'd appreciate it. I'm going to have to work through the night as it is.'

'Of course, my principal question is whether you can think of any reason why these threats are being made.'

He shook his head. 'God knows. Maybe it's a territorial question – you know, an Italian filmmaker feeling miffed that Hollywood's turned up in his backyard.'

'But *death* threats?'

'Like I say, who knows?'

After a few more questions, I released him to get on with his rewrite and called the last of the people on site not involved with the filming in the Palazzo Vecchio. This was Anna Galardo, the historical advisor, and both Oscar and I took an immediate liking to her. She arrived wearing a fine long dress in a deep-red colour that suited her complexion and fitted her perfectly. Clearly she had been luckier with the wardrobe department than the writer had been. She sat down opposite me and while she ruffled Oscar's ears, I took a closer look at her. She was a good-looking woman – well, a very good-looking woman really – and she might have been in her late forties or a little older. There were lines and wrinkles at her eyes that spoke of past trauma, but I was a fine one to talk about wrinkles. Helen, my ex-wife, often described the area around my eyes as looking like the sand after the tide's gone out. Transferring her attention from my dog to me, Anna Galardo produced a smile and addressed me in English.

'So you're the famous English private eye.' Her English was very fluent, virtually without accent.

'Definitely not the "famous" part but, yes, I've been hired to look into these threats.' I thought I might as well pop the question straight away. 'Have you any idea what's going on?'

She shook her head. 'I wish I did. It's so unexpected. It's not as if the movie's controversial; it's a pretty conventional thriller with a historical element, and not a particularly major element either.' Her English really was amazingly good.

'Dizzy told me they're only filming here for a couple of weeks. No chance any of the locals might be up in arms about it?' When she shook her head again, I added, 'What about the big names? Might there still be descendants of the Medici or some of the other families who might resent the intrusion?'

'There are still some distant descendants of most of Florence's great families around but, like I say, there's nothing derogatory or contentious in the film. The historical part is only really an offshoot of the modern-day thriller.'

I went on to ask her about herself and she told me she lived in Florence now but was originally from a village in the hills to the north of the city. She was probably older than I'd first thought – maybe not far off my own age – and she told me she'd spent twenty years of her life lecturing at Bath university, during which time she had married a Brit. That marriage, like my own, had ended in divorce – in her case ten years earlier – after which she'd returned to Florence to work at the university here. Her current historical adviser role was similar to that of Massimo Fornace, the security guard, in that she was supplementing her salary by dividing her time for a couple of weeks between her university commitments and her job here.

We were having a friendly chat about the Renaissance when a glance at my watch told me I needed to be heading for Signor Dante's favourite restaurant with my camera. As a final question, I asked if she had any suspicions, but all she could do was shrug her shoulders.

'I'm not here full time and, seeing as I'm living at home, I don't mingle much with the others socially. There's clearly a bit of bad feeling between Selena Gardner and both the director and the producer, but I don't know what that's about. But why we should be getting these sorts of threats is a mystery to me.'

After she had left the trailer, I glanced down at my dog, who was staring at her retreating back with regret. 'I know how you feel, Oscar. She's a nice lady.'

Of course, I reminded myself, for now she was a potential suspect in this case so I would do well not to get too close to her.

3

TUESDAY EARLY AFTERNOON

The restaurant chosen by Signor Dante and his girlfriend was just on the edge of the pedestrians-only *centro storico*, presumably so that he could drive in from Prato and park his car nearby. The buildings here were a lot newer than in the centre, but it was still a very stylish area, although the cars parked nose to tail rather spoilt the overall impression. As for the restaurant, I had never eaten there, but I'd passed it a few times and I knew that it specialised in seafood.

From my point of view it was ideal: there were tables outside on a terrace and from my observation post on a bench on the far side of the road at the edge of a little park I had a clear view of all the diners, in particular Mr Dante and Ms Napolitano. I had just shot off a few photos of them smiling lovingly at each other over a starter of oysters when my phone rang. It was Signor Dante's wife and she wasted little time with formalities.

'Is my husband at the restaurant with that little tramp?'

'Good afternoon, Signora Dante, yes, they're just eating their antipasti now.'

'The bastard!'

'I've taken some photos of them for you.'

'Doing what?'

'Holding hands and whispering sweet nothings to each other.'

'The bastard! What's the name of the restaurant?'

'Il Riccio Marino, near Porta al Prato.' I heard an intake of breath.

'The bastard! I've been asking him to take me there for years, but he never has. What're they eating?'

This seemed a trivial question to ask considering the far more serious matter of her husband drooling over his lunch guest, but I provided the answer. 'It looks like oysters.'

'Oysters... the bastard!'

For the sake of complete disclosure, I added a bit more information. 'And they're drinking French champagne.' Through the lens of my camera, I could read the label.

'The bastard!' It appeared that Signora Dante had a tendency to be repetitive, but I couldn't really blame her under the circumstances. Her voice rose and I had to hold the phone away from my ear. 'Right! I'm coming straight down there now.'

'I don't think that's a very good idea...'

But she'd rung off. I glanced down at my dog, sprawled at my feet. 'Get ready for fireworks, Oscar.'

He opened one eye, checked there was no food on offer, and relapsed into sleep in the shade at my feet.

Signora Dante must have been close by, because she turned up just as her husband and Ms Napolitano had been served their pasta course. This was *spaghetti alle vongole* by the look of the clam shells amid the piles of pasta on their plates. The outraged wife stormed through the tables towards him, and Dante only saw her at the last moment. Through the camera lens I distinctly saw the look of panic that spread across his face as he opened his lips to say something, but she was in no mood for cordiality. As the other diners looked on in astonishment, she grabbed his plate of pasta and splattered it in his face before turning towards the stunned Ms Napolitano and doing the same to her. I'm no lip-reader, but my knowledge of Italian invective was broad enough by that time for me to feel pretty sure I could make out some very juicy insults from the outraged wife before she spun around and stormed off. I took a couple of photos for my own sake but decided it was probably just as well if I didn't flash them about. A good lawyer could probably construct a case of assault, which wouldn't help the unhappy wife's cause.

A minute or two later, Signor Dante and his lady got up and left, still dripping pasta on the ground as they retreated. A pair of waiters immediately appeared with cloths and brushes and set about removing all trace of the incident. Sight of the food reminded me that I was hungry so, never one to waste an opportunity, I crossed the road with my dog and asked if I could take over the freshly laid table. Ten minutes later I was tucking into a plateful of *spaghetti alle vongole* – hopefully not recently scraped off Signor Dante and his mistress – and it was excellent. At my feet, Oscar had already devoured two packets of grissini and the remaining strands of pasta overlooked by the clean-up team, so I was sure he agreed with me that the food here was good.

I relaxed as I ate and let my mind return to the book I was writing. This was my second whodunnit and I knew that I would have to submit it to my publisher early in the new year, which gave me barely three months to finish writing it. Only a few months earlier I had received the unbelievable news I had been offered a two-book deal and so I was hard at work on this one, which was just over halfway written now. The good news was that I had finally worked out who the killer was after changing my mind two or three times already. I thought back to the scene I had just witnessed with the spaghetti and resolved to include a scene of that nature in the book. Somehow, however, I didn't think I would be including stripy pantaloons and bows and arrows in this one.

At two o'clock, I went back to the trailer park and picked up where I had left off.

A number of the crewmembers, all decked out in the regulation red and yellow stripes, had drifted back from the Palazzo Vecchio by this time and I gradually managed to interview most of them, but they provided little more information. Nobody had a clue as to what was going on or who might be behind it and I found myself wondering if this might all be a waste of time – the work of the sort of moron who dials the emergency services about non-existent fires or bombs. After them it was the turn of the people no longer needed on set, who ranged from bit-part actors to locally recruited extras, and after I had finished with them, of course, I knew I would have to speak to the main protagonists. None of these had come back from the Palazzo Vecchio yet and I wondered if I should go over there to look for them. When I suggested this to Dizzy, she shook her head and advised me to wait until shooting had finished for the day.

'We've only got access to the Palazzo Vecchio until four o'clock, so Emmy will be rushing to get things finished in time. Why don't you grab yourself a coffee and wait? It's gone three-thirty, so they won't be long.'

I asked her to look into the possibility of getting CCTV cameras installed and she took my request in her stride, telling me she would contact the local security company and see if this might be feasible, even as soon as tonight. Clumsy she might be, but I could see why the film company had employed her. Leaving her to make the call, I took her advice and went over to the truck belonging to an outside catering company and asked the guy behind the counter – also, bizarrely, wearing a medieval tunic – for a coffee. All around were tables filled with crewmembers or bit-part actors, all dressed in the obligatory tights and stripes. I spotted Big Jim making short work of a doughnut with sprinkles – I didn't even know these existed in Italy – and the writer, Martin Taylor, with his nose in his laptop and no fewer than three empty coffee cups in front of him. I felt sorry for him.

When I got my coffee, I offered to pay, but was told that it was all free and I almost regretted not asking for a doughnut to share with Oscar while I was at it. I could read disappointment in my dog's eyes and settled for a tiny packet of biscuits, which brightened his expression in an instant. Labradors, as I knew so well after cohabiting with Oscar for over a year now, live for food and would happily eat until they explode. As he crunched up his biscuits, I took a seat in the shade of an ancient umbrella pine and ran through the list of people I still needed to interview – basically, the most important people involved in making the movie.

The main players essentially added up to six people: first there was Selena Gardner, the world-renowned actress whose appearance in a movie directed by a newcomer would have been somewhat surprising if I hadn't heard that she and the director used to be an item. It came as no surprise to learn that, now that this relationship had ended, things weren't too rosy between them.

And then there was Miss Gardner's onscreen paramour played by American actor Scott Norris. Although I had heard of him and even seen a couple of his movies before, he was definitely in a lower league than Miss Gardner and probably playing alongside her represented a step up for him. From Dizzy's cast list I could see that there were two other major players: a rising British star called Charles Vincent, famous already for appearances on UK television, making his debut here in a big-time movie, and the actor who played the character described by Dizzy as the 'bad guy'. This was Douglas Ogilvie, whose name sounded familiar, even if I couldn't immediately picture him.

Last but not least were Emiliano Donizetti, the director, who had allegedly been Miss Gardner's offscreen partner, and Gabriel Lyons, the producer. From what I had been hearing it wouldn't have surprised me if Emmy turned out to be an arrogant and self-centred character, considering the way he had allegedly used Selena Gardner to further his career. As for the producer, from what Dizzy had said, Gabriel Lyons was likely to be irascible and domineering. I wasn't looking forward to either interview, but they had to be done.

For these more senior figures, Dizzy explained that protocol dictated that I should go to visit *them* rather than calling them to see *me*, so when a couple of limos and a minibus returned with them, I set out for the first on my list. I decided I would start with Douglas Ogilvie, the 'bad guy', and work my way up the pecking order from there. I found him sprawled back on a couch in his luxurious caravan with a glass of what smelt like Scotch in his hand. He was dressed from head to toe in black satin and with his D'Artagnan beard he looked a most convincing movie villain. As he waved me into a nearby seat, our eyes met and we both did a double take. He was the first to react.

'I know you. You're Inspector Armstrong, aren't you? How could I forget? Well, well, well, who'd have thought it?' I immediately recognised both his face and his fruity accent.

'Duggie Ogilvie! I knew I'd heard that name before. I'm delighted to see you doing so well. Star billing in a Hollywood movie, no less.'

He sighed. 'Not top-line star billing, but Stephen would have been so pleased for me.' He reached down to pat Oscar while my brain worked hard to retrieve the information from my memory banks.

It all started coming back to me. I had come across Duggie Ogilvie about fifteen years earlier when he had still been a struggling young actor, hoping for his big break. His long-term boyfriend, Stephen Something-or-other, had been found dead in their flat, ostensibly of a cocaine overdose. The finger of suspicion for at least supplying, if not administering, the drug had pointed at Duggie, but I'd had my doubts from the start. As a recently promoted detective inspector I'd had to fight hard to stop my then superior from arresting him on the spot. It had taken a lot of legwork and a few sleepless nights, but I'd finally traced the drugs to another of Stephen's boyfriends, whose existence had been unknown to Duggie Ogilvie or to my boss. I was able to prove that this man had killed Stephen in a fit of jealous rage and that Duggie was innocent on all counts. I filed away the thought that Stephen's killer would almost certainly be out of jail by now, having been convicted of the lesser charge of manslaughter, rather than premeditated murder. Might this bitter rival be behind the menacing notes?

After reminiscing for a few minutes and turning down the offer of a glass of whisky, I brought the conversation around to the present day and he came up with his theory.

'You want to know what I think, Inspector? I think it's the Mafia.'

'The Mafia? And it's just Dan these days, not Inspector.' As we were in Italy I'd been waiting for this hypothesis to surface. The fact that we were in Florence, which is almost a thousand kilometres from the Mafia heartland of Sicily, made this unlikely but it had to be borne in mind. I prodded him to explain his rationale and he carried on.

'It's Emmy; he's half Sicilian and he comes from the rough part of New York. I reckon he's done something to upset the local Don over here, and this arrow nonsense is them looking for payback.'

I decided to pour a certain amount of cold water on this idea. 'First, I seriously doubt that Florence has a resident Mafia boss but, even if there is one, Cosa Nostra have moved on from bows and arrows. This whole thing strikes me as very amateur – handwritten notes and random arrows? – and nobody could accuse the Mafia of being amateur. What about closer to home? Couldn't it be somebody in the cast or crew with a grudge?'

He looked disappointed at my debunking of his organised-crime theory, but he didn't object. I saw him mull the question over for a few seconds before responding.

'As far as a grudge is concerned, it's hard to know.' He leant forward and lowered his voice. 'You haven't heard this from me, right? The fact is that the whole movie's a bloody soap opera. The director and the producer are at loggerheads: Emmy hates Gabriel – you know, Gabriel Lyons, the producer – and Gabriel despises Emmy as a director. Then there's the *cherchez la femme* element: Gabriel lusts after Selena, but Selena barely tolerates Gabriel. Scott, that's Scott Norris, Selena's onscreen partner, would like to have an amorous relationship with her offscreen as well, but Selena's just come out of a relationship with Emmy so she's playing it cool.' He paused for effect. 'Or so she would like us to believe...'

He took a sip of Scotch and settled further back on the couch, clearly enjoying his role as raconteur. 'Add in a bit of old-fashioned jealousy, Scott hates Charles because he's younger and prettier than him, and Charles positively drools over Emmy. Oh, yes, and the woman scorned: Selena thought Emmy was in love with her, but she's now convinced that he was just using her. As for me, I hate the lot of them but it's work, and, like you say, a Hollywood movie always looks good on the old CV.'

I was scribbling as he spoke and I hoped that I'd be able to make sense of all this information – or at least gossip. Part of a detective's job is to work out what's true and what's imaginary, and over the years I had often been confronted by witnesses with fertile imaginations. I took what Duggie said with a pinch of salt but felt sure there was more than a grain of truth in there. Without being able to put a face to many of these names, it was a bit confusing. Whatever the full truth of it, it was clear that there was a lot bubbling away in the background to the set of *Lust for Power*. The thing I couldn't get my head around was why any of these internal feuds could have escalated to murder threats and expressed themselves in such a primitive, if cinematographic, way.

4

TUESDAY AFTERNOON

I left Duggie to his second Scotch and headed for the trailer housing the male lead, Scott Norris. He greeted me affably and invited me in. He made no objection to the presence of Oscar, but he didn't go out of his way to make a fuss of him. He also gave me a piece of advice.

'Make sure you keep the dog away from Gabriel. He'll be terrified of him; not of being bitten, but of getting sick. He's one of those germophobes who's constantly afraid of catching something, and he steers clear of all animals. He told me that's one of the main reasons he's never made a western.'

As he was talking, I checked him out. He was tall, maybe six three or four, and it was clear that he kept himself in shape. A treadmill and a set of weights over in the corner confirmed my supposition. He fell perfectly into the Hollywood film-star mould as a tanned Adonis with a very un-medieval set of perfect white teeth. I could remember Helen, my ex-wife, murmuring dreamily about him, and I felt sure she would envy my being here with him. He was still in his Renaissance costume, the same fancy red and yellow striped tunic, pantaloons and red tights as everybody else, but he managed to wear all this without looking ridiculous – something I felt sure wouldn't happen to me when I, too, pulled on a pair of tights. I was increasingly convinced that I would look a complete buffoon and I hoped no photos of me in costume would get out. I could well imagine the mirth an outfit like this would provoke among my former colleagues at Scotland Yard and the inmates of a number of His Majesty's prisons if they ever saw me in pantaloons.

I started by asking Scott where he was staying and it came as no surprise to hear that he, along with Selena Gardner, the director, and the producer, was housed in one of the dozen or so five-star hotels dotted around Florence's *centro storico*. I nodded approvingly. Security in a place like that was likely to be pretty tight. In fact, from what he told me, these four top people were protected not only by hotel security but by bodyguards from a private security firm as well. It sounded as though anybody with a grudge against one or more of them would have to assault them away from the hotel and that meant here or on set. All the more reason for getting CCTV set up as soon as possible. I then moved on to the threatening notes and he looked remarkably unfazed.

'Happens all the time. I was filming in Paris last year and we started getting bomb threats. Nothing happened, of course, it was just some crazy.' He shook his head ruefully. 'There are lots of crazies out there.'

'So you don't think I should be concerned.'

'You do your job, but don't be surprised if all you find at the end of it is some little old lady who thinks my pants are too tight.' He stretched uncomfortably and winced. 'And they are.'

Doing my best to ignore what looked like another disadvantage of my new costume, I continued with my questions. 'What about here among the cast and crew, how are things? Any animosity?'

He paused for thought. 'Hard to say. Gabriel and Emmy seem to be at each other's throats most of the time, but I fail to see how firing an arrow through Selena's door would have anything to do with that.'

'Why *are* they at each other's throats?' I'd already heard about this, but it was always good to get corroboration.

'Emmy only got the job because Selena bulldozed Gabriel into hiring him and then, of course, after she'd got her way, she realised Emmy had just been using her so she dumped him. Everybody knows that he's only here because of her, but the fact of the matter is that he's a good director, even if he is a bit young still, but that doesn't stop Gabriel taking every opportunity to find fault with him.'

'So Gabriel resents the fact that he was bullied into hiring Emmy, and Emmy resents the fact that the producer's constantly on his back. I see. Can you think of any other friction among the cast or crew?'

'Well, there's our English friend, Douglas. He's got the hots for young Charles, but Charles isn't interested.'

'Presumably Charles isn't gay?'

'Oh, I reckon he's gay all right, although he hasn't come out yet.' He grinned at me. 'It's supposed to be a secret, but to me it's all too obvious. You should see him with Emmy. Talk about spaniel eyes.'

By the time I left Scott Norris's trailer, my head was spinning. There really were an awful lot of sub-plots bubbling away beneath the surface here, but the fact of the matter was that so far I hadn't heard anything that led me to suspect any of the people I had seen of contemplating murder. A few harsh words or a slap in the face, maybe, but murder?

My next appointment was with Charles Vincent, the up-and-coming young movie star in the making. I found him in his caravan. This was visibly a bit less spacious and less luxurious than the others, but he looked quite happy. He invited me in and made a terrific fuss of Oscar while I started the questioning. He told me he was twenty-nine and his movie career was just taking off. I recognised his face immediately from a murder-mystery TV series back in the UK that had been very popular although, to an ex-detective like me, it had been littered with inaccuracies. Show me a police station where all the female officers are drop-dead gorgeous and their male counterparts similarly stunningly handsome – with the exception of a handful of bald, overweight and irascible senior officers. Charles told me that although he had had bit parts in movies before, this was the first time he'd broken into a Hollywood big-budget film, and he was clearly eager to do well and terrified of making a mess of things.

He was a very good-looking guy with a youthful face that made him look ten years younger than his real age. He appeared to have an open and friendly personality, although I got the feeling he maybe wasn't all that sincere. I could see where Scott was coming from with his theory that he might be gay, but I had my doubts. What I found strange was that if he really was gay, I couldn't see why he hadn't acknowledged it. In this day and age, and in his chosen field in particular, the days of stigma were surely long gone. He was wearing the same red and yellow striped pantaloons as Scott and the others, but this time accompanied by a baggy white linen blouse-like garment that gaped open to expose his hairless chest, and I could see the appeal he might have to members of either sex.

I asked him the same questions I had asked the others, but he was unable, or unwilling, to dish any dirt on any of his fellow actors or the crew. I didn't blame him. He was just starting out in the movies after all, and he needed to keep everybody onside. We chatted for a while, but I got nothing out of him.

By the time I had finished with him, it was almost five o'clock and I remembered the note on Dizzy's schedule about Selena Gardner's hair appointment. I decided to try her now in the hope of getting to her before the appointment started but as it turned out, I was too late. When I got to her trailer, I found somebody else waiting patiently outside the door. This was a young woman with tattooed forearms and some of the longest fingernails I had ever seen, carrying a hefty bag in one hand. She told me in a low voice that she was the hairstylist and that she was waiting to be admitted. As we spoke it became clear that Miss Gardner was engaged in what sounded like a furious argument with somebody inside her trailer and, from what I'd just been told, I had little doubt that it was likely to be the director, Emmy. I decided that the best course of action was a strategic retreat, so I set off in search of the producer, but not before I had inspected the neat hole punched in Miss Gardner's door by the arrow discovered the previous morning.

I found a similar hole punched in the side of the producer's trailer. I was just about to knock on the door when I remembered what Scott Norris had told me about the producer's germ phobia and dislike of animals, so I went over to Dizzy's place to ask if she could keep an eye on Oscar for a few minutes. The door was ajar, so I just tapped on it and looked in. To my surprise, I found she was not alone. Young heartthrob, Charles Vincent, had relinquished his trailer and was perched on the table in front of her and they appeared to be deep in conversation. As I opened the door, I saw a familiar look flash across both faces. I've seen enough looks like that in my time to recognise it as guilt.

'Sorry to disturb you, Dizzy, but would you mind looking after Oscar for me while I go and see the producer?'

She agreed readily and I left the happy Labrador being fussed over by both of them. As I walked back to Gabriel Lyons's trailer, I reflected on that momentary flash of guilt on their faces. Could it be that these two had something to do with the arrows and the threats, or might Charles not be gay after all, and I had interrupted a lovers' tryst? Alternatively, maybe they had just been slagging off some other member of the crew – or me – and had been afraid of being overheard.

When I got to the producer's trailer, I knocked and had to wait almost a minute for a reply, although I could hear him moving around inside. Finally, just as I was about to knock again, the door opened, and I was confronted by a figure who corresponded far more closely to my idea of what a Hollywood producer should look like. He was short, chubby, red-faced and he looked stressed. He didn't have a cigar, but I felt sure he was the kind of guy who would have smoked them – although maybe I was just subscribing to a stereotype. Unlike his staff, he was wearing a modern suit, collar and tie. Evidently the directive to wear Renaissance costume at all times didn't apply to the boss. He stared down at me for a second or two with thinly veiled lack of interest.

'Yes?' Not a lot of the milk of human kindness in his greeting.

'My name's Dan Armstrong. I've been hired to investigate the arrows and the threats.'

'Okay, so investigate.' He stepped back and it looked as though he was about to slam the door in my face, so I acted quickly.

'I wonder if I could ask you a few questions, Mr Lyons. I'll try to be as quick as I can.'

I heard him sigh. 'Okay, come in. Just make it quick.'

I did as ordered and was about to sit down on the plush-looking sofa – probably best not to refer to it as a casting couch – when he tut-tutted and pointed to an upright chair over to one side. It was clear that he wanted me to keep my distance and to remember my place. I sat down and tried to get through the questions as fast as I could so I could get away. First impressions count, and my first impression of the producer had not endeared him to me one bit.

'Can I ask, Mr Lyons, if you have any idea why you're getting these threats?'

'No idea.'

'None at all?'

'I said no, and I meant no. That's what you're here to find out.'

I'd come up against many much harder-nosed people in my time and I knew that two could play at that game, so I stood up. 'Right, well, thank you for your time, Mr Lyons. I'll leave you alone. I must admit that I'm surprised, though.'

'Surprised, why?'

'In your position I'd be worried, very worried. It's not every day that people receive death threats. Anyway, if you don't want to cooperate that's your funeral... at least, I hope it won't be.'

He stopped me before I reached the door. 'Okay, okay, I hear what you're saying. Sit the hell back down and I'll answer your questions. Do what you have to do but make it quick. I have a lot on my plate.'

I deliberately sat down on the sofa rather than the chair and took a closer look at him. He certainly looked stressed, and I wondered if that just came with the job or whether there was something in particular troubling him. I decided to give him a series of yes/no questions to speed things along.

'You've been filming here for barely a week and you're leaving at the end of next week?'

'Yes.'

'But you've had people over here for a month or so, getting things ready?'

'Yes.'

'But the threats have only started since you started filming?'

'Yes.'

'As far as you're aware, the only threats have been these five that came attached to arrows?'

'Yes.'

'And you have no idea who might be behind them?'

'No.'

I moved on to something a bit more involved. 'Would you say this is a happy set?'

'Happy, in what way?'

'Are your actors and crew happy here? Is there any friction?'

'What the hell's that got to do with anything? Are you trying to imply that these crazy arrows have been fired by somebody on the movie?'

'I'm not ruling anything out. I'll ask you again – is this a happy bunch of people?' Seeing that he was looking as though he was going to tell me to mind my own business, I added, 'Because from what I've been hearing, it isn't.'

'What's that supposed to mean?'

'How about relations between you and the director, for example? Would you say they're friendly?'

'Has he said something to you?'

'I haven't interviewed him yet.' I gave him a second or two. 'So, do you two get on well?'

'We work together. We don't need to love each other.'

'And what about the actors? Are you aware of any tensions among them?'

'No, none.' This came out a bit too quickly and he probably heard it himself as he immediately qualified his statement. 'Selena and Emmy aren't doing so well. They broke up just before we started filming back in the States.'

'Anybody else? Maybe one of the other crewmembers, not just the actors?'

'Like who?'

'Like your writer, Mr Taylor, for example. Is he happy?'

'I couldn't care less whether he's happy or not. I pay him to do a job and he has to get on with it.' He looked at his watch and his voice went up an octave. 'And, come to think of it, I'm paying you to do your job and you're wasting my valuable time, so I suggest you go off and pester somebody else.'

There was no point in flogging a dead horse, so I stood up and thanked him. He made no reply and ostentatiously returned his attention to the papers on his desk. I left him to it.

5

TUESDAY LATE AFTERNOON

This left me with the director and Selena Gardner still to be seen. I hoped that I would get more out of them. I now knew quite a lot more about the movie business than I had done this morning but had learnt precious little that might shine a light on who or what might be behind these threats.

As the big star was presumably still getting her hair done, I decided to collect my dog from Dizzy and head for the director's trailer first. I found Dizzy on her own, sitting on the couch in the trailer with the Labrador sprawled across her. Oscar had a broad canine smile on his face and looked equally happy. He wagged his tail when he saw me, but he made no attempt to get off his new friend. As I say, he's always liked the ladies. Dizzy gave me a little wave.

'Hi, Dan, please can I have your dog? I've fallen in love with him.'

'From the look on his face I reckon the feeling's mutual but, no, I'm afraid that's not going to be possible. He's my best buddy and where I go, he goes. On that note, I'm off to see the director and I thought I could relieve you of the burden of looking after Oscar first.'

'Let me keep him a bit longer. Please, pretty please...' She put her palms together and pleaded like a little girl. 'It's so nice to have someone so warm and friendly and not shouting at me to do something.'

I gave her a comforting smile. 'I suppose you get a lot of that.'

'From dawn to dusk.' She sighed.

'And who shouts the loudest?'

'Mr Lyons without question, although since Emmy and Selena are always rowing, they've both been in a foul mood most of the time.'

'On that subject, it sounds to me as though Selena dumped Emmy, rather than the other way round; is that right?'

'You're probably right. That would explain why he's so uptight.'

Hell hath no fury like a film director scorned, maybe? Had these crazy arrows been a way of scaring his ex-girlfriend... or worse?

'I'm on my way to see Emmy now.'

'You couldn't do me a favour first, could you?' Dizzy waved her hands over the Labrador snoozing happily on her lap. 'I'm dying for a coffee but I don't want to disturb Oscar as he's so settled.' Settled? He looked as if he had put down roots, but I let her go on. 'You wouldn't be a dear and get me a double espresso, would you? With Mr Lyons coming soon I need a bit of a booster.'

'Of course. Sugar? None? Okay.'

I went out and made my way across to the refreshment truck, which was still doing good business with a crowd of mainly men in medieval costumes sitting around it. I was in the queue, waiting to order Dizzy's coffee, when there was a thud, followed by an outburst of shouts and at least one scream. I pushed through the handful of stunned spectators and found Duggie Ogilvie rooted to the spot by the food truck's blackboard with today's specials written on it. Alongside him were Charles Vincent and Martin Taylor and all three had their eyes fixed on the blackboard. Bang in the middle of it was a steel crossbow bolt with blue and yellow flights. It had struck with enough force to drive it right into the timber and if it had hit Duggie, or any of the others, it could have been lethal.

I checked the angle at which the arrow had struck the board and looked back along the path it must have travelled. The perimeter fence was only about thirty yards from here and I scanned the area closely to see if there was any sign of the archer. All I could see was a young mother with a child in a buggy and an elderly man with an equally elderly-looking pug on a lead. In front of them was a small red and white striped tent, presumably belonging to workmen who were digging up the pavement. As my eyes landed on it I thought I caught a movement in the canvas. There wasn't a breath of wind so I set off towards it at a run.

Needless to say, my progress was halted when I reached the fence. I was looking around for a ladder, a table or anything to use as a means of climbing over it when I caught sight of a figure disappearing into the distance, clearly attempting to use the labourers' tent as a shield. He or she was only in my line of sight for a second or two before reaching a narrow alley between two buildings and disappearing. What I had seen, however, was a bulky object in the figure's hand – presumably the crossbow. I looked around me but there was no sign of security guards and a glance back in the direction of the food truck showed the tables empty as the film actors and crew who had been clustering around it had wisely taken to their heels. I looked back through the wire fence but knew that by the time I ran around to the main gate and back again, the archer would be long gone. I gave a frustrated snort and made my way back to Dizzy's caravan.

This time Oscar's beauty sleep was rudely interrupted as Dizzy immediately extricated herself from under him when I told her what had happened. I asked her to spread the word that there had been another attack while I made for the main entrance. Once there, I told Big Jim to do a careful check of the whole site and a headcount and list of names of everybody on the lot so as to be sure that the mystery attacker hadn't hit anybody else. I then went out and hurried around to the workmen's tent. It was immediately obvious that this was indeed the spot from which the arrow had been fired. The workmen had closed up for the day but somebody had slit the leather straps that closed the tent door. The inside was empty and an open manhole indicated where they had been working. Of particular interest to me was a slit cut in the canvas wall, looking out towards the film encampment from where he or she must have fired.

I made a close search of the inside of the tent without finding anything. The bare earth around the manhole contained numerous boot prints but nothing out of the ordinary in a working environment. Unable to find any clues inside, I went out and stood with my back to the slit in the tent wall and looked directly at the refreshment van where two or three people were beginning to reassemble. One thing was immediately obvious: firing from here would have involved ensuring that the crossbow arrow went through one of the narrow gaps between the wires of the fence. No mean feat.

I did a rough calculation and stepped over to check the fence in the area through which the arrow must have passed. Sure enough, there was a slight, but distinctly brand new, shiny nick in the metal at the right height, which indicated to me that the arrow had just caught the wire as it was fired and this had presumably affected the precision of the aim. It was a sobering thought that, without that slightest of touches, the arrow might have gone straight into the chest of any one of the people by the van – including me. Murder had been averted by a whisker.

One thing was for sure: I no longer had any doubts as to whether or not this whole bow-and-arrow story was a hoax. Whoever had done this had intended to kill.

For now, there was little I could do so I decided to finish off with interviewing the remaining members of the film company in the hope of unearthing some reason why these attacks were happening. I saw Max at the gate on my way back inside the compound and asked him to ensure that I got a copy of the list of names of people on site, just in case the attacker had been a member of the cast or crew who had slipped out.

I headed for the director's trailer. When I got there, I found the door open and saw Emiliano Donizetti, wearing the same yellow and red striped clothing as the others. He looked as if he was in his late thirties or early forties, with dark hair and a tanned complexion. He was crouching down, reaching into his fridge for something and not finding it. As I was about to announce my presence, he slammed the fridge door in frustration, muttered a couple of expletives and stood up, turning towards me and seeing me for the first time.

'Are you looking for somebody?' Less acerbic than the greeting I had received from the producer, but not exactly welcoming. Mind you, if he had just come out of a massive argument with his ex-girlfriend, I could sympathise.

'Hi, Mr Donizetti, my name's Dan Armstrong and I'm investigating the death threats.'

I saw him take a long, calming breath before replying and when he did, it was in a less confrontational tone. 'Yes, of course. Dizzy told me to expect you. Come in and make yourself comfortable. I would offer you a glass of ice water but there doesn't appear to be any.'

'That's kind, but I'm fine, thanks.' I had a feeling Dizzy would be getting another earbashing about the lack of cold water. Concentrating on the interview, I told him about the recent attack and he looked genuinely appalled.

'Another arrow? And you say it just missed a whole bunch of people? That's unbelievable.'

I asked him if he had any idea who might be behind the death threats. His answer didn't differ from what the others had said, so I tried another tack. 'Does it seem strange to you that the threatening notes are written in English rather than Italian? We are in Italy, after all.'

He shook his head. 'Not really. There are very few Italian speakers among us. Presumably whoever's been writing these threats wants to be sure we get the message.'

'What about you? You have an Italian name. Do you speak the language?'

He smiled. 'I picked up a smattering of Sicilian dialect from my grandparents when I was growing up in the Bronx, but apart from ordering pizza, I'm useless. Luckily most everybody here in Florence speaks English – or, at least, the ones working in hotels and restaurants do.'

'I believe you and the producer don't get on.'

'Is that what he said?' I almost smiled to hear him have the same reaction as his boss.

'No, just stuff I've picked up while interviewing the others.'

There was a brief pause before he nodded. 'All right, so we don't have a warm cosy relationship, but I get the job done and he can't say I don't.'

'Talking of warm cosy relationships, I went past Selena Gardner's trailer a little while ago and I couldn't help hearing an argument taking place. How's that relationship going?'

His expression hardened. 'These are some pretty personal

questions you're asking there, buddy. Are they really important or are you just looking for some juicy gossip to sell to the press?'

'My lips are sealed. I guarantee that. I've been hired to investigate these death threats and I need to have full knowledge of the background to this movie and everybody involved in it. I'm sorry to ask difficult questions, but I used to be a detective inspector and it's hard to break the habits of a lifetime.'

To my surprise and relief, he smiled. 'Got it. I could tell you were a cop or an ex-cop. Anyway, you're right, Selena and I used to be a couple. We split up not that long ago and things between us can get a bit tense on occasions.' He caught and held my eye for a moment. 'But that stays between you and me, right?'

'Of course, and I'm sorry to hear that. One or two people told me that she thinks you used her to get you this job. Any truth in that?'

He shook his head. 'No truth that I used her. She gave me her backing and of course that helped, but I didn't ask for it; she offered. I liked her a lot – I still do – and I thought the relationship might go the distance. Yes, she's a bit older than me, but *I* felt we were good together.'

'But that's not what she thought?'

He shrugged. 'Apparently not. It's tough being a household name. I get that. She's constantly surrounded by sycophants and vultures and the longer you spend in that world, the more your barriers go up and the less you trust people's true motives. For some reason she convinced herself that I was just another leech, feeding off her, and it hurt.' He looked up and produced a little smile. 'But I'm a big boy. I'll get over it. Besides, I have a movie to make.'

I gave him a smile in return. 'Thank you for your honesty, Mr Donizetti, and, like I say, I'm sorry how things have worked out for you.'

'Emmy. Everybody calls me Emmy.'

I stood up. 'Thanks for your time, Emmy. I'm off to see Miss Gardner now. Should I be wearing armour?'

'She's a very good actress. Trust me, she'll be delightful. She has a lot of experience at hiding her feelings.'

6

TUESDAY LATE AFTERNOON / EVENING

The director was right. Although I found the famous actress in curlers, she gave me a welcoming smile and invited me in. If I hadn't heard the argument a few minutes earlier with my own ears and hadn't learnt that she had recently split up from her partner, I wouldn't have believed her to be anything but relaxed and happy. Yes, she really was a good actress. She sent the hair stylist off to get herself a coffee and asked me to sit down. Considering she was wearing what looked like a dressing gown, she was still stunningly beautiful, and the curlers actually accentuated, rather than diminished, her beauty. The skin of her face and neck could have been that of a twenty-year-old and her eyes, in particular, were almost magnetic with a weird blue-green shimmer to them. A quick check on Google had told me that she was fifty-three, only three years younger than I was, but she could have passed for half that age – and that was more than could be said about me.

I told her what had just happened and then explained that I was interviewing everybody in the hope of working out who might be behind the arrows, and her expression mirrored that of the director.

'Another arrow! What on earth is going on? The arrow that hit my door scared the life out of me. It came right through, you know.' She extended an elegant finger towards the door, and I could see the hole where the crossbow bolt had penetrated through from outside to inside. 'If that'd been me, rather than the door, it could have killed me. Tell me, do you think it's somebody here on the lot who's responsible? Presumably if today's arrow came from outside it seems likely it was somebody unconnected with the movie, doesn't it?'

I answered honestly. 'At this stage, I really don't know, but my gut feeling is that it's got to be somebody connected with the movie in some way. I don't yet know who was inside and who was outside the compound just now, but it could of course be somebody acting on behalf of somebody here.'

'But why? Surely it's in everybody's interests to get the movie made. These threats could have the opposite effect. Isn't it more likely that they come from somebody who wants the movie to fail?'

She had a point. This thought had already occurred to me, and I had been struggling to find a motive for anybody here to want to slow or even stop the film's progress. 'I know what you mean. It's a real puzzle. Can you think of anybody around here or any person or group of people outside who might benefit from the film failing?'

She paused for thought. 'Other filmmakers might get a wry laugh out of it if we had to quit, but death threats are no laughing matter. Otherwise, who?'

'Gabriel Lyons is the producer and so I suppose he's got the most to lose if the film fails. Can you think of anybody who might have a grudge against him in particular?'

'Gabriel can be a pain at times but I can't think of any specific enemies he might have in the industry. No, it's a real mystery.'

I decided not to broach the subject of her defunct relationship with the director and returned her to the hands of the hair stylist. On the way back to Dizzy's trailer, I couldn't help thinking how surreal it was to have been in the presence of a cinema goddess, and I was already mentally making a few changes to my current manuscript to include a ravishing beauty like Selena.

By the time I got back to collect my dog, it was almost six and Dizzy was already bustling about, getting everything ready for the rushes meeting. Oscar was sprawled on the couch like a Roman emperor, clearly enjoying the pampering he had been receiving. He gave me a lazy wag of the tail but didn't deign to get up. I noticed that Dizzy had opened all the windows, presumably to remove any lingering aroma of Labrador before the producer arrived. I thanked her and queried if I could join the crew on set the following day. Her answer indicated that she had already heard from Martin Taylor, the writer.

'Of course you can, but it's all change for tomorrow. We're going to be filming around one the Medici castles out in the country north of here.' She checked her clipboard. 'I don't know how you pronounce it: Cafaggiolo. We were scheduled to go there next Monday but it's been brought forward.'

That sounded good. I'd heard of this famous castle but had never been to see it. 'Terrific, and it's pronounced *Ca*, like cat, *fagg* like badge and *iolo* at the end like raviolo, the singular of ravioli. What time should I get there?'

She repeated the name a couple of times in a creditable Italian accent and then answered. 'For location shooting the crew normally leaves from here early so they have time to get set up, and the cast and director will follow on, leaving here at nine, be there around half nine.'

'If anything happens between now and then please ring me – you have my number – and I'll come right away. I'd like to think that the attacker has been scared off – at least for now – but we can't take any risks. If nothing more happens I'll meet you at Cafaggiolo in the morning. I'll try and get up there ahead of the cast so I can check the place out.'

'Great. By the way, the guys from the local security company are coming any time now to rig up CCTV cameras around the perimeter. Hopefully they'll pick up anything that might happen tonight. Now I have something for you.' Dizzy swung round to set down her clipboard, but in so doing managed to hit the carafe of water she had just placed on the table, tipping it over and flooding the tabletop. As we looked on, the carafe itself rolled inexorably over the edge and I was just able to make a dive and managed to catch it before it shattered on the floor.

'Oh, Dan, thank you. I'm so sorry.' Her face was bright red with embarrassment once again and I was beginning to understand how appropriate her nickname was. I realised that this sort of thing was probably a regular occurrence with this walking disaster. I helped mop up the water, which had miraculously missed most of the seats, until the scene was once more back to normal. I was about to leave her to it when she reached down and produced a bag and handed it to me.

'Your costume. It should fit but if it doesn't, just let me know and I'll get it altered.' She must have spotted the expression on my face. 'Don't worry. You've seen what it's like here: everybody else is in costume so you don't need to feel self-conscious.'

'That's easy for you to say; you haven't seen my knees.'

'You'll be just fine.'

'I wish I shared your confidence, but okay, I'll be wearing this get-up tomorrow. I'd better head off now as Oscar needs a walk. See you in the morning.' I gave her a wave and called my dog, who reluctantly relinquished his regal position on the couch. Dizzy caught my arm and gave it a friendly squeeze.

'Thanks, Dan, for all your help.'

'I haven't done a lot so far, but let's hope my presence here on the set dissuades the crazy archer from trying again.' Mind you, I told myself, a fat lot of good my presence here this afternoon had done.

Oscar and I had only just said goodbye to Big Jim at the gate and were making our way back to my office when my phone rang. It was Virgilio.

'*Ciao*, Dan. Fancy a drink?'

'Absolutely, and I can give you the latest news at the same time.'

We arranged to meet outside one of the cafés in the centre. We were already in the first week of October and the days were growing shorter. Although it was barely six o'clock, the shadows were already lengthening, but the sun during the day had raised the air temperature to a very acceptable level and my walk through the city's historic heart was a delight. Florence was still busy, but the overwhelming mass of humanity that had packed the city over the summer had greatly diminished, and my dog and I were now able to make our way through the streets without constantly having to stop and squeeze past groups of noisy tourists. For people who live and work in historic cities like Florence it's a double-edged sword: yes, you have beauty, culture and history all around you, but you also have the crowds.

Thought of swords – double-edged or not – made me think of our phantom archer again. What I still couldn't work out was what possible motivation there might be behind these threats. As Selena Gardner had said, there seemed little benefit to anybody involved with the production of the movie for it to be delayed or even abandoned, but who else might want to do something like that? I seriously doubted whether it might be organised crime or a competitor film company but if not them, then who? Maybe Scott

Norris had been right when he had put the threats down to what he referred to as crazies.

The café where we were to meet up wasn't far from the main San Lorenzo market. As I walked down there past buildings that had been standing for half a millennium, I found myself doing what I often did here in Florence: I tried imagining the city at the height of the Renaissance when legendary names like Michelangelo, Botticelli or Leonardo da Vinci had walked along these very same streets. It felt surreal to be following in the footsteps of these colossi and I was feeling quite far away for a few moments before my dog suddenly stopped to pee on a lamppost, almost jerking my arm out of its socket and returning me to the twenty-first century with a bang.

The café was directly behind the impressive bulk of the Medici Chapel, built onto the far end of the basilica of San Lorenzo. This vast stone edifice boasted of the wealth and power of the Medici family and this thought took my mind back yet again to the movie. One thing was for sure; the Medici would have instantly identified with the jealousies, rivalries and intrigue on the film set. After all, Niccolò Machiavelli himself once worked in Florence and dedicated his famous book, *The Prince*, to members of the Medici family. In those days, arguments were often resolved by means of the sword, the dagger or the arrow.

Maybe nothing much had changed.

I was shaken out of my meditations when Oscar suddenly spotted Virgilio sitting at a table outside the café and started off at a gallop, dragging me across the street towards him. Virgilio shook hands with me with his left hand while his right was occupied in dissuading Oscar from climbing onto his lap. Oscar was good friends with the police inspector and so was I.

'*Ciao*, Dan. I ordered two beers. If you don't want one, I'll happily drink both. It's been one of those days.'

'A beer sounds great, thanks, and I'll buy the next round.' I picked up a bottle, clinked it against his, and took a very welcome mouthful as I stretched my legs and leant back. 'So tell me, what's been causing you grief today?'

'We've had a visit from a group of VIPs from the ministry in Rome. The *questore* himself has been clucking around like a broody hen and it's been impossible to get on with any work.' Virgilio worked at the main police station, the *questura*, and the *questore* was the equivalent of the chief constable in the UK, so a very big cheese. Virgilio took a big mouthful of beer. 'How're things with you?'

'I've been to the movies; well, to see the people involved in making the movie.'

'What did you think of our friend Miss Hindenburg?'

'She's a nice kid and she lived up to her disastrous name, but she's very efficient.'

'How did it go? Have you cracked the case yet?'

'It was interesting, more for the different squabbles and rival-ries going on between the different members of the cast and crew, but I'm no closer to knowing who's behind the threats.' I went on to tell him about this afternoon's attack and saw his expression harden.

'That's getting a bit close for comfort. I wish I could spare you a couple of my officers but we're stretched as it is. Any idea who the figure you saw might have been?'

'None at all. Before starting my interviews I had a hunch that the culprit would turn out to be somebody I would speak to today, but that's looking less and less likely, and not just because of that figure I saw.

'Why can't it be one of them or somebody employed by one of them?'

'Firstly, from the list I just got from the security guards, all the major players were *inside* the compound when this afternoon's arrow struck but, apart from that, I'm struggling for motive. As far as I can tell, it's in everybody's interests to get the movie made.'

We chatted some more, and he reminded me that I'd promised to play tennis with him on Sunday. I invited him and Lina to come out to my place for a barbecue afterwards. I'd recently bought a little house in the hills to the south of Florence and I was still basking in the first flush of enjoyment of its beauty and antiquity – it was at least several hundred years old – and its location on a hill amid iconic Tuscan cypress trees. As for the barbecue, my talents in the kitchen had improved since my divorce but I had no illusions about ever appearing on *MasterChef*. At least with a barbie I was on fairly safe ground – I just needed to try not to burn the meat, and everything should work out fine. Lots of Chianti would also help.

7

WEDNESDAY MORNING

Next morning, I checked my messages but there was nothing from Dizzy, so I hoped this meant there had been no further arrows or threats. After taking Oscar for a walk, I reluctantly pulled on my tights and pantaloons and immediately discovered I had a problem. These things had no pockets, so the compromise I came up with was to put on my tennis shorts underneath and resign myself to having to grope around in my pants for my car keys, phone or a tissue. This also made that area of my anatomy pretty warm, and I began to see what Scott Norris had meant about discomfort.

Still, the clothes fitted remarkably well, including the tunic, which buttoned up the front –needless to say, zips hadn't existed in Renaissance days – and I even found the tights unexpectedly comfortable. The ensemble included a floppy flat black hat that drooped down to one side but was quite comfy. I discarded my trainers in favour of a pair of slip-on brown leather loafers and had to admit that the final result looked surprisingly authentic; totally ridiculous to a twenty-first-century eye, but authentic. I took a photo of my reflection in the mirror and sent it to Tricia back in England. Somehow, I had a feeling my appearance would appeal to my daughter's warped sense of humour. No prizes for guessing where she got that from.

I loaded Oscar into the car, and drove north, desperately praying that I didn't get a puncture on the way. Changing a tyre while dressed like one of Henry VIII's lackies wasn't an appealing prospect. Thankfully it wasn't too far. From my place it took half an hour to get to the autostrada turn-off and another ten minutes from there to the Medici castle of Cafaggiolo.

The previous night I'd called Paul Wilson, my former sergeant, now promoted to inspector, and asked him if he could take a look at the file dealing with the killing of Duggie Ogilvie's boyfriend. He asked me how my new career as a private eye was working out, and I told him about the pasta-throwing incident at lunchtime and the red tights. Once he'd stopped laughing, he picked up on what I'd said about the movie.

'They were saying on the TV that Selena Gardner's over in Florence shooting a movie right now. It's not the film you're involved with by any chance, is it? I don't suppose you've been lucky enough to see her, have you?'

'Funny you should say that, Paul, I was sitting in her trailer with her only a few hours ago.'

'Wow, some people get all the luck! Is she as gorgeous in real life as she is in the movies? I've had a crush on her since school.' Paul was quite a bit younger than me, so he apparently had the same attraction for older women as Emmy– although in Selena's case, a very special older woman. 'And how did you manage to get to see her?'

I gave him a brief rundown of the arrows and threats and he sounded amazed. 'Gabriel Lyons is a respected producer, and everybody loves Selena Gardner. I can't believe anybody would want to kill them. Who do you think's behind it?'

'I wish I knew. Scott Norris told me that threats aren't uncommon, so maybe it's just some crazy person.'

'By coincidence we had a murder here a month ago that was done with a crossbow bolt. They can be lethal. We nailed the perpetrator by checking where he got the arrows from. Our forensics people found a batch number on the plastic vanes and traced the stock back to a little importer in Sheffield'

'Vanes?'

'You know, the flights that make the bolt fly straight. Technical term I learnt recently.'

'I'm afraid that won't work for us. The bolts used here have feather vanes. No maker's name.'

'Feathers, eh? That's fancy. Shame. Well, you make sure you keep Selena Gardner safe. I'm counting on you. And if you could get me a photo or an autograph, I'll be in your debt. If you can get me a date with her, you can have my car.'

'If you can check out the Ogilvie file, I'm the one who'll be in your debt.'

The Medici castle at Cafaggiolo was stunning. I'm a sucker for medieval and Renaissance architecture and this was one of the finest castles I'd seen since I'd been over here in Italy. Set on a flat site among the tree-covered foothills of the Apennines, it had been built in the middle of the fifteenth century and had allegedly been one of Lorenzo the Magnificent's favourite residences, particularly when he and his entourage wanted to escape the stifling heat of summer down in Florence. It was a masterpiece of mighty stone walls, crenelations and arches, with an imposing tower rising above the entrance. As I drove past it, I could imagine the colour and grandeur of the medieval court and I definitely approved of the choice of Cafaggiolo as the backdrop for the movie. The murder mystery I was writing was set over here in Tuscany so I very quickly decided to include this place in it. It was too good to leave out.

The film crew were already there when I arrived at half past eight in the morning and I found them busy setting up. A broad grassy area sandwiched between the castle and the steeply sloping woods was evidently where the action was going to take place. I spared a thought for Martin Taylor, the writer, and hoped he'd been able to rewrite the scene without having to burn too much midnight oil. The edge of the field, alongside a dirt track, was lined with almost a dozen vehicles, from vans disgorging cameras and other technical movie equipment, to horseboxes and a truck delivering portable toilets.

I parked at the end of the line and opened the back door to let Oscar out into the fresh air. A team was erecting a pair of small marquees over towards the wooded hillside and others were unloading chairs and tables. I was beginning to appreciate just why it is that movies cost so many millions to produce. Crew swarmed all over the scene and the ubiquitous food van was already there, hard at work providing free breakfasts to everybody. Not wishing to be left out, I went over and queued with Oscar for a coffee for me, and a biscuit or two for him. I could have had a bacon and egg roll if I'd asked for it, but I thought I should set a good example for my dog.

The good news as far as I was concerned was that virtually all the men I could see were wearing the same yellow and red costumes. Although I was still feeling pretty foolish, nobody appeared to notice my outfit and I soon began to relax. A bit.

I spotted Max, the young Italian security guard, and he had a bit of news for me. 'I thought you might be interested in something I just heard this morning as I was coming on duty. I know Elvis, one of the night team, pretty well.'

'Elvis?'

Max grinned. 'His parents refused to give him a catholic name, so he says it was a choice between Beelzebub and Elvis. He got off lightly. Anyway, he told me that around midnight he spotted a figure over on the far side of the lot, just on the other side of the fence. He went over to see what the guy was doing but as soon as the man caught sight of Elvis, he turned and disappeared.'

'Didn't he think to tell somebody about that?'

'He told his supervisor, but as the man hadn't done anything wrong and had gone off straight away, they decided it was unimportant. Maybe it was just some guy out for a walk or somebody curious to see what was going on with all the trailers. I'm afraid nobody told them about the figure you saw yesterday, and I was wondering if it might be the same man.'

'Or woman. I didn't get a good look at the person I saw. Are you sure what your friend saw was a man?.'

He shook his head. 'Now you come to mention it, I've a feeling Elvis was unsure about that as well. It was dark of course, but he said it was a big person.'

I thanked him for passing on the information and found myself wondering if last night's CCTV footage would reveal this figure or whether it had just been a coincidence. Maybe it hadn't even been the same person who had fired the arrow at the food truck. It was probably common knowledge around the area that the parking lot was being used by a film company and that was bound to arouse curiosity. Still, it did add credence to the possibility of the bowman being from outside the film company.

Hank, one of the crewmembers I'd interviewed yesterday, was standing by the van in the same medieval garb, and he talked me through what was going to happen today. I remembered suppressing a smile the previous day when he'd told me that his title on the set was 'best boy'. Considering that he looked older than I was, I thought that was pushing it a bit. He apparently worked for the 'gaffer', who was in charge of lighting, and when I remarked that today's cloudless sky and bright sunshine would probably render artificial lighting superfluous, he was quick to set me straight.

'Lighting's vital. You can have too much as well as too little light. We're setting up over there.' He stretched out his arm and pointed towards the edge of the wooded hillside. 'In an hour or so that area will be in shade, and we need to have everything rigged in readiness for the action.'

'And the action's going to consist of what? I gather this is a brand-new scene.'

'Not completely new; we were scheduled to come here next week, but Emmy decided to bring it forward and to change some of the action and some of the lines. I believe somebody's going to be shot with an arrow.' He hastened to clarify. 'Not in real life, you understand. By the way, any developments in your investigation?'

'None so far. I didn't get a call overnight so maybe yesterday's archer has thought twice about carrying on. They say that art imitates life – well, I hope life doesn't start imitating art. People being shot with arrows in the movies is all well and good, but not when it's for real. Tell me more about what's planned for today.'

'The main characters are out hunting, and there's an assassination attempt on the main man – that's Scott's character. We're just waiting for the horses now, God help us.' He grinned at me. 'Remember the old saying: never work with animals or children. I'm just hoping none of them decide to charge our equipment. I've seen horses do all manner of damage in my time.'

In the distance, I spotted a minibus bumping down the track towards us, and when it stopped, the first person to emerge from it was Dizzy in her medieval robe, followed by a dozen of the minor actors, all decked out in red and yellow. I swallowed the last of my coffee, said farewell to Hank, and headed across to ask the all-important question.

'Morning, Dizzy. Any more arrows or threats? Anything on the CCTV? Max said the night guards saw a big figure lurking in the shadows.'

'No, nobody said anything about that. I assume the camera didn't pick him or her up. The security company have been monitoring it and they say there was nothing untoward going on, but I'll give them a call and get them to check with their guy just in case. Let's hope that's the end of it.' I saw her take a good hard look at me in my gaudy clothes. 'The costume fits well. You really look the part. I'll ask Emmy to make sure you appear in some of the scenes.' She pointed downwards. 'Just two things to remember: make sure your phone's on mute and take your watch off. Have you found the side pocket for your valuables?'

When I shook my head, she pointed out a tight little fissure set into the side seam, which I hadn't spotted. This opened into a tiny pocket just big enough for my watch and car keys. However, I knew that if I felt my phone vibrate, I would have to start fiddling about in my pants. Just to reinforce the message, my phone started ringing and I scrabbled to retrieve it, doing my best to ignore the amused look on Dizzy's face. It was Tricia calling from England. My daughter and I usually spoke once a week.

'Hi, Dad, or should I call you milord? Thanks for the photo. You certainly look the part. Does this mean you're going to be in the movies?'

I told her that I might appear in the background of one or two of the shots, but not to start telling everybody her father was Hollywood's latest discovery. We chatted and she asked me how I was getting on with the new book and then she gave me a progress report on her life. She and Shaun had recently got engaged and all looked rosy on that front, and she also mentioned that she'd seen Helen, her mum. Relations between me and my ex-wife had remained reasonably amicable now that we had both accepted the finality of the divorce. By the sound of it she might have found herself a new man, and I wished them well. I really did. Whether there was a new woman out there for *me* remained to be seen.

8

WEDNESDAY LATE MORNING

In the course of the morning, the scene was set. The producer, director and the big-name actors arrived and took their places. Cameras, lights and sound-recording equipment were prepared and Emmy finally called, 'Action' through a loudhailer. From behind the castle, three horsemen appeared and galloped towards us, the hooves drumming on the grassy surface of the field into which Monday night's rain had already disappeared almost without trace. When they were about fifty yards away, they gradually slowed, and I was surprised to hear Emmy shout, 'Cut' through his loudhailer. The three horsemen reined in and climbed off their mounts.

Scott Norris, Charles Vincent and the 'bad guy', Duggie Ogilvie, emerged from their seats in the shade, walked over and took the places of the stuntmen on horseback, and the scene restarted. As the three of them trotted sedately towards the cameras, I was impressed to see Duggie managing to look quite at home on the horse. He was, as before, dressed all in black, while the other two were in red and yellow, and the three of them looked indistinguishable from the riders they had replaced. All three horses were also decked in very convincing brightly coloured medieval livery and behaved themselves impeccably – for now. I spared a thought for Hank and his expensive lighting equipment and hoped none of the horses would decide to misbehave.

The scenes continued one after another, and a bit later, Selena appeared on a beautiful white horse. She was riding side-saddle, which always looks to me as if the rider is about to topple off backwards, but she made it seem easy. She looked as beautiful as ever and I felt sure Paul back in London would have approved. I pulled out my phone and took a couple of photos to send to him. I had just pressed 'Send' when I heard my name. It was Dizzy.

'It's your big moment, Dan. Emmy wants you in the crowd for this next scene. I'll look after Oscar while you go and do what the director orders.'

Feeling remarkably apprehensive, I checked that my phone was on mute, stuffed it into the shorts beneath my pantaloons along with my watch, adjusted the rakish angle of my hat and walked out into the open along with another dozen or so extras and bit-part actors and a few of the crew, where we were instructed to form a reception committee for Selena. The instructions from the director were for 'adulation' and 'adoration'. I did my best to join in the roar and waved excitedly no fewer than five times before Emmy declared himself satisfied and moved on to another scene. I had had my moment in the sun.

A bit later that morning, a car arrived, bringing a reporter and a photographer from the celebrity magazine. At that point Donny Lopez, the PR director, took over. I had yet to interview him – he had been in Rome the previous day doing the round of the media outlets – but I recognised him from Dizzy's description: a tall man around my age with black hair, greying at the temples, and an infectious smile, positively exuding bonhomie. He and Loredana, his glamorous blonde assistant, stuck to the two journalists like limpets and were clearly doing their best to impress them. Of course, I reminded myself, publicity was the lifeblood of the movie industry, and it brought to mind an uncharitable thought I had already had before yesterday's attack, that maybe all these arrows and threats might just have been some form of publicity stunt. I now knew better but I resolved to interview Mr Lopez later on to see whether he had any idea that might help identify the mystery bowman.

I looked on as Donny and Loredana set up interviews with Scott and Selena, as well as with the director and producer, but from what Martin Taylor had told me it was unlikely the writer would be introduced to the journalists. Considering that without him the movie wouldn't exist, I could understand his frustration. It occurred to me that over my years at the Met, I had come across cases where intense frustration had led to something more serious, including threats – although never delivered attached to arrows. Might the source of the threats be Taylor? But he had been among those so nearly hit by the arrow yesterday. Thought of writing reminded me that my first whodunnit would be coming out in the spring and I would then finally be able to call myself a published author. It felt good.

Lunch was served at one o'clock and Dizzy informed me that they only had a handful of scenes left to shoot that afternoon. They had made good progress in the course of the morning and even Gabriel Lyons was looking less stressed.

Lunch itself was an interesting indication of the pecking order and the divided loyalties on set. There were a dozen separate tables, and the seating plan was instructive. Gabriel Lyons and Dizzy occupied one table, Dizzy scribbling orders onto a pad, as the producer fired them at her. From the amount of notetaking going on, I had a feeling her food was likely to get cold before she had a chance to eat it, but the producer appeared not to notice. Or maybe he did, but he just didn't care. Selena Gardner and Scott Norris were on their own at another table while Emmy was on a third table, flanked by Charles Vincent and Duggie Ogilvie. Clearly relations between Emmy and Selena hadn't improved overnight. The remaining tables were occupied by other members of the cast and crew. As for me, I decided to get some food and take a seat as far away from the producer as possible, for fear that he might object to Oscar's presence.

The choices of food, too, were interesting. Selena, I noticed, just had salad. And when I say salad, I mean just lettuce, celery and a lone tomato, accompanied by a glass of water and some dry wafers. Charles and Scott were also remarkably careful in their choice of food but, of course, I reminded myself, staying in perfect physical condition for the cameras demands sacrifice. In spite of being in Italy, there was no sign of wine on the tables and all the actors looked as if they were being most abstemious – at least while shooting was taking place. I felt sure Duggie would be reaching for the Scotch once he got back to his hotel room.

As far as I could see, most of the crew were less concerned about their waistlines and were tucking into burgers and fries, accompanied by cold beers. Having long since given up worrying about my waistline I did the same. I looked for a quiet table and ended up sitting next to Martin Taylor and I asked him how the writing had gone last night. He ran a weary hand across his fore-head and sighed.

'I finished writing everything by about midnight, but then I had to send the scripts to be copied and delivered to Emmy, Gabriel and the actors. I finally got off to sleep some time around two or three o'clock.'

'That means you only got a few hours' sleep?'

'Par for the course. You'd be amazed how many rewrites there can be. I've got a bit more writing to do after lunch, and then I'm going to find myself a cool place in the woods this afternoon and catch up on my sleep.'

He told me that he'd decided to make today's assassination attempt the work of a lone bowman and he even managed a little smile. 'There actually was a real assassination attempt on Lorenzo the Magnificent. This took place inside the duomo, where a bunch of men fell on him and his group with swords and daggers, rather than arrows. That's what we were going to reproduce as an interior scene until Emmy changed his mind. Seeing as today's scene is completely made up, I thought I'd make it bows and arrows rather than swords, seeing as we're out here. At least with everything that's been happening back in the trailer park, I was able to draw on recent experience. By the way, I gather there haven't been any more arrows. Let's hope our very own crossbowman has given up.'

'I'm keeping my fingers crossed.'

A few minutes later he left me and went off to finish his work and then presumably to look for a quiet place for a snooze. His place at my table was taken shortly afterwards by Anna Galardo, the historical consultant for Florence University. Both Oscar and I were very pleased to see her. Being out in the fresh air had given her a bit of colour in her face and she was looking most appealing, probably more appealing than a potential suspect in a criminal investigation should look. She gave me a bright smile as she approached.

'Hi, can I join you?'

'Please do. I've got a few questions for you anyway.'

'That doesn't come as a surprise. Did I hear somebody say you used to be a detective inspector? Presumably you never stop asking questions.'

'Sorry, I should have specified that the only questions I have for you today are historical ones.' I went on to tell her about my attempt to write a book set at the time of the Medici but which I had subsequently ditched halfway through, although my interest in the Florentine Renaissance remained. She appeared interested.

'So did you write something else?'

'Yes, a whodunnit, set over here in Tuscany.'

'And has it been published?'

'I'm delighted to say that it's coming out next spring. A publisher in London has offered me a two-book contract.'

'Good for you. I'll have to look out for it. What's it going to be called?'

This was a bit of a sore topic. The publishers had poo-pooed my original title and were now trying to decide on something punchier that would appeal to the market. 'No title yet. Hopefully that'll be decided before long.'

'I'll have to give you my contact details. Let me know when it's coming out and I'll buy a copy.'

'Thanks, that's very kind.'

'Have you started writing the second book yet? Are you going to be able to meet the deadline?'

'I started a couple of months ago and I'm probably about half-way, so fingers crossed. What about you? Have you published anything?'

'Non-fiction only. I wrote a book about the history of Florence that came out a couple of years ago.'

'That's fascinating. What's the title?'

'It's a bit of a mouthful: *Lorenzo the Magnificent, Hero or Villain of the Medici Family.*'

'Sounds interesting.'

She smiled a charming, friendly smile that lit up her face. 'Well, it got me this job so I can't complain. I was contacted by the film company a few months back and they asked me to act as historical consultant.'

'And does your book reflect the events of the film?'

She shook her head. 'Hardly at all. My book's purely non-fiction while the film's 90 per cent a modern-day thriller and the bits they're shooting over here are little more than cameos.' She grinned. 'Besides, I've already worked out that Hollywood has a fairly flexible approach when it comes to the true historical facts.'

'Martin Taylor gave me that impression.'

She grinned again. 'Martin knows less about history than I do about detective work.'

'He certainly didn't sound too enamoured of it. So where can I buy your book? I'd very much like to read it.'

'I can give you a copy if you like. The publisher sent me a boxful, but as it's a UK publisher and the books are in English, not too many of my friends over here are able to read it.'

I protested that it was only fair I should pay for it and then an idea occurred to me. 'I tell you what; I'll accept a free copy as long as you let me take you out for dinner once I've read it so we can discuss it.' As I spoke, I could almost see my old superintendent wagging an admonitory finger at me and warning me that Anna was still a suspect. I reminded myself that I was no longer a police officer and, anyway, by the time I'd finished reading the book, this investigation should be well and truly finished.

She looked up from her focaccia sandwich. 'I'd like that, Inspector, thanks.'

'Then it's a deal. And it's just Dan these days.'

'I'll bring you a copy tomorrow, just Dan.'

We chatted freely about medieval history over our lunch, and I had to make a conscious effort to concentrate less on her face and more on what she was saying. There was no getting away from it: she was a very attractive woman and we appeared to have a surprising amount in common… but that didn't alter the fact that she was still potentially a suspect.

9

WEDNESDAY AFTERNOON

The filming continued after lunch and included the climactic scene where the unknown killer fired at Lorenzo the Magnificent from a hiding place in the trees. Cameras were set up along the edge of the forest and the horsemen came riding past three or four times until Emmy was satisfied. Each time they did so, there was a sound like the twang of a bow and the stuntman playing the role of Lorenzo clutched his shoulder and fell spectacularly off his horse onto the ground. Emmy then shouted, 'Cut,' the stuntman casually got up again after a fall of at least six feet onto his back and climbed onto his horse without even a grimace. Rather him than me.

There was no sign of an arrow, but I was told that that would be added at the post-production stage. I was amazed to hear from Dizzy that post-production, with all the editing, the addition of special effects, Computer Generated Imagery, music and so on, could easily take far longer than the actual two weeks on location. Yes, making movies was an expensive business all right.

By four o'clock, it was all over, and everybody began to pack up. Tents were taken down and all the props, equipment and other paraphernalia, from cameras to toilets, were hauled back onto trucks and into vans remarkably quickly. Within an hour, the only people I could see were Dizzy with her clipboard and the last remaining minibus, empty apart from its driver. I went over to see if she needed anything before I, too, went off and I saw at once that she was looking troubled.

'What's the matter, Dizzy? Lost something?'

'*Somebody*, to be honest: Donny Lopez, our PR director.'

'Maybe he went for a walk.' I remembered what the writer had told me at lunchtime. 'I don't know about your PR man, but Martin Taylor said he was going to find himself a nice cool, quiet spot in the trees for a snooze. Maybe Mr Lopez did the same after his magazine people left. Oscar and I'll go and look for him. I bet we find him in the woods.'

We did.

After less than ten minutes wandering through the trees along the edge of the forest, with Oscar pottering happily about picking up sticks for me to throw for him, I pushed through a thicket of holly and came across the missing man. There, stretched out on the soft ground with his cheek resting comfortably on his forearm, was a figure wearing the regulation Renaissance costume. He looked very tranquil, as if he had just settled down for a rest and drifted off to sleep. His face was turned towards me and even from here I could see that this was Donny Lopez.

The trouble was that he wasn't asleep and the familiar deep blue and yellow vanes of a crossbow bolt were just visible, protruding from the middle of his back. I felt sure he was stone dead and the first feeling to flood through me – apart from pity for the victim – was one of guilt. This man had died on my watch and I had been unable to prevent it from happening. What was the point of having me here if I was to prove to be so ineffectual? Yesterday's near miss should have warned me that the killer meant business. Maybe I should have spoken to the producer and director and advised them to stop filming, although whether they would have listened was of course another matter. Giving myself a mental shaking by the scruff of the neck, I did my best to avoid wallowing in guilt and self-pity and switched my detective brain back on.

There was very little blood on his clothes or around him, and from what I could see the arrow must have penetrated straight to the heart, killing him instantly. This must have been either a shot fired by an expert marksman or, more probably, one fired at close range. Very carefully, I made my way over and pressed a finger against the victim's carotid artery, confirming what I had already seen. There was no pulse, and the skin of his throat was cold to the touch. There was no question about it: he was dead. I retreated as carefully as I had come, not wanting to encroach on what was now a crime scene.

I didn't need to call Oscar to me. As if he knew I wanted as little disturbance as possible, he came padding back to me with his tail between his legs. He knew a dead body when he saw one. I pulled out my phone and the first person I called was Virgilio, closely followed by Dizzy. She was understandably shocked and appalled.

'Donny, dead? I can hardly believe it.' Her voice was tremulous. 'Are you coming back? We're all alone here. Do you think we're in danger?'

'I've called the police and they'll be here before long. Oscar and I'll wait for them. Why don't you get the driver to take you back to Florence and, while you're at it, make a few calls? Speak to Gabriel Lyons first and ask him to make sure that everybody stays put until we can question them. Nobody to go back to their hotels for now. Tell them what's happened and instruct them to stay in the trailer park and I'll ask the police to put some of their men on the gate alongside Big Jim.'

'Are you going to be all right? Do be careful, Dan.'

'I'll be fine, thanks. My car's parked just up the track a bit so I can leave whenever I want. Go on, just get in the van and go.'

I felt I should stay at the crime scene although the thought that there might well be a killer loose somewhere in the woods didn't do a lot for my confidence. Hopefully the murderer would be long gone by now but, to be on the safe side, I found the biggest tree in the area and pressed my back against its massive trunk. This way, if there was a killer on the loose, at least he wouldn't be able to shoot me in the back like Lopez. One thing was now definite: any thoughts I might have had of Lopez being responsible for organising the arrows as a publicity stunt were dead in the water.

I glanced down at my dog. Now that we were a bit further away from the dead body, he was sitting at my feet, idly scratching his ear with his back paw and looking relaxed. Hopefully he would alert me if somebody tried to sneak up on us. As I stood there and counted off the minutes until the police arrived, I found I could see down to where most of the action had been taking place earlier. It occurred to me that it was possible that the cameras in the field might have been able to pick up the face of the murderer among the leaves and branches. Somebody would definitely need to check through today's footage at the end of the day with a fine-tooth comb.

Apart from this, the main question going through my head was who could have done it? Had this murder been the work of an unknown assassin who had followed the convoy from Florence, lain in wait for the PR man, killed him and then melted into the forest to make his, or her, escape? Was this the same person who had fired at the food truck or the big figure Max's friend Elvis had spotted outside the trailer park fence? Or was our killer known to us? Was it possible that Donny Lopez had been killed by somebody involved with the new movie, somebody I'd interviewed yesterday? Some of the people at the trailer park had been nicer than others, but none had struck me as a potential murderer. The other thought plaguing me was why? Why had this man been killed?

I was roused from my speculation by the familiar sound of sirens, and through the branches I saw vehicles approaching. As they drew nearer, I hurried down the barely twenty or thirty metres or so to the edge of the wood and waved to attract their attention. There were three police cars and an ambulance. As soon as I was sure they'd seen me, I went back to the crime scene and took up my sentry post again. Lopez's body was still in the same position, and nothing looked as if it had been touched. Hopefully nobody had sneaked up to disturb things while I'd been away.

Only a minute or two later, I heard approaching feet and called out to direct them up to me. The first to arrive was Virgilio's faithful sergeant, Marco Innocenti. We knew each other well by now and as we shook hands I could see him struggling to keep a grin off his face. This had nothing to do with the body at our feet. This was all about me and my pantaloons. In the heat of the moment, I'd forgotten about my Renaissance costume.

'*Ciao*, Dan. You look… different.' He spoke very little English so we always spoke Italian together.

'*Ciao*, Marco. Yes, I know I look like an idiot, but it's called blending in.' I hastened to return to the matter in hand rather than my ridiculous appearance. 'One dead body and no sign of the perpetrator.' At that moment Virgilio himself appeared, together with half a dozen uniformed officers, so I addressed myself to him. True professional that he was, he didn't bat an eyelid at my bizarre appearance, although the other officers were clearly struggling to keep a straight face. I ignored their quizzical looks and carried on.

'*Ciao*, Virgilio. Victim is Donny Lopez, PR director for the film, killed with a crossbow bolt between the shoulder blades.'

Virgilio came over and shook my hand while Oscar nuzzled his leg. 'Thanks, Dan. Any idea who might have done this?'

'I haven't a clue. I've been trying to work out if it might have been an inside job, committed by somebody in the crew or cast, or whether it was somebody from outside.' I went on to tell him what Max had told me earlier about a big, shadowy figure prowling around the perimeter of the trailer park, but, without a face and a name, we both knew this to be of little help. 'Maybe forensics will help.'

Virgilio nodded and walked carefully over to check on the body of the victim. After squatting down and studying the murdered man carefully for a few moments, he straightened up and issued orders to his officers. 'Right, listen up. I want you to cordon off this area. Spread out and search a radius of a hundred metres or so all around the crime scene. Innocenti, call in dog handlers and see if they can find any trace of the perpetrator. Pick up and bag anything you find that doesn't belong here in the woods, from cigarette ends to shotgun cartridges: everything. In particular, check to see if you come across any fresh footprints – the soil's still slightly damp in places – and anywhere the murderer might have been hiding or the path he might have used to make his escape.'

The familiar face of Gianni, the pathologist, appeared behind Virgilio and I gave him a little wave. He came over and shook my hand.

'Got a new tailor, have you, Dan? Very fetching. Tell me – why is it I keep seeing you at crime scenes? Haven't you got better things to do with your time?'

'To be honest, I was here to try to stop something like this happening. I rather think I might be out of a job after this.'

He gave me a grim smile and headed towards the corpse. He was accompanied by three members of his forensic team, all dressed in disposable overalls, and Virgilio nodded for them to start work. '*Ciao*, Gianni. Thanks for getting here so fast. I'd like to know when the death occurred and anything you can tell us that might help us with our investigation. Answers in the next five minutes would be helpful.' He gave Gianni a smile. 'Or as soon as possible.'

'I'll do what I can.' Gianni gave him a long-suffering smile in return and surveyed the body. 'One thing I can tell you straight off is that this wasn't suicide. Shooting yourself in the middle of the back with an arrow is physically impossible.' He managed a wry little smile. 'But an experienced detective like you has probably already worked that out. Now clear off out of my crime scene and let me and my people get on with our work.'

Virgilio and I walked back down through the trees to the edge of the wood. As we walked, I filled him in as best I could on who had been where today. I told him I'd seen the victim at lunchtime with the journalists and he'd looked full of beans, certainly not showing any signs of fear or distress. When and why he had then gone into the woods remained a mystery. I also told Virgilio my idea that there might even be a glimpse of the murderer captured on film and he promised to get all today's footage studied closely. We leant against the bonnet of his car, and I took Virgilio and Innocenti through the various members of the cast and crew until they had a reasonable idea of the make-up of the film personnel. Virgilio then repeated his original question. I'd been asking myself ever since finding the body.

'And you've no idea who might have done it?'

'I wish I knew. I think it's less likely that it was an inside job – not impossible, just less likely. We'll have to interview everybody who was here today so we can find out who might have had opportunity. Hardly any of them speak Italian so I'll be happy to help out if you want me. By the way, I've asked for them all to stay at the trailer park in Florence and I said I'd ask you to send a couple of officers along to help guard the perimeter just in case. It'll be interesting to see where everybody was at the time of the murder. I'm pretty sure the director and producer were where I could see them all afternoon, as were most of the lighting and sound people along with the camera crews.'

'What about the actors?'

'It's difficult. The big four – Selena Gardner, Scott Norris, Charles Vincent and Duggie Ogilvie – were all involved in the action today but not all of them all of the time. There were two small marquees set up where they went to rest and rehearse their lines between takes and there were portable toilets set up by the edge of the trees. I suppose one or more of them might have been able to slip out this afternoon unobserved for long enough to commit the murder, but it would have been difficult.'

'What about the assistant producer, our friend Miss Hindenburg? Was she there all the time?'

'I honestly can't remember. I saw her at lunchtime, but I can't recall seeing her again after that. She's normally at the side of the producer, ready to run errands for him, but until we speak to Gabriel Lyons himself, we don't really know. I suppose she might have slipped off into the woods and killed Lopez, but I have serious doubts about whether she's the type. Apart from anything else, she's so clumsy she'd probably have shot herself in the foot.'

'You don't think she and Lopez might have gone into the woods for a bit of... you know what?' Virgilio made the unmistakable Italian gesture involving a raised forearm that indicates hanky-panky. I shook my head.

'I would think it's very unlikely. The only person I've seen her with – and it could have been perfectly innocent – was Charles

Vincent, the young actor, and as far as I'm aware he was on set all afternoon.'

'What do you think made Lopez go into the woods?'

'I have no idea. Maybe he wanted a rest after talking all morning, maybe he was looking for mushrooms, who knows? Quite possibly he was taking publicity shots of the actors from his position among the trees. From the murder scene it's just possible to get glimpses of where the action was taking place. If he's still got his phone on him, somebody should check to see what photos he took.'

'Right, I suggest we head back to Florence and start the questions. If you're sure you don't mind helping out, I'd be grateful.' Virgilio turned to his sergeant. 'Innocenti, you're in charge here until uniform take over. I can travel back to Florence with Dan, and I'll leave you the car. You join us for the interviews at the trailer park as soon as you can and for God's sake don't let uniform destroy any evidence. Make sure if they find footprints leading to or from the scene you get them to make plaster casts. Okay, we're off.'

10

WEDNESDAY EVENING

Virgilio, Innocenti and I discussed the results of the ensuing four hours of intensive interviews over dinner in a pizzeria not far from the Uffizi. My appearance dressed in red and yellow striped pantaloons caused considerable amusement among our fellow diners but they soon settled down. As for me, tonight I had more important things on my mind than my dignity. A man had been killed on my watch, and I felt a personal responsibility to help bring the perpetrator to justice as soon as possible.

The restaurant had tables outside in a little piazza and, even though it was gone nine o'clock and there were fewer tourists in the city than in the summer, the place was packed. Luckily some people left just as we arrived, and we were able to take their spot. My dog reminded me with a few insistent nudges of his nose that he was getting hungry by this time, but a solution was to hand. Marco Innocenti knew the proprietor well and got him to rustle up a plate of leftover pizza crusts for the Labrador. These served as an excellent *amuse bouche* for Oscar until I could get him home for a proper feed. He polished off the food in a matter of seconds and then subsided onto the flagstones under the table while Virgilio,

Innocenti and I tucked into pizzas. I chose a simple, but enormous, pizza margherita, accompanied by a welcome glass of cold beer.

We were about halfway through when Virgilio's phone rang. It was the pathologist with his report and Virgilio relayed it to us at the end of the brief conversation. 'Gianni says time of death was between three and four this afternoon. The victim, Donald Lopez, was hit by a single arrow in the middle of the back and it went straight to the heart. He died instantly and he probably didn't feel a thing. There was no sign of a struggle or a fall, so Lopez was probably already lying on the ground at the time. Gianni reckons the murderer sneaked up on him as he was lying down and killed him just like that.'

'So he was maybe asleep... or drugged? No sinister substances in him?'

'Not unless you count burger and fries as sinister.'

Tricia, my daughter, is a veggie so she probably would have agreed with that assessment of the PR man's last meal. 'And any clues? Fragments of hair, fingernails, anything at all?'

'Nothing.'

'Not exactly a lot to work on, is it?'

'You can say that again. They checked his phone and there were a number of photos of the actors on horseback so, like you thought, that's presumably why he went to the woods and then ended up taking a nap. What we've got to work out is whether his killer was somebody connected with the movie or somebody completely different.'

'Nothing more of any help? What about the search in the woods?'

'We *might* have a lead there. The dogs sniffed out and followed what could be the track taken by the killer, although it might just have been a mushroom hunter. It's prime porcini season at the moment and the hills are alive with people. The trail led up the hill and over into the next valley where there's a quiet country road. Apparently it only took them just over fifteen minutes to walk from the crime scene to the road. They've taken casts of some fresh shoe prints as well as of recent tyre marks in the earth where somebody left a car or a van at the side of the road, but first reaction is that there doesn't appear to be anything too memorable about any of them. No guarantee that this was our murderer, but it could be.'

'What about the film footage? Any sign of the perpetrator hiding in the trees?'

'The director's given us a copy and my people will sift through it properly tomorrow, but first impressions aren't too hopeful. Apparently the cameras were mostly positioned close to the trees, looking away from the crime scene back towards the castle.'

'I suppose we still have to consider the possibility that the murderer was one of the people involved with the movie who managed to slip off unnoticed.'

'Anything's possible.' Virgilio was looking pensive. 'Could the murder have been committed by somebody we've just interviewed or was it by person or persons unknown? What about your runaway archer or the mysterious big figure the security guard saw? What do we think? Did any of our interviewees attract your attention, arouse any suspicions?' After throwing out the questions he returned his attention to his rapidly cooling pizza.

I had almost finished my food, so I was able to take my time before replying. 'If it's somebody we've interviewed, it's clear that only a handful of them had the opportunity to commit the murders without being missed, although a few more might just about have managed to get away and back again without being seen. Let's see if we can whittle it down.' I took a sip of the blissfully cool beer. In spite of the fact that it was now October and the sun had set two hours earlier, the evening was still pleasantly warm. Setting the glass down, I started listing the possible suspects.

'There's only one person who was definitely in the woods at the time and that's the writer, Martin Taylor. I saw him at lunchtime, and he told me he was exhausted after a very late night rewriting the scene. He said he had some more work to finish and then he was going off to find a quiet spot in the woods for a snooze. In fairness, he told me that was where he was going, and he admitted it freely when we spoke to him at the trailer park this afternoon, so that was strange behaviour if he really did set out to kill Lopez.'

Virgilio grunted. 'Could be a double bluff, of course. That still makes him arguably our prime suspect, just from an opportunity point of view. Nobody else admits to having been in the woods. Anyway, forgetting about him for a moment, if we rule out all the technical people and anybody who was tied to a job all afternoon, who are we left with? Innocenti, what've you got?'

Innocenti's notebook was already open on the table in front of him. 'The majority of the bit-part actors were ferried back to Florence by minibus shortly after two so they're in the clear – unless one of them jumped into a car and came zooming back to commit the murder.'

I hadn't thought of that. 'I suppose that's a possibility. If they left Cafaggiolo just after two they would have been back in Florence well before three, so it's just possible somebody had a car waiting and drove straight back up here. After parking in the next valley, he or she then ran the fifteen minutes over the hill to the murder scene and carried out the crime before four o'clock, but they would have been cutting it very fine. Besides, how were they to know that Lopez would be lying there at that time?'

Virgilio nodded. 'I agree, it's possible but not likely, but we'd better interview all of them a second time just in case. Who else do you have, Innocenti?'

'In terms of people who were still here and had ample time and opportunity, realistically there are only very few: Martin Taylor, like Dan just said, and then there's Rachel Hindenburg, although when we were interviewing her, she managed to knock over her chair and step on your dog, Dan. I seriously doubt whether she would have been able to shoot Taylor so accurately in the heart. Like you said, it's more likely she would have shot herself.'

Virgilio and I both nodded in agreement and Innocenti went on.

'The other three people with ample time – by which I mean people whose absence for half an hour or so wouldn't have been noticed – are the two security guards and Anna Galardo, the historical consultant.'

'What about Lopez's assistant, the gorgeous blonde, what was her name?'

'Loredana Belluno; she was in a car on the way to the station with the two people from the magazine. They left at two-thirty so she's definitely out of it.'

'And people who *might* have been able to sneak off unnoticed for a short while? What about the actors?'

'Any one of the top four: Selena Gardner, Scott Norris, Charles Vincent or Douglas Ogilvie. They weren't all involved in every scene, and they mostly went back to the VIP tent in between takes, but nobody can swear that they were in sight all afternoon.'

'What about the producer and director?'

'I think we can assume the director's in the clear. Nobody remembers him leaving his seat all afternoon, apart from once or twice to walk onto the set and talk to the actors. The producer admits that he went off to take and make a few calls in the course of the afternoon, but nobody saw him sneaking into the woods. I can't see what possible motive he might have for committing the murder, but we'd better keep him on our list for now.'

'Anybody else?'

'Not really. The tech people work in teams, and, unless they were all in it together, none of them report any of their number going off for more than a quick pee.'

'So that gives us eight people, nine if we include the producer, who had opportunity of some kind: four actors and four or maybe five others.' Virgilio looked pensive. 'As far as the murder weapon's concerned, the crossbow bolt's identical to all the others and Gianni says it could well be the same crossbow that shot the original arrows, but there's no way of being sure. If it is, then that sort of weapon comes apart and folds up and wouldn't have occupied much space; easy enough to conceal among all the crates of stuff that came with them or to carry in a bag.'

'And like you say that leaves us with the problem of finding a motive.' I shook my head slowly. 'And that's where I'm struggling; in fact, I've been struggling since yesterday. It's surely in everybody's interests to get the movie made. Certainly, I can't see that any of the actors had anything to gain from doing something like this.' I took another mouthful of beer and looked across the table at the two of them. 'And, unless the murderer was specifically targeting Lopez for some reason, it seems to me that whoever is behind these arrows is trying to stop them filming. I don't know what's going to happen now. I wonder if the film company will opt to carry on over here. Hopefully the producer will tell us in the next twenty-four hours.'

Our interview with Gabriel Lyons earlier that evening had been a far different affair from the caustic few minutes he had grudgingly granted me the previous day. We had found him deflated, puzzled and above all apprehensive – for two reasons. The first was for himself.

'Do you think the killer's still out to get us? Is this just the start, or do you think he was specifically after Donny?' His fingers were drumming nervously on the desk, he was perspiring heavily, and a vein in his forehead was throbbing. He was flushed and he didn't look a well man. 'Why Donny? I've known him and worked with him for almost ten years and he's... he was... a stand-up guy. What if this was just a random killing and the murderer plans to strike again, to kill somebody else... me, even?'

Virgilio had done his best to calm the producer down, but the fact was that we had no way of knowing what might be going on inside the killer's head. Could this be the beginning of a random killing spree or had Lopez been specifically targeted? When Lyons started talking again, the other reason for his apprehension was rapidly revealed.

'I don't know what's going to happen next. I've been in touch with the company back in LA, and we've scheduled a Zoom meeting tonight to decide whether to press on with the movie or to scrap the Italian part of it and head home.'

'Wouldn't that ruin the movie?'

'I need to sit down and talk to Emmy and Taylor. Maybe we can use what we've already got in the can from this week and mock up a few interiors when we're back in LA. I don't know.'

'So you wouldn't need to scrap the whole movie?'

'I sure hope not. If we do that, we lose millions, not just in what we've spent so far but in contracts to be honoured and, of course, the wasted time when we could have been making other movies.'

'Don't you have insurance?'

'For cancellation due to fire, flood or theft, yes, but not for murder. No, if we decide to pull the plug on the whole thing, it'll cost us a fortune.'

'Could the company stand to lose that much?' A vague idea was forming in my head that the intention might have been to bankrupt the film company. Maybe an unscrupulous rival company?

'Yeah, we have reserves. We could weather the storm, but it wouldn't be pretty. No, I don't see us scrapping the whole movie. Like I say, if necessary, we'll have to make do with the Italian footage we already have and hope we can still make the movie work.'

'What happens short term? Can you carry on without Lopez?' I felt sure that everybody on the lot wanted to know what the future held for them.

'That's not a problem. Donny's assistant, Loredana, can take over the PR side of things for a day or two. If we decide to stay on over here, I might get somebody to send a replacement for him – and PR's our number one priority now – but she's good at her job and she'll need to be. When this news hits the fan, there'll be journalists and photographers climbing all over us. This will need managing and managing good.'

'I thought all publicity was good publicity.' Virgilio said what I had been thinking.

'Not this sort of publicity. If it isn't handled right, it could spell disaster for the movie and damage the reputation of the company.'

Virgilio nodded. 'I see. Tell me about Donald Lopez. You say he was a good guy. Can you think of anybody who might have had a grudge against him?'

The producer shook his head. 'I can't. Everybody liked Donny. I don't think I ever saw him without a smile on his face.'

'What about family? Was he married?'

'He was, until about three, maybe four years ago, when his wife divorced him.'

'Was there bad feeling there?'

'Not more than in any divorce. His job took him away a lot and she met somebody else. I think it hurt him at the time but, like I say, he was soon smiling again.'

This made me think of my own recent divorce. I certainly hadn't done a lot of smiling at the time. I threw in a question of my own. 'And now, since the divorce, did he have a new woman in his life? What about his assistant maybe? She looked very distressed when we interviewed her.'

'We're all distressed. I'm not aware of anybody in particular, and I've no idea about Loredana. The thing is, she hadn't really known him for very long. She was locally recruited in August to help out with the language, so they'd only been working together for six weeks or so. If there was anything between them it would have been very new. Otherwise, I don't know of a special woman in his life, but other people might know more. You should ask Dizzy. She knows everything about everybody.'

'What about Dizzy, Miss Hindenburg herself? Might she and Lopez have been...?' Virgilio was still hypothesising.

'Dizzy?' The producer actually laughed. 'You must be joking. No, I'm sure there wasn't anything between the two of them. Yes, she liked him, but we all liked Donny.'

The interview came to an end and Virgilio stood up and held out his hand. 'Thank you very much, Mr Lyons. When do you think you'll make a decision on whether or not to carry on filming?'

'For now, we're taking a timeout. Definitely nothing doing tomorrow. As soon as you guys have finished your questioning, I'll send everybody off. They can go back to their separate hotels and tomorrow they can all take the day off while we decide what happens from now on.'

At the pizzeria, Virgilio carried on trawling through the possible perpetrators.

'If it wasn't one of the actors, that only leaves the lady with the blue glasses, the history consultant, the security guards or, of course, the writer who admits being in the woods at the time. And then there's Gabriel Lyons himself. The guards certainly look tough enough, but one's a university student on a short-term contract, and there doesn't seem to be any other connection between him and the movie. His partner, the big guy, has worked for the company for years, so why start killing now? I must admit I didn't see either of them as a murderer. Besides, if it was one of them, why?' Virgilio finished his pizza and handed down the last bit of crust to my canine waste-disposal unit under the table. 'And what about the two ladies: Anna Galardo and Hindenburg? I don't see either of them as cold-blooded killers, and we're definitely talking about cold-blooded killers here. To commit a murder, you need a strong stomach.'

Innocenti and I both agreed, and Virgilio proceeded.

'And I can't see the producer deliberately torpedoing his own movie. It makes no sense. That only really leaves us with the writer, Taylor, but I tended to believe him when he said he'd just been sleeping in the woods. Either that or he's such a good actor he should be starring in the movie. One thing's for sure: we're going to be keeping a close eye on him.' He dropped his fork onto his plate and looked across at Innocenti. 'I need to know every single thing there is to know about Donald Lopez just in case there's a link to somebody here, particularly Taylor. Tomorrow I'll sit down with Miss Hindenburg again and see if she really does know everything about everybody, and then I'll have another go at Taylor. Maybe the experts will pick up a glimpse of the killer from the footage shot today, but I'm not holding my breath. For now, let's keep an open mind until we get all the background checks done, but it's looking more and more likely that the murderer is an outsider –

whether it's the man or woman spotted outside the fence last night or the one who fired at the crowd by the food wagon, or somebody completely different. It could be that Lopez was a target picked at random and that the killer has his sights on the movie rather than this particular man. And we all know what that means.'

'He could well be prepared to kill again.' Innocenti got there just before me.

'Or she...' They both nodded. We just didn't know.

The idea of yet another person being murdered, particularly now that I had got to know the cast and crew quite well, was grim but there was no getting away from it. It had to be considered as a strong possibility and I was just nodding in agreement when my phone rang. I didn't recognise the number, but I immediately recognised the voice at the other end.

'Mr Armstrong, it's Selena.'

'Miss Gardner, good evening.' I glanced up to see Virgilio's eyes open a bit wider. 'How can I help?'

'I'm at my hotel and I've just been talking to Anna, Anna Galardo. You've probably heard that we have a day off tomorrow. You can't imagine how good that sounds to me. My schedule's been jam-packed ever since I arrived in Italy, and a day all to myself sounds great – although it's just so sad that it has to be in these terrible circumstances. Anyway, I've asked Anna if she'd be prepared to take me around and show me some interesting bits of Tuscany, outside of Florence itself. She's so knowledgeable about the history of the area. She's agreed but I'd feel happier if you felt like coming along to keep an eye on us, if you could manage it. Do bring your lovely dog with you if you like. Anna's been telling me about him, and we both love dogs. Would you be prepared to do that?'

'Of course, but shouldn't that be the job of the company's security guards? I wouldn't want to put their noses out of joint.' Not least as they could pound me to a pulp if they felt like it.

'They're lovely guys, but they stick out a mile.' She was right there. Man-mountain Big Jim with his dark clothes, dreadlocks and dark glasses probably wasn't an everyday sighting here in Tuscany. 'Do say you'll come. I'm sure you'll be what's needed.'

I agreed readily and we arranged that I would come and pick Selena up from the hotel at 9 a.m. I told her I thought it would be better if we took my car in view of the fact that we would have Oscar with us. Also, my anonymous VW minibus would attract far less attention than a big limo. As I rang off, I couldn't help wondering how much use as a bodyguard I was going to be. After all, I'd been with them at Cafaggiolo today and that hadn't stopped there being a brutal murder. Still, the idea of a day out with a world-famous film star had distinct appeal, and the thought of spending time with Anna Galardo sounded even more attractive. Paul over in London probably wouldn't have shared my priorities, but there was definitely something very appealing about Anna. Once again, I had to remind myself that both ladies were potential suspects in a murder enquiry.

11

THURSDAY MORNING

Next morning I awoke feeling weary after a late night. I had been trying to keep up a regular schedule of writing at least a thousand words a day and it had taken me until well past midnight to finish my quota. Interestingly, I had not only invented a new, stunningly beautiful blonde character inspired by Selena but somehow another female character had also materialised on the pages who bore an uncanny resemblance to Anna Galardo. Write about what you know is the received wisdom for writers and nobody could say I wasn't doing that.

I checked my messages and found an email from Paul with a summary of the file relating to the death of Stephen Sinclair, Duggie Ogilvie's boyfriend, fifteen years earlier. As I had surmised, the killer, George or Georgie Bennett, had been released from jail earlier this year and his last known address was in Brighton. I would dearly have liked to find out whether he was still there now or whether he had left the country, but I didn't want to give my former employers extra work. Although I felt sure Paul would check this if I asked him, I stopped short of putting in a request, mainly because I could see no possible reason why Georgie

Bennett could have wanted to kill Lopez – Duggie Ogilvie, possibly, but surely there was no way Bennett could have known the other man.

After a walk with Oscar, I took a shower and changed into fresh clothes – definitely not striped pantaloons – for my day out with the two beautiful ladies. Before going into the shower, I sent Paul an email thanking him for the files and attaching a photo I had taken the previous day of Selena in her Renaissance finery. To wind him up I added a casual comment to the effect that I was to be spending all day today driving around Tuscany with her. When I emerged from the bathroom, I found an email from him complaining about how unfair it was that I always got the good jobs while he got the unpleasant ones, reminding me of the time I'd sent him into a sewer pipe to hunt for a murder weapon – which he'd found. I decided not to tell him of my hours in the pouring rain outside Signor Dante's hotel the other night. If Paul wanted to imagine me living the high life, who was I to disabuse him?

I got a surprise when I picked Selena up from her hotel. She emerged wearing jeans and a baggy sweatshirt that did a remarkably good job of concealing her identity and her femininity. On her head she had a baseball cap with a ponytail emerging from the back of it. With her sunglasses it added up to a very effective disguise as an anonymous tourist and, if I hadn't been expecting her, I wouldn't have given her a second glance.

Before climbing into the car, she insisted on being introduced to Oscar, who was standing in the boot space wagging his tail. He gave her a warm welcome but, as already established, he likes the ladies. For her part, Selena appeared enchanted to meet him and made a real fuss of him before finally getting into the car alongside me. She took off the sunglasses and gave me a beaming smile. If Paul had been driving, he would have melted on the spot. As it was, I almost had to pinch myself as the realisation dawned that I was sitting next to one of the most famous and beautiful women in the world. For a moment I wondered what my ex-wife would have said if she had known. Back in the day she would have been jealous, but now I knew she no longer cared.

'Hi, Mr Armstrong. Thanks for doing this. I'm really looking forward to it.'

'You're very welcome, Miss Gardner.'

'Selena, please.'

'Thanks, and I'm Dan, by the way.'

'I know. Dizzy told me. You used to be a top cop at Scotland Yard, didn't you?'

'Hardly a top anything. I was too insubordinate for that. I was a chief inspector in the murder squad, but I came over to Tuscany last year and now I live here and I've set up my own investigation agency.'

'That sounds like a major step. I wonder why you did that...' She subjected me to a searching stare. 'Don't tell me, let me guess: you were trying to get away from some woman?'

This stopped me in my tracks, and I nodded at her in admiration. 'Have you ever thought of becoming a detective? That's very close to the truth. To be honest, it was in part because I was getting away from an unhappy marriage; at least, it was unhappy as far as my ex-wife was concerned. I'm afraid being married to a police officer isn't always a bundle of fun.' This was getting a bit close up and personal, so I changed the subject. 'But it was also because I've fallen in love with Tuscany. Anyway, where are we picking Anna up?'

'She said she'd be waiting at the gate of the trailer park.' Selena must have got the message that I didn't want to talk about my ex-wife, and we chatted about trivia as I threaded my way through the traffic along the *viali* to the trailer park. When we got there, we found Anna waiting at the gate, chatting to Big Jim. Like Selena, she was also wearing jeans today, but she had chosen a colourful top that highlighted, rather than concealed, her femininity, and she looked good. After Anna had climbed into the back seat, Selena was the first to comment.

'Hey, Anna, that's a gorgeous top. You look great.' To my embarrassment she then prodded me in the ribs with her elbow and dragged me into the conversation. 'She really does look great, doesn't she, Dan?' I caught her eye for a second and I couldn't miss the mischievous twinkle there. I had a feeling Selena might be playing Cupid, and I wondered if this was because of something she had noticed on my face, or maybe something she had heard from Anna. Doing my best not to blush like a teenager, I hastened to agree.

'Yes, Anna, you look lovely. You both do.'

'Thank you, that's very kind.' She sounded as uncomfortable as I did at Selena's machinations, and I hoped this wasn't going to develop into an awkward day. Fortunately, Oscar chose that moment to try to climb over the back seat to kiss Anna, and she was fully occupied for a while persuading him to settle for a few cuddles and stay where he was. When she sank back into her seat again, I did my best to sound business-like.

'Right, Anna, you're the guide. Where are we heading?'

'I think we should take Selena to see San Gimignano. I know it's a touristy place, but it is something rather special. Do you agree?'

'Definitely. I know what you mean by touristy, but at least it's October now so the summer crowds should have disappeared.'

'Tell me about San Gimignano, Anna.' As we set off, Selena twisted around in her seat so as to talk to her. 'What's it like?'

'Think towers, lots of them. It's on top of a ridge in the hills not far from Siena and there are no fewer than fourteen towers, some over fifty metres tall.' For the sake of an American unfamiliar with the metric system she added, 'That's equivalent to the height of a ten-storey building, but with a much narrower base. But on the way there I'd like to take you to visit a couple of less well-known places that just ooze Tuscan charm. Sound good?'

Selena settled back in her seat with a happy smile on her face. 'That sounds just perfect.'

I glanced in the mirror and had to smile as Oscar did his best to kiss Anna's ear. He has good taste, my dog.

I made my way out through the traffic and turned onto a series of more minor roads as we headed into the hills. Although Florence is a world-renowned city, it doesn't take long to get out into the country from the centre. In fact, the route Anna chose took us close to my house and I was able to point it out to them on the hillside above us, the roof just visible for a few seconds between the cypress trees. Both ladies looked impressed and Selena, in particular, expressed great interest.

'How wonderful to live in a place like this. Dan, I can see now why you decided to come and live here. It's a dream come true.'

I decided not to tell her that last winter without central heating had not been for the faint-hearted – it can get very cold in Tuscany – and accepted the praise.

'I love it to bits and it's perfect for my four-legged friend.'

'Would you think it awfully rude if I asked if maybe we could swing past your house on the way home, just so I can see it and check out the view? It'll give me something to dream about when I'm back in LA.'

'Of course, you'll be very welcome, but it's nothing special. I'm sure you'll find it far too ordinary for your tastes.'

'Chauffeurs, pools and private tennis courts aren't as glam-orous as you might think. I know it's a forlorn hope for me, but you've no idea how much I long for the chance to live somewhere plain and simple without all the bling.' She turned and shot us both a grin. 'Don't get me wrong. I love my life, I love LA, and I love my house in Beverly Hills, but it can get a bit much sometimes. Having a bolthole somewhere like this would be amazing, somewhere I could live a normal life again, even just for a few days at a time.'

A bit later on, the conversation inevitably turned to the murder. Both ladies expressed amazement that Donny Lopez should have been targeted. Selena, in particular, had clearly known him well.

'Donny was a sweetie. He wouldn't have hurt a fly. Everybody on set loved him and when the police inspector was asking yesterday if I could think of anybody who might have wanted to kill him, I couldn't even think of anybody who didn't like him, let alone wished him harm. It's just so baffling.'

I nodded in agreement. 'I'm afraid that's the conclusion the police are coming around to. Maybe Lopez was chosen by chance.' I decided not to add the obvious corollary that if the PR man had been nothing more than an opportunistic target then that might well mean the killer would try again. I thought it better not to worry them any more than necessary, but, as it turned out, Anna had already reached that conclusion.

'The thing is, unless the police can unearth somebody who hated Donny enough to want to murder him, then it sounds to me as though the killer selected him at random when he happened to find him in the woods. I have a horrible feeling it might just as easily have been anybody else connected with the film. Maybe Donny was just in the wrong place at the wrong time. Next time it might be one of us.'

'Next time?' Selena reached out and gripped my arm for a few seconds. 'Is that what you think, Dan? Might we all be in danger?'

I waited until I had overtaken one of those quaint narrow tractors that are specially designed to squeeze between the rows of vines in the vineyards before answering. This battered red vehicle was driven by a gnarled old man with a face the colour of a chestnut. On his lap was a scruffy brown and white terrier that looked so comfortable there that it could probably have taken over the driving if need be. In reply to Selena's question, I decided to tell them the truth. There was no point denying it.

'We just don't know. The police are doing all sorts of background checks but, yes, I suppose we have to accept the possibility that Donny's death was sheer chance, and the murderer might be prepared to kill again in order to shut down the movie for whatever reason. After all, that's what the threatening notes have been saying all along.' I could almost feel the shiver of fear that ran through the car, so I made an attempt to lighten the atmosphere. 'But at least for today we three are safe as houses. Nobody knows where we are and I'm sure we haven't been followed so let's enjoy the day. *Carpe diem* and all that. Besides, don't forget we have a guard dog.'

The fact that the guard dog was snoring noisily at the rear of the car didn't bode well if he were ever to be needed in that role, but it brought a smile to the ladies' faces. I decided to keep up the positive reinforcement.

'And talking of enjoying ourselves, why don't we stop at lunchtime in a little restaurant I know out in the depths of the Chianti vineyards? The owner makes his own wine and bakes his own bread among other things.'

'That sounds wonderful. I'd love to experience a bit of the real Tuscany.'

I was pleased to hear Selena sounding a bit more cheerful, although a glance in the mirror at Anna's face told me she was still worried. And quite rightly so. Nevertheless, I decided to keep up the cheerful chatter as I pointed out the vineyards to Selena.

'It was a particularly hot summer and the *vendemmia*, the grape harvest, was early this year. Around this area it was all finished a couple of weeks ago. It's just as well or we'd probably be stuck behind tractor after tractor on these little roads. Here in Chianti, wine takes priority over everything else when it's *vendemmia* time.'

Anna caught my eye in the mirror and summoned a little smile, but I knew how she felt. It was a creepy feeling knowing that there might still be a murderer out there.

12

THURSDAY

The first place Anna took us to was Montaione. I'd heard the name and seen it on signs, but I'd never been here, in spite of having lived less than half an hour away for over a year now. It turned out to be a charming little Tuscan hilltop town, its centre almost entirely composed of picturesque medieval buildings. I found a parking space at the side of the road, and we wandered into the *centro storico*, making our way through the narrow streets and alleys, through stone arches and alongside the ancient castle walls until we came to the fifteenth-century Palazzo Pretorio. This fine stone building was studded with enamelled coats of arms of the families who had ruled the town in centuries gone by. I queried with our history expert if she recognised any of the names and she reeled off half a dozen. It came as no surprise to hear that this whole area had been in the hands of the all-powerful Medici family for many years. Thought of the Medici returned my mind to the movie. When we sat down in the shade outside a little café for mid-morning coffee, I still had the movie on my mind. It soon emerged that my guests did too.

'Do you think the company will carry on with the film after what's happened?' Anna addressed her question to Selena, who shrugged helplessly and directed her answer to both of us.

'I honestly don't know. I'm pretty sure the movie itself will go ahead. Dan, you probably know by now that it's essentially a contemporary drama set in LA. We're only here shooting cutaways to highlight the similarities between the ruthlessness of Scott's character, Lawrence Mead, and Lorenzo, the famous Medici man. We've already filmed well over half of the action back in the States. What they might do is cut short the location shooting over here and send us all back to California, where we should be safe. I'm sure they could make it work – like I say, I don't think the Italian stuff's really vital.' She took a sip of coffee and looked across the quaint little piazza with its cobbles and flagstones. 'Personally, I hope we carry on. I love Tuscany.'

'In spite of the possible danger?' I was mildly surprised.

'There's danger in everything we do. There's danger just crossing the road or in a flight back to the US. I'd be prepared to take my chances for the sake of another few days over here.'

Anna turned to me. 'What do you think, Dan? Should they go ahead with filming?'

'It's a tough call. Like we were saying in the car, I reckon there might still be a risk, so maybe the sensible thing to do would be to cut and run, as long as it doesn't spoil the whole movie. Dizzy told me there's only another week or so of filming over here to go, so maybe the answer they choose will be a compromise: cut some scenes out and condense what's left into two or three days, heighten security and power through, so as to leave as soon as possible.' I reached out and scratched my dog's tummy with the toe of my shoe. 'I'm glad I'm not the one having to take the decision.'

On our way across to San Gimignano, we stopped off to give Oscar a walk in the woods on what was described as the Sacred Mount of San Vivaldo. In among the trees, we found a monastery and a series of buildings created in the fifteenth century as a miniature reproduction of the holy city of Jerusalem. We were the only visitors, and it was fascinating to walk around the collection of little chapels, roofed with sun-scorched red tiles, that made up the old monastery. I'd never heard of this place before and it was yet another of those spectacular surprises seemingly hiding around every corner here in the Tuscan countryside. I really did love Tuscany, even if there was still a killer on the loose back in Florence.

We didn't spend too long at San Gimignano. I'd already been here several times and I liked the place, but I disliked the crowds and the way the village had effectively prostituted itself to tourism. Virtually every shop along the main street – a stone-paved, pedestrians-only street – offered San Gimignano baseball caps, T-shirts, mugs and postcards alongside olive oil, olives in jars and, of course, bottles of wine. The place was thronged with visitors, but it was nothing like as bad as it would have been a couple of months earlier. Outside I had counted only three coaches in the coach park, although finding a free space for the car had still been tricky. At least now we could walk around freely without being crushed by the crowds.

Still, even the commercialisation of the place couldn't mask the stunning beauty of this medieval gem. The towers reached high into the sky, some unbelievably slim for their height, and it was testimony to the ability of the original architects that so many were still standing. Selena's disguise worked well, and I didn't spot any knowing looks or other signs of recognition on the faces of the people we passed. Even so, I was pleased when we emerged unscathed and returned to the car. Selena climbed in and sat down with a contented sigh.

'Beautiful, absolutely beautiful. Thank you both so much; Dan for doing all the driving and looking out for us, and Anna for all the historical stuff. I've seen and learnt a lot. Now, how about lunch? My treat.'

I took them for lunch to the place I had discovered quite by chance back in the spring. It was at the end of a potholed track that wound its way into the forest – no doubt teeming with wildlife and mushrooms – about ten kilometres from San Gimignano, and the only indication of its existence was a faded wooden sign with the word *Ristorante* painted on it. A local hunter had blown one corner off the sign, and it looked far from prepossessing. However, when we got to the little restaurant, the place was as good as I remembered and the even better news was that we were the only guests so Selena didn't have to worry about being exposed. The elderly owner showed us to a table outside his ancient, crumbling farmhouse, and we sat in the shade of a wooden pergola swathed in vines. The leaves were already starting to turn brown as autumn advanced, even though the temperature gauge in the car had told me that today was a very pleasant twenty-three degrees. The view back down over the tops of the trees towards the towers of San Gimignano was delightful and I sat down and relaxed.

I wondered if Selena would stick to her rabbit-food diet, but she surprised me by announcing that she was letting herself off the leash today, and she joined Anna and me in ordering a mixed grill. Remembering the quantity of meat I'd been served on my previous visit, I convinced the others to accept my advice just to have a few slices of luscious, orange-fleshed melon and freshly carved ham as a starter, and we turned down the offer of a pasta course before the main.

Over lunch we chatted, and I learnt more about the life of a superstar – and it didn't sound like a bed of roses with the intrusion of the media and the constrictions of always having a perfect image to maintain and the sacrifices that this involved. True, being so famous had considerable compensations, which went a long way towards offsetting the loss of freedom, but it sounded like a strange life. I looked down at my dog, who was pretending to sleep while keeping one eye on what was happening on the table above him, his nostrils checking the size, weight and tastiness of every bit of meat that arrived for us. Yes, I was happy with my life as it was and had no desire ever to ascend to superstar status – which was just as well because even Oscar knew that that wasn't going to happen.

As for Anna, I gradually learnt more and more about her, and I liked what I discovered. She sounded like a very grounded person with a good brain and enough experience of life – both good and bad – to make her excellent company. I was interested to learn that she had a daughter only a year or two younger than my own daughter and who was also living in the UK. Add to that the fact that Anna was divorced like me, and we certainly had a lot in common. Once again I had to remind myself that she remained a suspect in a murder case. Do not get involved with suspects – I'd drummed it into the heads of the officers under my command at the Met often enough – but I knew it was easier said than done.

At one point Anna revealed to Selena what I had told her about my publishing contract and the megastar sounded genuinely interested. She then came up with a fascinating proposal.

'Remind me to give you my address before we leave Italy and when your book comes out, do please send me a copy. I'll read it and I'm sure I'll like it and, unless you have any objections, if I think it would make a good movie, I could talk to a few people in

Hollywood.' She gave me a grin. 'You never know, if there's a character in there for me, who knows? I might find myself acting in a movie that you wrote.'

I thanked her profusely and decided to give the new Selena character I had just invented a more prominent role just in case. I also did my best to temper my excitement. A lot of water would have to pass under the bridge before I could see one of my books turned into a movie. First it would depend whether Selena liked it, then whether she could convince any of her Hollywood contacts to take it on and, most importantly of all, it would depend entirely on her emerging from this murder investigation unscathed and innocent. Still, it's good to dream, isn't it?

In the afternoon we visited the wonderfully preserved walled town of Monteriggioni with its fourteen watchtowers that had earned it a mention in Dante's *Divine Comedy*, and where we had wonderful home-made ice creams. After that, we stopped off at the small but heavily fortified castle in Staggia before taking a tour through the Chianti vineyards. All traces of the *vendemmia* had disappeared by now, although there was a lingering aroma of alcohol as we passed through some of the tiny villages around Greve in Chianti.

Finally we called in at a winery alongside a fine old Renaissance villa and tasted their red and white wines along with their special Vin Santo. This strong honey-coloured wine was made from grapes left to dry on straw mats until they reduced to the size and shape of raisins containing a very sweet, and alcoholic, residue. Selena insisted on buying two cases of Chianti and giving one each to Anna and me as thank you gifts. It was a most pleasant day in excellent company.

On the way back to Florence, as promised, I drove them up the bumpy white gravel *strada bianca* to my house. Oscar got very excited as we neared home and Selena became even more excited.

I gave them a very quick tour of the little house with its two bedrooms upstairs and big downstairs room that served as kitchen, living room and dining room. Thankfully Maria, the cleaner, had been in for her weekly clean only yesterday and the place was pretty presentable. Since getting divorced, I had been getting a lot tidier and, apart from a couple of chewed sticks on Oscar's rug in front of the big empty fireplace, the place looked okay.

I offered them tea and we drank it outside under the shade of the *loggia*, a lovely, covered terrace on the side of the house, from where we could look down over the vines and olive trees to the valley below and the distant Apennines on the horizon. I never tired of the view and the two ladies sounded as if they felt the same way. Selena took a load of photos and I managed to get a good close-up shot of her to send to Paul, and a close-up shot of Anna for myself.

After dropping Selena at her hotel and being rewarded with kisses from her – not just air kisses but real smackers on my cheeks – I delivered Anna and her case of wine back to her home. I discovered that she lived in an apartment inside an even older building than my office just over on the far side of the River Arno, a stone's throw from the Ponte Vecchio. This medieval town house was in a narrow street and there was no way I could stop the car for long, so I just had to drop her off. Before she left with her carton of wine she reached into her bag and produced a copy of her book.

'Don't feel you need to read it all. It isn't homework. I promise I won't be quizzing you on it.'

For a moment it almost looked as though she might even be about to lean in and kiss me, but a white van behind me reminded me with a toot of his horn that he was in a hurry, so I could only give her a wave and set off again. As we drove off, I exchanged glances with my faithful hound, whose head was resting on the seat back behind me. He didn't say a word, but I could see he was thinking the same thing that I was: Anna Galardo was a very nice lady.

And a suspect.

13

THURSDAY EVENING

Before going home, I drove back to my office to check if I had any mail. Squeezing the car in through the arched entranceway that had been designed for carriages rather than modern vehicles, I parked in the courtyard while I checked the mailbox. It was empty apart from the usual adverts and I was just going back to the car when I spotted old Signor Rufina, the picture framer, sitting outside the door of his studio enjoying the last of the afternoon sunshine before the surrounding walls cast the whole courtyard into the shade. He was reading a copy of the local newspaper, *La Nazione*, and he waved me over.

'*Buona sera, Signor Armstrong.*' He always pronounced my name as if it consisted of four syllables, *Arm-e-stron-ga.*

'Good evening, Signor Rufina, had a busy day?'

'Not too busy.' He pointed to the newspaper in his other hand. 'Here, you're a detective, what do you make of this murder out at Cafaggiolo? Didn't you say that you're doing something with the film company?'

I nodded. 'Yes, I've been investigating a series of threats they've been getting, and now one of them has come true.'

'It says here the man was killed with an arrow.'

'A crossbow bolt, actually.' I held out my hands to show him how much smaller than a traditional arrow it had been. 'Not that long. Several of them have been found in the film company's trailer park over the past few days.'

He looked interested. 'Is that so? In the paper it said that the one that killed the man at Cafaggiolo had feathered vanes. That's unusual for a crossbow bolt.'

'All of the bolts we've found so far had flights made with feathers. Do you know about crossbows?' This might be interesting.

He stood up and beckoned. 'I know all about bows. Come and I'll show you something.'

He led me into his workshop that smelt, as always, of freshly cut timber and glue. The floor was piled with pictures and frames, and on his workbench I spotted a particularly fine ornate gilded frame that he had obviously just finished making. Even without a painting in it, it was a work of art. He pointed proudly at a framed document on one wall, so I went across to read it. Beneath an impressive logo of a longbow and quiver of arrows, the formal-looking document attested to the fact that Arnaldo Rufina had been bestowed the rank of *Cavaliere del'Arco*, literally a Knight of the Bow. I cast him an interrogative look and he explained.

'I've been an archer all my life and chairman of the local archery society for almost twenty years, so when I finally gave up the position, they made me a *cavaliere* and gave me this.'

'Congratulations, *cavaliere*. I'm most impressed.'

'I don't suppose you have a photo of one of the crossbow bolts, have you? I'd be interested to see it.'

I thought quickly. This guy was clearly an expert so maybe he might be able to spot something that the police forensics people had missed. There was nothing compromising or secret about the bolt and I felt sure Virgilio would have no objections if I let Signor

Rufina give it the once-over. 'I can do better than that. I've got one of the bolts upstairs in my office. I can go and get it, if you like.'

'Please do. That sounds marvellous.' He looked as enthusiastic as he sounded.

Leaving Oscar in the car with the windows open, although by now the temperature had dropped considerably, I hurried upstairs, retrieved the crossbow bolt and brought it down to Signor Rufina. I handed him the plastic bag and he took it gingerly before looking up.

'Can I take it out of the bag? Is it all right to touch it or might there be fingerprints on it?'

'Take it out and touch it all you want. Lots of fingers already have.'

He removed it from the bag, and I watched him turn it over reverently in his hands for almost a minute before picking up a magnifying glass and studying the feathered vanes in minute detail. When he had subjected it to intense all-over scrutiny he straightened up, set the magnifying glass and arrow down on his workbench, and delivered his verdict.

'Somebody's gone to a lot of trouble with this bolt. They've cut off the old plastic vanes and replaced them with feathers. From the look of them, I'd say maybe pigeon or chicken – nothing fancy. What *is* fancy is that whoever did it has then taken the trouble to dye them blue and to add the yellow detail.'

'Yes, what is that? Are they just yellow squiggles or is there more to them than squiggles?'

He stood there for a few moments, lost in thought, before turning and walking across to a bookshelf. He removed a well-thumbed hard-backed tome and brought it over to the workbench. I saw that the title translated to *Shields and Insignia*. He set the book down and leafed through it. As he did so, a little cloud of dust flew into the air and hung in the last rays of the dying sun coming through a window high in the end wall. After a short search, he found what he was looking for and beckoned for me to come and take a look.

There on the page was a full colour plate showing a curiously sculpted blue heraldic shield, its shape not dissimilar to a jigsaw puzzle piece, the decoration on it consisting of five crosses and two long thin yellow fish or eels. The shape of the two fish looked similar to the yellow squiggles on the crossbow flights.

'Bright yellow on a field of deep blue. It fits.' Signor Rufina sounded very pleased with himself. 'I bet that's what the man who made these vanes was trying to replicate.'

'What's the significance of the two eels?'

'Not eels, they're dolphins.' He caught my eye for a moment. 'Artists back in the Middle Ages weren't too precise about depictions of animals.'

'The Middle Ages? So does this belong to one of the old Florentine families?'

He nodded. '*I Pazzi.*'

'*I pazzi?*' I could hear the bewilderment in my own voice. What he'd just said translated as 'the crazy people'.

He saw my confusion and explained. 'Pazzi with a capital P. The Pazzi family were one of the most powerful and influential families in fifteenth-century Florence and they were bitter enemies of the Medici.'

My mind was racing. Could it be that these arrows had been the work of an embittered rival family? No sooner did the idea cross my mind than I felt highly sceptical. After a wait of over five hundred years, as a motive for murder it was tenuous in the extreme. 'So do you think this Pazzi family might be behind these arrows and even the murder?'

Signor Rufina shook his head. 'Definitely not. They no longer exist.' He paused and then corrected himself. 'Well, there may be a few people still alive today who can trace their history that far back, but only in a very roundabout and distant way and I have no doubt none of them would stoop to murder.'

'Why are there so few descendants left?'

'Because Lorenzo de' Medici wiped the family off the face of the earth.' He leant against the workbench and launched into a bit of historical explanation. 'Things got so bad between the two families that in 1478 the Pazzi attempted to murder Lorenzo the Magnificent inside the duomo itself, of all places.' This sounded familiar and it chimed with what Martin Taylor, the writer, had told me. 'Lorenzo's brother, Giuliano, was killed in the attack and Lorenzo himself was injured. Lorenzo's vengeance was savage. He had the culprits caught, tortured and hanged from the Palazzo della Signoria until their bodies rotted. The whole Pazzi family were banned from Florence and their property confiscated. The family name and coat-of-arms were also banned, and anybody called Pazzi had to change to a different name. Within a matter of years, the Pazzi ceased to exist. Although some remnants of the family returned to Florence at the end of the fifteenth century, the Pazzi line effectively ended in 1478.'

'Wow.' I also leant against the workbench as I mulled over this tale of rivalry, intrigue and brutal revenge. 'Lorenzo the Magnificent wasn't a man to be trifled with, was he?' This wasn't completely new to me, but I hadn't realised the full extent of Lorenzo's ruthlessness. When I had been planning to write a thriller set around that famous family, I had concentrated on the early days, as they were rising to power, rather than the most famous of the Medici, Lorenzo. I stood there for a minute or two, turning over in my head the ramifications of the possible connection these arrows might have with a long-defunct noble Florentine family, and wondered, yet again, just how this might be linked to the murder of an American PR man in the twenty-first century.

I was finally roused by a woof from the courtyard where Oscar was reminding me that he was still in the car and, needless to say, hungry. I thanked Signor Rufina, retrieved the arrow from him, and went back out to my dog. Before going back home, I decided to go round to the *questura* to see Virgilio and relay to him what I'd just been told.

By now Oscar and I were a familiar sight at Florence's main police station, and we were allowed to climb the stairs to Virgilio's office unchallenged. As usual, the inspector was at his desk. On the whiteboard over to one side of the office there were photos of Donny Lopez: one of him alive with a smile on his face, and the other of his dead body, stretched out in the woods. The names and photos of the film people who might have been able to slip away and commit the murder were marked below, some with arrows linking them together. The actors' photos were clearly promotional shots, and it was unsettling to see so many smiling faces in a murder investigation. Even the producer was smiling, and I couldn't remember ever seeing him smiling before. It looked vaguely creepy.

Virgilio operated a traffic-light system with his marker pens for suspects and I saw that nobody had so far been transferred into the red or 'most likely' category, although the writer, Martin Taylor, had a big question mark alongside his name. Halfway down the board was a stick figure and a question mark, with the words 'Big Prowler' below it and, alongside it, another stick figure marked 'Figure seen by Dan'. Both of these had been written in orange ink. I was pleased to see my own name a bit lower down the board in green. It's always good to stay on the right side of a murder investigation. However, I was less amused to see that he had pinned up a photo of me in my stripy pantaloons, which reinforced my feeling that this was a look to be avoided at all costs. The photo of Anna, on the other hand, was very flattering and I found my eyes lingering on it. Virgilio looked up from his paper-work and gave me a little wave of greeting.

'*Ciao*, Dan and *ciao*, Oscar. How was your day out with Holly-wood royalty?'

'It was a great day.' While he petted the dog, I gave him a brief summary of where I'd been with the two ladies and then told him what Signor Rufina had told me about the possible significance of the blue and yellow vanes on the arrows. He listened intently, but his response was disappointing.

'It doesn't really help us very much, partly because I doubt, like your Signor Rufina said, that there are any descendants of the Pazzi left in Florence, and any who may still be around will be awfully distant. The other reason it doesn't help much is that most Italian schoolkids learn about the Medici and the Pazzi conspiracy at school, so anybody with half a brain could take that information and use it to muddy the waters of the investigation by making us think the murderer has to be a historian. Besides, I think the Pazzi conspiracy found its way into books and even video games, so it's far too well known. Still, you never know.' He looked up and caught my eye. 'Of course, if it *is* a history specialist, we have two among our list of suspects who might have been able to sneak off and kill Lopez: one of them being Martin Taylor, the writer, and...' he gave me a little grin, '...you've just spent the day driving around Tuscany with the other one.'

The same thought had already occurred to me, but I couldn't see Anna as a serious contender for the role of cold-blooded killer, and the fact that her name was written in green on the board showed that Virgilio didn't either. Still, even as I thought it, I couldn't help reminding myself that stranger things had happened. *Never rule anybody out* had been one of my mottos at Scotland Yard. As for Martin Taylor, he didn't exactly strike me as a potential Jack the Ripper either, and, from what I'd heard from him and Anna, history wasn't his strong suit. He had probably never even heard of the Pazzi family, let alone considered fiddling about with scissors and glue trying to duplicate their coat of arms on crossbow vanes. Virgilio waved towards a vacant seat.

'Anyway, thanks for the information and I'll bear it in mind. I'm glad you've come. Come and sit down. We've just received background information on the victim and the main suspects. It's mostly in English and I've made sense of much of it, but there are a few things I'm not so sure about.'

I sat down while he took me through what he'd received. He started with a bit more background information from the UK about Duggie Ogilvie and Charles Vincent. Neither produced any surprises apart from indicating that Scott Norris's assumption about Vincent's sexuality appeared to be unfounded. The report on the young actor included a long list of former female partners, but no boyfriends, and a number of the women had even taken to social media to lament the way they felt they'd been used and discarded by him. Duggie Ogilvie continued to get a clean bill of health, as did the other Brit in the group, Martin Taylor, the writer. No previous convictions.

Taylor was listed as divorced, but I wouldn't hold that against him. It can happen to anybody – as I knew to my cost – and Virgilio's second interview of the writer had been no more fruitful. When Virgilio had interviewed him again that afternoon, Taylor had sworn on his mother's life that he had only gone into the woods for a rest and nothing more. He hadn't seen Lopez or anybody else and he had heard nothing. Virgilio told me that he tended to believe him, but this didn't prevent him from continuing to keep a close eye on Taylor all the same. The writer still remained our most likely suspect here among the movie people, but there was nothing in the new information to suggest a violent or unstable history or any motive for killing Lopez.

Rachel Hindenburg, aka Dizzy, also had no criminal record. She was clearly a bright girl and had graduated *summa cum laude* from Yale, no less. She was unmarried and had been working for the film company for six years now. Virgilio's long talk with her that afternoon had shed no further light on the events of the previous day, although at the end of the interview she had managed to drop her pen into her coffee while showing him out. A necessary requirement for all good archers is a steady hand and, somehow, Dizzy just didn't fit into that category.

Selena Gardner had no criminal history. She didn't even have a parking ticket. She had notched up three divorces in her fifty-three years, but none were listed as particularly acrimonious. Certainly it seemed highly unlikely that any of her ex-husbands might be trying to kill her off.

Scott Norris had a minor offence involving possession of cannabis in his youth but nothing substantial. To my surprise I saw that he was listed as currently married, so if he was lusting after Selena, he shouldn't have been.

Gabriel Lyons had a few speeding fines but otherwise appeared to be an upright citizen although he, too, was described as married, so if the stories that he also had the hots for Selena were true, he wasn't living up to his marriage vows either.

I listened intently when the report on Anna Galardo was read out, but there was nothing there that she hadn't already told me. She had been married to a lecturer at Bristol University by the name of Alexander McGregor for ten years as she had said, but had kept her own name, and she was the mother of a daughter aged twenty-eight. No criminal record of any kind.

Emiliano Donizetti, the director, was slightly more interesting. He had a conviction for abusive and threatening behaviour and a number of minor offences, principally petty theft, while in his teens, but over the past twenty years he appeared to have lived a blameless life. He was unmarried and, like the rest of the suspects, he appeared to have no financial problems.

As for the victim, Donald Henry Lopez, he had been divorced, no convictions, and a healthy bank balance. People who knew him agreed with the general opinion of the people we had interviewed here that he had been a popular guy. There seemed no conceivable reason why he should have been targeted. I looked across the desk at Virgilio and shrugged my shoulders.

'I don't know about you, Virgilio, but in spite of my original hunch that it might have been an inside job, I'm now definitely leaning more towards the theory that the murderer came from outside the group and that the choice of Lopez was purely opportunistic. Whether the killer was the one who hit the food van or the shadowy figure seen by Elvis the other night – or they might be the same person – remains uncertain, but at this stage we have to consider all possibilities, however flimsy. I haven't heard anything from Dizzy today, so I assume the CCTV footage for last night didn't throw up any further sightings of him or her. Whoever it was, I'm coming round to thinking that he or she wanted to kill somebody, anybody, in order to stop the movie, and Lopez had the bad luck to be taking an afternoon nap in the wrong place.' Something occurred to me. 'By the way, any joy from the film footage? Any sign of the murderer in the woods?'

He shook his head. 'Nothing at all, mainly because the cameras were concentrating on the action taking place out in the fields most of the time. But from what we know so far, I totally agree that it's looking more and more likely that the murderer wasn't part of the group.' Virgilio glanced at his watch and gave a heartfelt sigh. 'I've been in this office for ten hours and my brain's scrambled. I need to go home. But first I need a drink. Fancy a beer?'

We walked out and around the corner to our usual café where

we found a table under a parasol and ordered two cold beers. October was turning out to be warmer than normal here in Florence and it occurred to me that a day like today would have been considered a perfect summer day back in England. As it was, it was six o'clock and autumn was already upon us and yet I could still feel residual warmth radiating up at me from the pavement beneath my feet. This appeared to suit Oscar who, after accepting the last remaining biscuit from the pack I'd picked up on set the previous day, settled down on the warm stone with a grunt of satisfaction.

The beers arrived and I had barely taken a sip of mine when my phone started ringing. It was Dizzy and she had news.

'Hi, Dan, I've just heard from Mr Lyons that we're going to carry on filming. We're going to shorten things, work through the weekend, and condense the last few days so as to be out of here by close of play on Monday.'

Today was Thursday so that meant only four more days of filming. Hopefully this wouldn't be long enough for our murderer to strike again. I thanked her and queried where filming would be taking place in the morning. She told me the company had been granted access to a section of the Boboli Gardens, not far from the top of the hill, so that there would be good views over the roofs of Florence as the backdrop to the action. I frowned as I heard this. Although it no doubt made sound cinematographic sense, I was well acquainted with that area – this was in fact not far from where my two Florentine councillors had been frolicking a couple of months earlier – and it offered numerous spots where a would-be assassin could hide with impunity. When I relayed the information to Virgilio at the end of the call, he shared my concern.

'I'll get some of my men to do a sweep of the area in the morning before the film crew start setting up. Hopefully if the killer's still on the loose, the sight of a bunch of uniformed officers will dissuade him from doing anything.'

'Or her...'

'Indeed, or her.'

But surely, if it was a woman, it couldn't be Anna, could it?

14

FRIDAY MORNING

Next morning, once more wearing tights and pantaloons, I was at the Boboli Gardens with my dog at eight o'clock, and we arrived at the same time as a police minibus disgorged half a dozen officers, who set about making a sweep of the area. It was another gorgeous day and the air was crystal clear, allowing some spectacular views over the roofs, spires, towers and cupolas of the city. At this time of the morning, I could feel a first hint of an autumn chill in the air, but I knew that the sun would make short work of warming things up. I followed the police officers into the gardens, and Oscar and I joined in the sweep, but we found nobody lying in wait. Hopefully the cast and crew would be safe today.

The gardens themselves were a delight and, at this time of the day with nobody else there, it was doubly pleasant to walk up between the lines of carefully trimmed hedges, past statues, grottoes and classical style temples. I came across, not only the ubiquitous Florentine pigeons in abundance, but also two beautiful brown, black and white hoopoes. These unusual birds with their crests and long curved beaks were remarkably unconcerned to see me and my dog, no doubt used to all the tourists in the gardens.

I remembered reading that the gardens themselves had been created on the orders of the Medici family for their own exclusive use, but this had been well after the death of Lorenzo the Magnificent. They had been constructed by his successors, so at the time of the events of this movie, they would not have existed. This historical inaccuracy didn't appear to bother the movie people and I was reminded of what Anna had said about the writer's fairly cavalier approach to historical facts. There was no doubt, however, that they formed a magnificent backdrop to today's scenes, and had it not been for the possibility of a murderer lying in hiding somewhere, this morning's walk in the gardens with my dog would have been absolutely charming.

A couple of uniformed officers stayed on the gate with the company's security people to ensure that it remained closed to the general public. It was just as well that they were there as the reports of the Donny Lopez murder had hit the national and international media by now and there was a scrum of journalists and paparazzi at the gate clamouring to get in. However it was that the news had got out, word that filming was taking place here today must have spread like wildfire, and I couldn't help thinking that this meant it might well have also reached the ears of our killer. Of course, as with Wednesday's shooting out at Cafaggiolo, all it would have needed would have been for the murderer to lurk somewhere near the trailer park and then simply follow the vans and trucks as they left there.

At eight-thirty, this same convoy began arriving at the Boboli Gardens and a swarm of crewmembers set about the laborious process of getting everything ready. At just after nine, a series of anonymous cars ferried in the actors and filming started.

As the morning progressed, I was once more called on to take part as an extra, albeit hidden away at the back of the crowd. Emmy instructed us all through his loudhailer to look first 'in amazement' and then 'in silent appreciation' at what was happening before us. I found the first facial expression easy enough but the second was more difficult until I tried imagining Anna down there looking gorgeous. That definitely worked for me. While I was doing this, I left my dog with Big Jim, who had two bacon cheeseburgers and a pile of fries on a plate in front of him. When I returned, all trace of both burgers and every single chip had disappeared, but I noticed that Oscar was still licking his lips. Another few days like this and he was going to need to go on a diet.

Around mid-morning, Emmy called a break, and I sat down for a coffee with Anna. Trestle tables had been set up near the top of the gardens on a flat gravelled area around a delightful Renaissance fountain in the middle of a circular pool. A chubby cherub sat in a wide stone bowl on a pillar in the middle of the water, while carved stone monkeys guarded the base. From up here we could look in both directions: north across the roofs of Florence but also to the south away from the city towards a panorama of green hills topped by cypresses, olive trees, and magnificent villas painted in that wonderful sandy light ochre colour so common here in Tuscany.

It was a charming view – and Anna looked as attractive as usual as she made a fuss of Oscar. We were joined after a few minutes by the director and the writer, and I had to dismiss a feeling of annoyance at the intrusion. I had been enjoying Anna's company and wished I could keep her all to myself. To make matters worse, only a minute or two later, Scott and Selena also came and sat down with us. Seeing as the intimacy had been spoiled, I reverted to doing my job.

'Tell me, you history experts.' I was addressing this principally to Anna, but I thought it only polite to include the others, particularly the writer and the director. 'What's this I've been hearing about the Pazzi conspiracy? How come the two families were at daggers drawn?'

Predictably, the others deferred to the history professor and Anna did her best to explain it to me – and to the others. 'During the Florentine Renaissance, there were many big, important family names, but the most famous of them all were the Medici. They were bankers but, like some members of the banking fraternity today, they sometimes made their money by questionable means. Along the way they made powerful enemies, and top of the list were the Pazzi.'

'Were they bankers too?'

'Yes, and, until the Medici came along, they were among the richest and most powerful here in Florence. The Medici managed to take over the top spot from them – not always by legitimate means – and were soon ruling the roost.'

'That can't have gone down too well with the Pazzi family.'

'It definitely didn't. That's why they finally decided to get rid of the Medici, starting with the ruthless and all-powerful Lorenzo the Magnificent. By the way, nobody knows who first started calling him "Magnificent", but it wouldn't surprise me for a moment if it was Lorenzo himself. If he were around today, I'm sure he would be branded a narcissist. As for the conspiracy, that's what this movie's loosely based on.'

This was the signal for the director to join in. '*Very* loosely. *Lust for Power* is principally a modern-day thriller. Martin's screenplay references an imaginary conspiracy with imaginary names. The Pazzi don't come into it as far as we're concerned.'

Martin Taylor nodded in agreement. 'So as to avoid any possible complications, just in case there might be any descendants of any of the old families left around, I deliberately invented a totally fictitious family with a different name. You know: "any resemblance to actual persons, living or dead, is entirely coincidental".'

This was interesting. If Signor Rufina was right about the crossbow bolts bearing Pazzi colours, they made little sense. From what Emmy was saying, the Pazzi didn't get a mention in the movie, so even supposing this was the work of some disaffected long-lost relative, why go to all the trouble of cutting off the plastic vanes and going through the fiddly and time-consuming business of substituting them with coloured feathers? From what Signor Rufina had told me, it would have taken hours to do, and so it must have had real significance for the person who did it. But why?

As I was thinking, I saw Dizzy approaching bearing a tray. I pushed out a chair for her and she came across to sit down. As she did so, three things happened simultaneously: first, I felt Oscar jump to his feet as he recognised her and, second, Dizzy tripped over something – probably her own feet – and fell forwards, tipping her doughnut onto Emmy's lap and sending a shower of cappuccino over the rest of us. We all jumped back in unison, and it was at that precise moment that the third thing happened.

There was a sudden thwack and we stared in stunned shock at Emmy, all of us struggling to comprehend what had just happened. I found myself blinking several times before the penny dropped. An arrow was now firmly lodged in the director's upper arm. A second or two later, the frame unfroze. Emmy gave a howl of pain, Selena and Dizzy screamed, and most of us threw ourselves to the ground to take cover. I crouched on the gravel next to my clearly puzzled dog for a few more seconds before cautiously straightening up again and looking around. Most were still cowering alongside or under the table and Emmy was sprawled back in his chair, his right hand clasping his left bicep. His eyes were wide open, locked on the bloodstained arrow in his arm, and his breath was coming in rasping gasps. I caught sight of Big Jim on the next table and shouted to him.

'Jim! Get the police. Now!'

It took a moment or two, but then the security guard took in what had happened and heaved himself to his feet, setting off at a surprisingly swift pace downhill towards the gate. Inconsequentially, I found myself hoping he wouldn't barrel into anybody on the way or the results could have been lethal. Returning to the matter in hand, I went around the table to Emmy and gently prised his hand from the arrow and tore the cloth of his tunic to expose the wound. As I did so, I couldn't miss the fact that the flights of the arrow were a deep blue colour with those same bright yellow dolphin shapes painted on them. The arrow had wedged in his arm, which was twitching as his muscles contracted, but I was relieved to see that blood was oozing, rather than spurting, from the wound. Hopefully it had missed any significant blood vessels as it sliced into him.

I looked across at Dizzy, who was now upright again, an expression of utter horror on her face as she stared, spellbound, at the arrow. I had to wave my hand to attract her attention, and it took a moment or two before she could drag her eyes away from the scene.

I adopted my most comforting tone, not just for her benefit, but for all of the stunned onlookers and, indeed, the victim himself. 'It looks gruesome, but I don't think it's too bad. If you have a first-aid kit, it could be useful. I'll call for an ambulance.'

Comprehension dawned on Dizzy's face, and she rushed off towards the trucks. I made the call for an ambulance and then pulled a chair to Emmy's side and offered reassurance. At his feet, my dog disposed of the flying doughnut that had probably saved the director's life. I let him get on with it. It wasn't as if he were destroying evidence after all, although how it would sit on top of the bacon cheeseburger and fries Big Jim had given him earlier remained to be seen.

I carried on doing my best to provide reassurance. 'Emmy, you're going to be okay. It looks as though you've been very lucky. If you hadn't jumped back when Dizzy dropped her tray, the arrow might have hit you in the chest.'

He nodded and asked the obvious question. 'But I thought the police did a sweep. How could this have happened?' He was looking very pale, but he sounded once again in control, although the sight of the arrow sticking out of his arm must have been as disconcerting to him as it was to the rest of us. I studied it carefully.

'This arrow's a lot longer than the crossbow bolts and it's made of wood. Off the top of my head, it looks like this is a proper arrow, either fired from a traditional bow or from a far more serious crossbow than the other one. All I can assume is that whatever it was, it has a longer range.'

I did a quick calculation based on where Emmy had been sitting and the angle of entry of the arrow and looked back in the rough direction from which it must have come. The high stone wall surrounding the gardens was just visible in a few places through the trees and bushes and was probably at least fifty metres away. There was no sign of any intruder, but it wouldn't have been impossible for somebody with a bow to climb onto the top of the wall and fire from there. They could then have easily made their escape unseen and I had little doubt that he or she would be far away by now.

I called Virgilio to give him the news and I heard him groan. 'Okay, stay there. We're on our way.'

By this time news of what had happened must have spread throughout the cast and crew, and people started gathering. One of the first to arrive was Gabriel Lyons, out of breath after running up the hill.

'What the hell? Another arrow...? What the hell?' He stared in shock at Emmy's bloodstained arm, his eyes wide and his normally ruddy cheeks now the colour of a ripe tomato. After a few seconds he swung around towards me. 'How did this happen? Didn't the police check the area?'

I told him my theory about a long-distance archer, and he looked even more perplexed. 'What the hell?' He was getting a bit repetitive, but that was the shock. And the fear. 'What're we dealing with here: Robin frickin' Hood, for God's sake?'

Fortunately, two uniformed police officers appeared at that moment, and I told them my theory about a shooter on the wall. The sergeant nodded and spoke into his radio, asking for a patrol car to head around to the other side of the wall just in case the would-be killer was still in the area. In the distance I heard the familiar sirens of the emergency services.

15

FRIDAY LATE MORNING

It wasn't long before I saw Sergeant Innocenti come running up the hill, closely followed by his boss and a pair of paramedics. Leaving the medics to look after Emmy, I went over to greet Virgilio and outlined what had happened. He and Innocenti listened closely, and both agreed that in all likelihood Dizzy's trademark clumsiness had averted another murder. The uniformed officer's radio crackled, and he came over to report to the inspector.

'One of our cars is over on the other side of the wall now and they report that there's nobody to be seen, but there are fresh tracks of a big vehicle like a van in the scrub at the side of the track. They say the wall's about two and a half metres high, so somebody could easily have climbed it from the roof of a vehicle or even stood on the roof and fired from there.'

Virgilio nodded. 'Good work. Get Forensics to take plaster casts of the tyre marks just in case. We need to compare them with the tracks found at the side of that road over the hill from Cafaggiolo.'

We walked back over to find that the paramedics had snipped

the arrow off close to the entry and exit wounds and Emmy had
been bandaged with his arm secured in a sling as a temporary fix.
Sergeant Innocenti bagged the cut pieces and no doubt the
remaining section of the arrow would be removed at the hospital
under anaesthetic. Emmy was being accompanied down to the
ambulance by the paramedics and I was relieved to see him walk-
ing. There was no doubt about it. He had been very lucky indeed –
certainly a lot luckier than Donny Lopez.

Dizzy, Selena and Anna were still standing there alongside the
producer, the writer and Scott Norris, all of them looking shell-
shocked, although Selena still looked as beautiful as ever. Dizzy
recovered enough to tell us that the other two principal actors,
Charles Vincent and Duggie Ogilvie, hadn't been needed this
morning and so were out of harm's way back at their hotel. I
exchanged glances with Virgilio: back at the hotel or maybe on the
other side of the wall?

I translated while Innocenti took statements and then the
producer announced that filming was cancelled for the rest of the
day. I went and spoke to him afterwards as the crew set about
packing everything up again. He was obviously very upset; so
upset in fact that he didn't bat an eyelid when Oscar wandered
over and nuzzled his hand. He even ruffled the dog's ears in
response.

'What about tomorrow, Mr Lyons? Are you planning on doing
more filming?'

He shook his head. 'No, that's it as far as exteriors are
concerned. I would have liked to do a bit more, but I reckon we
can manage with what we've already got in the can. We still have a
few indoor scenes to shoot over the coming days, but hopefully
there'll be no opportunity for our crazy bowman to fire any more
arrows at anybody.' He gave me a pleading look. 'What the hell's

going on? Who's behind this and why? We're just making a movie, after all...'

'I share your frustration. I don't get it either.' I started to tell him about the Pazzi and the blue and yellow flights on the arrows, but I saw his eyes glaze over long before I got to the end. I cut it short and finished with a promise to do all I could to find the perpetrator, but I could see the scepticism on his face. I didn't blame him. He'd hired me to find the source of the threats and the only results so far had been a murder and an attempted murder. I thought the least I should do was ask him if he wanted to save the company some money and dispense with my services, but to my surprise he shook his head.

'No, you stick at it. I know it's not your fault, and my people – Selena in particular – need all the protection I can give them.'

I sat down for lunch with Virgilio in a little restaurant by the River Arno – Innocenti had gone back to the *questura* – and we discussed the events of the morning over *pappardelle alla lepre* – thick strips of pasta in a rich gamey sauce. Today I'd remembered to bring a change of clothing and had been able to slip out of my Renaissance costume before walking into the centre. There's a limit to how many times you want to be stopped by tourists asking for a selfie alongside them. As it was, I had a feeling that a number of photo albums from Tokyo to Tennessee would now forever contain my face and a pair of knobbly English knees.

A naturally suspicious person, I started with the two missing actors. 'Do we think Charles Vincent or Duggie Ogilvie might have done it? Unless they can come up with convincing evidence that they were nowhere near the Boboli Gardens this morning, we have to consider them as suspects, although they were both almost hit by the arrow that struck the food truck the other day.'

'Yes, we need to include them but it's pretty unlikely they were involved. Okay, it's just possible they got a third party to stage the food-truck attack, deliberately just missing them, and one or the other might have had the opportunity to kill Lopez out at Cafaggiolo, but it's complicated and we need a motive. I just can't see what possible benefit either of them could have got out of killing Lopez or the director.' He reached for his wine glass. 'And as far as I'm concerned, everything points towards it being the same perpetrator in all three cases and it's hard to pin it on anybody here among the cast or crew.'

'I agree that we're almost certainly just looking for one person, although I suppose it's possible this was a copycat attempted murder by somebody else. And there's another thing: I suppose we have to consider that Emmy might not have been the killer's intended target at all. When Dizzy tripped and spilled her coffee all over the place, everybody jumped. Maybe the real target was one of the others: Anna, Selena, Taylor, Scott or Dizzy herself?'

'Or you.' Virgilio's words took me by surprise.

'Me? Who on earth would want to kill me?' I'd had a few death threats over the years from villains I'd put behind bars, but was it credible that somebody would have come all the way to Italy to kill me, a year and a half after I'd retired?

'Cast your mind back, Dan. It might be worth racking your brains and asking Paul at Scotland Yard to check whether anybody from your past with a particular grudge against you has recently been released from prison.'

'Yes, but if they were after *me*, why did they kill Lopez the other day?'

'The more I think about it, the more I reckon Lopez was killed by mistake. Think about it. Almost all the men in the cast and crew were wearing the same stripy outfits as you. Lopez was about your height with dark hair like yours, and he'd been resting face-down on the ground, his head on his arm. What if the killer mistook him for you? Come to think of it, what if the intended victim was the writer, Taylor? He also looks pretty similar to Lopez and to you – at least from behind. Either way, I'm increasingly convinced that the murder of Lopez was either random or a mistake.'

'You may well be right.'

It was a sobering thought, although I couldn't see how I could be the intended target. The death threats aimed at the movie had been launched days before I had had any involvement with it. There was no way that anybody – myself included – could have imagined any connection between me and the movie at that stage. However, the fact was that the threats and Donny Lopez's death, and indeed my involvement in the investigation, were now common knowledge, and it could be that somebody had jumped at the chance to piggyback on the threats to the movie to get revenge on me, feeling confident that there would be no way they were likely to be linked to the investigation. I would have to search my memory banks.

I shook my head sadly. 'Poor Donny Lopez. Of course, there's another possibility. It could be that this morning's bowman just fired blindly in the direction of the film people, rather than picking out somebody specific, and the arrow just happened to hit Emmy. It's a long way from the wall to our table and it would have taken a skilled archer to pinpoint any one person from there.'

'That's been bothering me, too. Let's face it – there aren't too many people alive these days who know their way around bows and arrows.' He grinned. 'Back in Lorenzo the Magnificent's time it would have been a different matter.'

'What I could do is check with the old boy in the picture-framing workshop to see if he could let us have a list of names of members of his archery club, particularly the really good ones. Could you ask somebody in Forensics to take a couple of good quality photos of the pieces of the arrow removed from Emmy's arm and send them over for me to show to Signor Rufina? Maybe they could also provide the exact length of the arrow before it got chopped up as well. Signor Rufina might be able to shed some light on the weapon involved. I reckon it must have been a proper bow this time, rather than a crossbow.'

Virgilio nodded and called Forensics to ask for the arrow photos to be sent to him and was just putting the phone down again when it started ringing. Somebody at the other end then gave him a long report and all I heard for a couple of minutes were occasional grunts from Virgilio and a series of monosyllabic replies. He finished the conversation with a terse, 'I'll come right round.'

He drained his glass and shot me an apologetic glance. 'Sorry, Dan, but I have to go. We have a missing woman, possible abduction or maybe murder: traces of blood in her apartment but no body. It doesn't sound good. Would you be able to help Innocenti have another talk to the writer this afternoon? The more I think about it, the more I reckon Lopez was killed by mistake – and that means it was either just a random choice or he may have been mistaken for the writer or for you. As for you, I strongly advise you to have a long hard think about former customers of yours who might want to kill you.'

'I will, I promise, but there can't be many.'

'Just do it, for my sake. Now, this afternoon when you and Innocenti speak to Taylor, I need to know if there's anybody, anybody at all, who might have it in for him. I know we've asked all of them that already, but there's nothing like a near-death experience to focus the mind. At least today's assault would appear to clear him of any involvement in Lopez's murder – assuming the same person is responsible for both assaults – so that's one more off our list of suspects, along with the other people who were on your table this morning. As for today's victim, we'll leave him in peace until tomorrow, but you'd better question the other people who were with you again, just in case there's anything they might have forgotten to tell us. Do it on the phone by all means, rather than getting them to come back to the trailer park.' He caught my eye and winked. 'Innocenti can question Anna Galardo on his own. I imagine you might find it a bit embarrassing if she started talking about past lovers.'

I did my best to meet his eye. 'I'm a pro, Virgilio. She could tell me what colour underwear she's wearing, and I wouldn't blush.'

He gave me a sceptical look but he didn't comment. Instead, he got to his feet and headed for the cash desk. As I followed him, he glanced back at me. 'Let me know if you have any bright ideas or if your Signor Rufina can add anything when he sees the photos of the arrow. *Ciao*.'

16

FRIDAY AFTERNOON

That afternoon, Sergeant Innocenti and I met a still visibly shocked Martin Taylor at the trailer park. Dizzy had arranged the meeting and had been able to reassure us that not only was Emmy already out of hospital and back at his hotel, resting, but that he was determined to continue directing when they filmed the last remaining interior scenes over the next three days. With me translating and adding a few questions of my own as we went along, Innocenti quizzed the writer about any possible enemies he might have, and he shook his head and pleaded ignorance until we mentioned social media. When I queried whether he'd been involved in any online spats, at first he indicated he couldn't remember any, but when I reminded him that his life might be in danger, he finally opened up.

'Well... there was one. About six months ago, I started getting abusive tweets and messages from somebody on Twitter.'

'Who was this person? Did you know them?'

'Not at all. All I know is their Twitter handle. It was @author4261478.'

'You remember the full number?'

'There were a lot of tweets; sometimes twenty or thirty a day, all abusive. The name and number sort of imprinted themselves on my memory.'

'And it was a man?'

'I have no idea. I've assumed it was a man, but it could just as easily have been a woman. There's no photo on Twitter and no contact details. I tried asking Twitter but all they said was for me to block them, which I did.'

'And why was he or she being abusive?'

'The tweets were just ranting and raving and barely comprehensible, but I got the impression whoever it was thought I'd copied their work.'

'What sort of work?'

'They didn't specify, but I assumed they'd written something that they thought I'd plagiarised.'

'And had you?' My contract with the new publishers had contained a clause specifically about this kind of thing. It was definitely a no-no in the publishing world.

For a fraction of a second, I felt sure I spotted a flash of guilt on his face, but it disappeared in an instant. 'No, of course not. All my ideas are my own.'

'You're sure about that?'

'Yes, definitely.' I detected more than a hint of bluster, so I tried pressing him.

'What have you written, prior to this film?'

He reeled off a list of half a dozen books and screenplays – mainly contemporary thrillers, by the sound of them – followed by this one, which had a historical bent.

I tried again. 'And what made you write this particular screenplay? You already told me that history wasn't really your thing.'

'I read an article about Florence in an in-flight magazine on one of my trips to the States and it gave me the idea. But, like I told you, *Lust for Power* is a thriller, not a historical saga. The historical element is only a very minor part of it, and I got everything I needed off the Internet.'

When I translated this to Innocenti, I read the same scepticism in his eyes as I was feeling myself. 'You say this was six months ago. Has the Twitter person been in touch since?'

Taylor hesitated and then nodded reluctantly. 'Yes, back at the end of August, just after we started filming in the States. Although I'd blocked the original Twitter account, he or she started up again with the username @4261478author – they just inverted it – and seeing as they started going on about this movie, it was pretty clear the tweets were referring to the screenplay for *Lust for Power*.'

'And you didn't think this was worth mentioning to us when we first spoke to you?' There was something very smelly about this and I gave him my sternest chief inspector stare. He dropped his eyes to his fingers on the table in front of him, which were twisting nervously.

'I didn't think it was important.' Even he must have realised how feeble that sounded as he added, 'Besides, you know what Twitter's like: it's full of loonies.'

'And as far as you're concerned, there was no justification for these comments?' I kept my tone hard and sceptical.

'None at all. Like I said, all my ideas are my own.'

'And has this person continued to bombard you with Twitter messages since then?'

'No, I blocked them again.'

'Are you aware of another screenplay or maybe a book that could be construed as being similar to your screenplay?'

'Not at all. I even did an Internet search to see if there was something out there that would help me track down this character, but I could find nothing.'

By the time I came out of the interview, my opinion of Taylor had gone right down and Innocenti was feeling the same way. It looked clear that there was another writer out there who was convinced Taylor had stolen his or her work. This same person might have decided to scupper the movie by any means and yet Taylor hadn't thought it worth mentioning. It beggared belief. Discovering the identity of this person would be like looking for a needle in a haystack, but it was certainly a line of inquiry we had to follow up. Of course, there's a big difference between having a slanging match on social media and resorting to murder over a piece of professional plagiarism, but I agreed with Taylor on one thing: there were a lot of loonies on social media. And some of them were loony enough to start killing people.

After Martin Taylor had left, Innocenti and I spoke to the others, but without getting any new ideas. Dizzy herself was unable to add any suggestions either. It was getting really frustrating. Finally, I went over to the food van and helped myself to a cup of tea – I am English, and it was mid-afternoon after all – while Innocenti made the call to Anna. The sky was clouding over a bit and the temperature had dropped and I was able to sit at a table in the open without risking sunstroke. This also had the advantage of being out of earshot of anybody, so that when Innocenti returned we could talk freely. He told me how his interview with Anna had gone – again nothing of note to report – and pointed out what he considered to be the obvious conclusion to be drawn from today's events.

'At least it's clear now that Anna Galardo, Selena Gardner, Rachel Hindenburg, Scott Norris and Martin Taylor – plus the director with an arrow in his arm of course – can't be our murderers.' He grinned at me. 'And that clears you, too. I'm sure we need to look for somebody else.'

I'd been thinking about this and, although I tended to agree, I felt obliged to play devil's advocate. 'I suppose it's possible that there might be two perpetrators in it together, or maybe today was just a copycat attack by a totally unrelated person. The arrow story's been plastered all over the media and some lunatic might have done it just for the hell of it.'

'I suppose that could be the case, but if any of the people with you at the table were working with the person who fired the arrow, then they must have been very sure of his ability to hit the right target. I wouldn't like to trust the accuracy of a bow and arrow at fifty metres.'

'That's a good point. So if we exclude these people and exclude a crazy copycat, who are we left with?'

Innocenti checked his notebook. 'Assuming today's arrow was fired by the same person who killed Lopez, I feel it has to have been somebody unknown to us, like the driver of the vehicle that left its tyre tracks in the mud on the other side of the wall of the Boboli Gardens, for instance. I suppose it's just possible one or other of the two actors not on set this morning might be involved, but if they're responsible for all the attacks, how did they manage to be on the receiving end of the food-truck attack the other day? Then there's what Taylor's just told us. I'll get our people onto checking with Twitter in the hope that we can discover the identity of the person who's been harassing him, but I'm not holding my breath. It's so easy to hide behind a wall of anonymity on social media. Otherwise, everybody else was here in the Boboli Gardens and in such a small area, they couldn't have slipped away unnoticed.'

His phone bleeped and he interrupted his flow to check his messages. What he read made him jump to his feet.

'The boss wants me to check out something to do with the woman who went missing this morning. I have to go. Would you feel like sitting down with Charles Vincent and Douglas Ogilvie?

Find out where they were this morning and what they were doing. It's probably a waste of time but it needs to be done.'

I assured him I would get onto it, and he headed off to meet up with Virgilio. I went back to Dizzy and she greeted my dog with warm hugs and a handful of biscuits. She certainly knew her way to a Labrador's heart. Oscar was quite clearly a very happy boy, although I feared that the mix of cheeseburger, fries, doughnut and biscuits might produce unpleasant results later on. Once he had finally subsided onto his back on the floor at Dizzy's feet, I asked her to arrange for me to meet up with Ogilvie and Vincent, and she made the calls. As efficient as ever, she fixed up for me to see them in the city centre: Ogilvie at five o'clock at his hotel, and Charles Vincent at six in a bar close to the duomo.

Before I left, Dizzy gave me the address of a private villa on the way up the hill towards Fiesole where they would be shooting in the morning, and I promised to be there to keep an eye on proceedings – even if my track record so far as a bodyguard was lamentable.

17

FRIDAY LATE AFTERNOON

After a struggle to persuade Oscar to leave Dizzy and come with me, he and I set off for my office. First things first, I wanted to speak to Signor Rufina about the arrow, the photo and details of which were now on my phone. I found the old man hard at work, this time on a very intricate frame for what looked very much like an old master. I queried it and he nodded.

'It's a Botticelli – the portrait of Simonetta Vespucci.' Seeing my expression of alarm – this painting had to be worth millions and I knew for a fact that security here in Signor Rufina's workshop was non-existent – he grinned and explained. 'Don't worry, this is just a print. I reframe paintings for many galleries, including the Uffizi, but for obvious reasons they just give me a print on a board exactly the same size as the original. I make the frame and hand it over to them. It's all right, no cause for alarm.'

Reassured, I handed him my phone. 'I wonder if you can tell me anything about this arrow. It's over twice as long as the original crossbow bolts. The medics had to cut it into three pieces in order to remove it from the victim. There's a ruler alongside the pieces so you can see the total length.'

He studied the photos carefully for some time. 'Well, the first thing I can tell you is that this is indeed an arrow, not a crossbow bolt. I can see that it's made of wood. Crossbow bolts are made of metal and are much heavier. They were originally designed to be tough enough to penetrate steel armour. This was shot from a traditional bow, maybe even a longbow. I see it has the same blue and yellow flights as the crossbow bolts. Where did it come from?'

I told him it had been fired at a group of us that morning, wounding one person, and I told him I wanted to take advantage of his expertise. 'The distance from where the archer was standing to where we were sitting was something like fifty metres, maybe a tad more. How accurate could something like this be over such a distance?'

'In the right hands, very accurate. For example, Olympic archery contests are up to seventy metres and the best archers normally get their arrows close to the centre of the target almost every time. Did you say it hit somebody? Not fatally, I hope.'

'No, but it could so easily have done.' I went on to ask him how I could get hold of a list of archers in the Florence area who would be capable of hitting a target at that distance, and he directed me to the website of the Florence Archery Society. I thanked him and went up to my office, where I checked out the website on my computer and found lists of competitors in the monthly archery contests. In all, there were somewhere around a hundred names, but none of them were familiar to me. I printed off a copy for myself and sent the link across to Innocenti just in case. By this time, it was gone half past four, so I set off for Duggie Ogilvie's hotel. On the way there I received a very welcome call. It was Anna.

'*Ciao*, Dan. I've been talking to Selena, and we wondered if you were doing anything special this evening. There's the annual ceramics fair in Piazza Santa Croce today, and Selena's asked me if

I'd like to take a look and then maybe go out for dinner afterwards. Because of everything that's happening, she says she'd feel safer if you were with us and she'd enjoy your company.' There was a momentary pause before she added, 'And so would I.'

My immediate instinct was to say yes, but I hesitated. The idea of spending an evening with the two ladies was appealing, not least as an outdoor venue would mean I wouldn't have to rush home first and bribe Oscar to spend the evening on his own. The trouble was that a crowded festival environment would make it almost impossible for me to provide much in the way of body-guarding. Before I could express my reservations, Anna set about assuaging my concerns.

'Selena says to tell you that she'll wear a long black wig and a sack for a dress that should conceal her identity. Would that help?'

'Definitely. And of course I'd thoroughly enjoy your company... the company of both of you. It's just that I'm still a bit worried about your safety.' Or, if Virgilio was right, my own safety if some former London bad boy was on my trail. I hadn't had any success so far delving into my memory banks to see if any names came up, but I would keep trying, although I felt sure I couldn't be the intended target. If so, why all the charade with fancy arrows? Surely there had to be a link with the movie, not with a retired detective from London.

Anna was quick to offer reassurance. 'Selena said that would be your reaction, but not to worry; she isn't worried.'

'What about you, Anna? What do you think?'

'Life has to go on, Dan. I say let's do it.'

'Okay, it's a date.' As I said it, I reflected that an evening out with a woman, let alone two of them, was a real rarity for me. 'What time and where shall we meet?'

'I'll take a taxi to her hotel to collect her, so shall we say Piazza Santa Croce opposite the basilica at seven?'

'At the west end of the square, got it. See you there.'

I met Duggie Ogilvie at five as arranged. He was waiting for me in the lobby of his hotel, and he led me out onto an internal patio where we sat down at a table in one corner, out of earshot of anybody else, and concealed from curious eyes by a huge lemon tree in an ornate terracotta pot. I started by asking him about his former boyfriend's killer and he produced some new information.

'He's out of jail – but you maybe already know that – and I believe he's gone to South America. Needless to say, I've never met him, and I never want to, but I heard on the grapevine that he left the country almost as soon as they let him out of jail. He was a singer, so I imagine he'll end up in some sleazy nightclub.' He shook his head sadly. 'And good riddance.'

'And you're sure he's gone?'

'That's what I heard.'

I made a note to ask Paul in London to verify that just to be on the safe side. Assuming it was correct, it appeared to rule out an attempt on Duggie's life by his former lover's killer, so I moved on to more pressing matters. 'Listen, Duggie, Inspector Pisano's asked me to check where everybody was when Emmy was hit by the arrow. I gather you weren't wanted on set until the afternoon.'

'That's right. I had a lazy morning and then I went out for lunch with a friend. What time did Emmy get hurt?'

'At just after eleven-thirty.'

'At that time I was still in my room having breakfast.'

'Can anybody corroborate that?'

'The rather handsome young man from Room Service. He brought the tray in around that time.' He gave me a cheerful wink. 'I thought about asking him if he wanted to join me for breakfast in bed, but then I decided I'd better be a good boy. I have a reputation to maintain these days, but it's a pity, really; he was *very* attractive.'

That alibi sounded easy enough to confirm, and I was just wrapping up the interview when he changed the subject to me.

'I've been meaning to ask you: why did you leave the police? You were very good at your job. I thought you'd end up as Chief Constable.'

'That's kind of you, Duggie, but there was no way I'd ever get promoted that far up the ladder. I was far too much trouble for that.' As for the real reason I had retired at fifty-five, I decided to leave my ex-wife out of it. 'I left because I needed a change.'

'And why Tuscany?'

'Good food, good wine, good weather, beautiful scenery... what's not to love?'

'You have a point there. It *is* a gorgeous part of the world. I always thought if I hadn't become an actor, I would have made a wonderful art thief – you know, old masters and so on – and of course, for that, Florence has to be the best place to start.'

'Well, I can only say I'm glad you made the right career choice. I arrested the head of a worldwide art theft gang years ago and he ended up being put away for fifteen years. You wouldn't have enjoyed that.'

'No, I suppose you're right, but it does sound so dashing somehow.'

'There's nothing dashing about His Majesty's penitentiaries, I can tell you.'

'I suppose you're right.' But he didn't look convinced.

As I walked back towards the duomo for my appointment with Charles Vincent, I found myself thinking about the art thief. Antony 'Tonio' Fortunato had been his name, and he had belonged to a very dodgy Italo-English family of villains in Streatham, in the days before that part of London went upmarket. He had started out as an accountant and moved on from there to cooking the books for some of the most unsavoury members of the

UK underworld. He had subsequently made the leap into creating his own criminal empire and had proved to be very good at his chosen career. Catching him and rolling up his network had been a major feather in my cap, and I rated it as among my better arrests.

Interestingly, now I came to think of it, the last words I ever heard him speak had been in court after the judge had delivered his sentence and they had been a vituperative threat directed at me that had resulted in the judge threatening to add a year to his sentence. I'd shrugged it off at the time, but a quick calculation told me that if Fortunato had made parole, he would probably have been released from jail after eight years or so and, as far as I could remember, his arrest had been roughly that long ago. Could it be...?

I sat down on the stone steps outside one of Florence's innumerable churches and called Paul in London. A female officer whose name I didn't recognise but who knew mine told me that Inspector Wilson wasn't in his office, so I left a message with her to ask him to check Antonio Fortunato along with Duggie's boyfriend's killer. Thinking back to what Virgilio had said, it was probably worth checking up on both, but I couldn't believe that a character from Duggie's or my past could still be out for revenge after so long and, particularly, should have chosen to resort to all this medieval mumbo-jumbo with bows and arrows, but it made sense to be sure, if only to keep Virgilio happy.

I had to wait almost a quarter of an hour before Charles Vincent appeared. Oscar and I had found a table on the pavement outside the café, and I spent the time watching the world go by. Here in Florence, there were visitors from all around the globe; I never ceased to enjoy the spectacle and mentally recorded some of the more interesting faces to slip into my books. I started counting the number of people carrying bags of a suitable size in which to hide a folded crossbow and soon had to give up. The sheer number of these reinforced the scale of the task ahead of us, if our murderer was indeed somebody as yet unknown to us.

Finally, I caught sight of Charles Vincent emerging from the throng and on his arm, or, rather, wrapped round his arm, was a very pretty girl wearing a microskirt. When he saw me, he said something to her, and she pouted for a few seconds before kissing him as if her life depended on it and heading off towards the shops. I remembered the scene at the trailer park when I had caught Charles and Dizzy together and both had produced guilty looks. If Dizzy and he were romantically involved, I wondered whether she knew that she didn't occupy an exclusive place in his affections. I hoped she wouldn't end up with a broken heart when she found out. I liked Dizzy – maybe not quite as much as my four-legged friend did, but still quite a lot.

Charles made his way over to where I was sitting, acknowledging greetings from random members of the public who must have recognised him from his TV series as he threaded his way through the tables. One thing was for sure: he didn't appear to be making any effort to keep a low profile. Whether this was because he knew he was in no danger because he was the person responsible for the murder of Lopez and Emmy's attempted murder, or whether he was just irresponsible, remained to be established. Maybe he was just so young he still thought of himself as invulnerable and immortal. If so, I envied him his laid-back attitude to life and hoped it would serve him well.

I waved him into the vacant seat opposite me and asked him where he'd been at eleven-thirty this morning. Like Duggie Ogilvie, he claimed to have still been in his hotel room. I asked him if there was anybody who could provide him with an alibi, wondering if his friend in the short skirt might have been with him, but he shook his head.

'I'm afraid not. I got up late, probably around nine-thirty, went out for a run, and then I spent the rest of the morning learning my lines and working out.'

'And you were back at your hotel still doing your lines and exercises at eleven-thirty?'

'Yes, until about half past twelve. I work out most mornings – apart from the days when I'm on set.'

Although he couldn't provide me with an alibi, his story rang true. I knew that actors at this level – particularly ones for whom physical appearance was vital – took an inordinate amount of exercise to keep their bodies suitably toned for the cameras and the fans. The other thing was that to my way of thinking, his lack of an alibi actually worked in his favour. A cold-blooded murderer who took the trouble to make his own arrow flights would surely have organised an alibi for himself before setting off with his bow. I ticked Charles off in my head as still a possible suspect, but not really a serious contender. Apart from anything else, although I quizzed him, I couldn't come up with any kind of motive he might have for wanting to murder Lopez or Emmy. By the time I released him to return to his girlfriend, I was no closer to knowing who might be behind these attacks.

18

FRIDAY EVENING

I met up with Selena and Anna that evening in Piazza Santa Croce as arranged. The whole square was packed with stands where expert potters demonstrated their art alongside stalls selling pottery and, of course, vendors of food, wine and souvenirs. The magnificent white marble façade of the Basilica of Santa Croce formed a spectacular backdrop to the exhibition. Our resident history expert told us that construction of the church – the biggest in the city – had started at the end of the thirteenth century and had taken a century and a half to complete. I told them I'd come across a few builders back in London who worked at a similar rate. They would turn up late, make a pretence of a start, leave a few tools around to give the impression they were coming back, and then disappear off to another job.

Although the church was closed at this hour, I resolved to visit it sometime soon. According to Anna it housed the tombs of Michelangelo and Galileo along with a veritable rollcall of the great and the good of Italian history. My ears pricked up when Anna told us that one of the outstanding features of the church was the Cappella dei Pazzi, built in honour of the Pazzi family only a few years before the infamous conspiracy and the subsequent extinction of the whole line. Why did this name keep cropping up?

We spent almost an hour wandering around the ceramics exhibition, during which time Selena bought herself a charming lamp and asked for it to be sent to her hotel the next day. The stallholder had by this time recognised her and wasted no time in asking her to pose with him for a couple of shots, which would, no doubt, be used for promotional purposes in the years to come. Other people also recognised her and started taking photos and asking for autographs, and any chance I might have had of keeping her identity a secret and thus helping to protect her went out of the window. In consequence I spent the rest of our time there constantly looking over my shoulder. Fortunately, the murderer stayed away, and Selena and Anna emerged intact.

Finally, as the clocks started chiming eight o'clock, Selena surprised both Anna and me when she announced that she couldn't after all join us for dinner as she had a date. She gave both of us a knowing look as she broke the news and added her good wishes.

'It's lovely to see the two of you together. I'm sure you'll have plenty to talk about without me. I do hope you enjoy your date.' A black Mercedes with tinted windows appeared from nowhere and pulled up alongside her. As she opened the door, I recognised the man waiting for her inside the car. It was unmistakably Scott Norris.

Anna and I stood and watched as the car disappeared in the direction of the river before turning to face each other. Anna was the first to speak.

'I think the words are *fait accompli*. She's a schemer. I rather get the impression she thinks you and I should spend time together, Dan.'

'*Fait accompli* indeed.' I managed to look Anna in the eye. 'Still, she's not all wrong. I think we will enjoy our date – if that's what it is. At least, I know I will.'

She produced a big smile and caught hold of my arm. 'And so will I. Where are we going for dinner?'

'Anywhere you like. The only constraint is my four-legged friend here.'

'I know a very nice restaurant with tables outside on a lovely panoramic terrace not that far from here. It's about ten minutes on foot, just across the other side of Ponte alle Grazie. Oscar will be welcome there and the food's great. They offer traditional Tuscan cuisine, particularly lots of fish dishes, if you like that sort of thing.'

'Sounds perfect.'

We walked back to the river through the narrow streets of the *centro storico*. At this time of the evening it was almost completely dark and bats zoomed and swooped in the orange glow of the street lamps. It was delightful and romantic – or it would have been if I hadn't kept reminding myself that I was with somebody who was still a potential suspect in a murder case, however unlikely that might seem. We crossed the bridge and headed up an even narrower, winding road that climbed towards the panoramic Piazzale Michelangelo. The restaurant was only about halfway up the hill, but the view from here over the lights of the city was almost as good as from the top. Anna obviously knew the restaurant staff and, although it was busy, they found us a table for two plus the dog. This was over to one side of the gardens, beneath an olive tree, and slightly separated from the rest of the diners. As we walked past the kitchens, a tantalising aroma wafted out and Oscar wasn't the only one to start salivating.

On Anna's recommendation, we chose to share mixed seafood antipasti that arrived on a silver platter and consisted of all manner of crustaceans and molluscs, ranging from minute snail-like things – whose names escaped me both in Italian and in English – to oysters, plump prawns and delicious crab meat. We followed this with a mix of grilled fish accompanied by a simple salad, and the food was as delightful as the company. We talked a lot and increasingly freely about all sorts of things – but not the investigation – and even ended up discussing our various divorces. I learnt a lot about her and liked what I learnt. Under other circumstances I could really have seen this relationship developing, but the ever-present shadow of Donny Lopez's murder hung over both of us, and I could tell that she was feeling it as well. Neither of us had room for dessert after this feast and by the time we got onto the coffee, I felt relaxed enough to address the elephant in the room – or at least the one out here under the olive tree.

'It's a pity we had to meet like this Anna.'

She looked up from the cantuccini biscuit she was in the process of dipping in her coffee and nodded. 'I know what you mean. Until this whole murder thing's resolved, I suppose Inspector Pisano would prefer it if you and I didn't spend too much time together.'

I took a chance, feeling uncommonly nervous. 'Would you like to spend more time with me?'

'I would if you would.' She gave me a grin. 'It's solely because I've fallen in love with your dog, you understand.'

'He has that effect on people. He's a sweetie really.' No sooner had I spoken than a noxious cloud of near toxic gas came wafting up from beneath the table and I was quick to apologise – and clarify. 'I'm sorry, that was Oscar. The bacon cheeseburger and the doughnut he had today are making their presence felt.'

She was still smiling. 'Maybe that's fate warning us that we shouldn't get too close.'

'Do you believe in fate?'

Her expression became more serious. 'Maybe I do. If it wasn't fate that brought us together then what was it?'

'I'm assuming sheer chance is the wrong answer.'

'Who knows? Hopefully we'll find out one of these days.'

From the restaurant it was barely a fifteen-minute walk to her house and when we got there, we had a moment of indecision when my instincts were telling me to kiss her while the former DCI inside me reminded me that this would be a mistake. I felt pretty sure that she was similarly undecided. In the end, the Labrador's alimentary canal made the decision for us as further olfactory proof of the gastric maelstrom going on inside my dog made itself felt, and I stepped back apologetically.

'I rather think that fate has just told me that the sooner I get Oscar back home, the better.'

'You might be right. Never mind, there'll be another time, I'm sure.'

'I hope so.' And then, as I was about to hold out my hand towards her, she leant forward and kissed me softly on the cheeks.

'*Buona notte*, Dan.'

'*Buona notte*, Anna. I've enjoyed tonight.'

She smiled at me. 'So have I. Selena wasn't wrong, was she?'

As soon as Oscar and I got back home – with all the windows in the car wide open – I took him for a walk and a much-needed comfort break. It was dark up here on the hillside but, as ever, the black dog against the contrast of the *strada bianca* made it easy for me to follow him up through the cypress trees. Tonight, the scent of resin hung heavy in the air, and I breathed deeply, relishing the fresh feel after the heat of Florence. My head was full of thoughts of Anna. It had been a most enjoyable evening – probably one of the most enjoyable evenings I had spent with anybody since my divorce. Apart from the distinct physical attraction I felt for her, I realised that we had a considerable amount in common and I knew I wanted to spend more time with her. Of course, I also knew that was going to have to wait until this investigation was finally wrapped up.

As I walked, I also ran through in my head every villain I could remember from my past who might still harbour a serious grudge against me and came up with reassuringly very few. In the end I narrowed it down to only three, and two of them were almost certainly still in jail, and hopefully would remain there for the rest of their days. The third and final one was Tonio Fortunato, and I wondered what Paul would be able to tell me about the former art thief.

19

SATURDAY MORNING

I found out when I woke up next morning. Paul had been busy. The message from him made interesting reading.

Hi Dan. The killer of your friend Ogilvie's lover was released in July and left the UK for Rio di Janeiro on 3 August and hasn't returned. Antony Fortunato was also released from prison in July this year after serving seven and a half years. Parole Board recommended release as he's now considered reformed (you and I've both heard that before!). He left the UK on 10 August and is reported to be staying on the Italian coast near Castiglioncello, just south of Livorno. Here's the address. Hope that helps. P

I almost choked on my coffee as I realised that Tonio Fortunato was now living little more than an hour's drive from where I was sitting. Suddenly he had leapt from a vague possible to a definite threat. Could it really be that *I* had been the real target – at least since the death of Lopez? The fact remained that the death threats aimed at the movie had started long before I became involved so any attack on me must have been an opportunist attempt to cash in on the confusion caused by the Lopez murder, and it was hard to believe. Still, seeing as Fortunato was now living so close by, he definitely warranted further investigation.

I remembered Tonio as an intelligent man who would have been capable of putting together a plan like this at short notice but, in spite of his threats aimed at me eight years ago, I couldn't really see him as a murderer. Of course, it could be he'd subcontracted the job to somebody better equipped to carry out such an intricate and audacious attempt, but I had my doubts. I called Virgilio and gave him the news, which he took very seriously.

'Castiglioncello's out of my jurisdiction, so it'll take me a few hours to get authorisation sorted out to pay this guy a visit. I'll pick you up at eleven. Okay?'

'Could we make it a bit later on? I'm supposed to be keeping an eye on the film crew in Fiesole this morning.'

'Pick you up from your place at half past twelve, okay?'

Half an hour later, once again wearing my fifteenth-century costume, I drove up the winding road that links Florence with the charming and very exclusive suburb of Fiesole, searching for the villa where I would meet the film crew. With some difficulty I located a pair of wrought-iron gates set in a stone wall almost submerged beneath a near impenetrable barrier of bushes and trees. If I hadn't spotted the unmistakable form of Big Jim standing at the gate with his clipboard, I would never have imagined there could be a Renaissance villa hidden within this jungle. I pulled in and he gave me a lazy wave of his massive hand.

'Hi there, Dan.' Movement and a muted whine from behind me told me that Oscar had recognised his buddy who gave him beefburgers – and wind. Jim was quick to respond. 'Hi, Oscar, how you doing? Feeling hungry?'

'He's always feeling hungry, Jim. I think he overdid the food yesterday and almost asphyxiated me on the way home. Who's here this morning?'

'The crew have been setting up and I'm expecting Mr Lyons any minute now. Just drive on down to the house and park where you see the other vehicles. That way you'll be out of camera shot.'

I set off through the gates and along a gravel drive until I emerged from the thick undergrowth to a spectacular sight. There before me was one of the finest Tuscan villas I had ever seen, complete with a dovecot in the centre of the roof and the obligatory complement of cypress trees surrounding it. It wasn't enormous, but it was beautifully proportioned. The beautiful light ochre walls were punctuated by dusty green shutters and the red roof tiles had been bleached pink by the sun over centuries. In front of it was a long, paved terrace on which I could see the film crew busily engaged in setting up all of their paraphernalia. As a location for a film, it was beautifully chosen, and I wondered if Anna had had anything to do with selecting it.

I was just parking the car between a pair of trucks when I got a call from Virgilio.

'Hi, Dan, I'm afraid I need to be here all morning. We're still struggling to find this missing woman and everybody's beginning to get very concerned for her safety. I'll pick you up after lunch if that's okay.'

'Of course. That means I can take the dog for a walk when I get home and leave him to sleep this afternoon while we go for our trip to the seaside. Do you have any clues as to what's happened to your missing woman?'

'Precious few. We're doing a forensic search of her apartment this morning and I want to be there in case they miss anything. She has family but they're all down in Campania, south of Rome, and the only people who know her up here are her workmates, and none of them knows where she might have gone.'

'Well, good luck with it. Let me know if you need a hand. I'll see you after lunch.'

'We should be with you around two o'clock.'

Oscar and I went over to where Emmy was issuing orders. His left arm was still in a sling, but the colour had returned to his cheeks, and he looked as if he'd bounced back remarkably well from his near-death experience. Alongside him was Dizzy, so I made a beeline for her and queried what was going to be happening this morning. She bent down and made a fuss of Oscar while she gave me the information.

'First scenes will be outside on the terrace and then we move inside. You should see this place, it's amazing.'

'And it's privately owned? Some famous family?'

'It's private, but nobody lives here apart from a caretaker. It's owned by a hedge fund based in Lichtenstein. They rent it out for weddings, conferences and other special events or to people like us.'

'I can imagine that places like this don't come cheap. It's a shame to think of it as just part of an investment portfolio, but I suppose that's the way of the world nowadays.' I looked around at the well-maintained gardens and the belt of trees beyond the lawns. 'I'll take Oscar and check out the perimeter, just to be sure there aren't any more would-be assassins hiding in the bushes.'

'There shouldn't be anybody. This place has more security around it than Fort Knox. There are cameras all around the grounds and there's a bank of CCTV screens inside the villa. The caretaker told me the boundary wall has sensors all over the place but do check it out, by all means.'

My tour of the perimeter revealed nothing apart from the elec-tronic precautions Dizzy had listed. I felt reassured that nothing untoward was likely to happen here today, so it should be safe for me to take my trip to the coast this afternoon. When my dog and I returned from our walk it was to find that the big stars and the producer had all arrived, and shooting was about to begin. I spotted Anna standing to one side and made my way over to her. When she saw me, she gave me a sparkling smile that warmed the cockles of my heart – whatever they are.

'*Ciao*, Dan. Isn't this place amazing? I've never been here before. I was reading up about it last night and you'll never guess who it originally belonged to.'

'The Medici?'

'Almost – the Pazzi.'

That name again. 'This villa belonged to the Pazzi family?'

'It was built by them.'

I didn't like the way this name kept cropping up. It was all very well Martin Taylor assuring me that the Pazzi family didn't get a mention in his screenplay, but this business with the flights of the arrows bothered me. If it wasn't some long-lost member of the Pazzi family – and I accepted that they had been all but wiped off the face of the earth by Lorenzo the Magnificent – then all I could assume was that the murderer appeared to have a keen interest in and knowledge of Florentine history. The trouble, of course, was that the lady who had kissed me on the cheeks last night fell very neatly into that category. I did my best to stifle any suspicions and decided to take a chance.

'I was wondering if you felt like coming out to my place for dinner tomorrow night. I've got Virgilio Pisano and his wife coming for a barbecue, so you don't need to worry about finding yourself all alone with a strange man.'

'I wouldn't consider you that strange.' She grinned. 'All right, you're English so you probably do all the strange English things like drinking tea at five o'clock and driving on the wrong side of the road, but otherwise you're quite civilised. I'd love to come to dinner if you're sure the inspector won't mind. Aren't you maybe still worried that I might be a murderer?'

There was no doubt about it. I liked this lady.

'I'm prepared to take my chances.'

20

SATURDAY AFTERNOON

Oscar and I had a good walk at lunchtime and when Virgilio and Innocenti arrived to pick me up in an unmarked black Alfa at two o'clock, I left the dog sleeping peacefully in his basket. In the car, the two detectives were discussing their missing person case and it transpired that they might have found a clue.

'What about the American?' As always, Innocenti's nose was buried in his notebook.

'Ah, yes, the American.' Virgilio had opted to drive for a change, and he glanced across at me as he explained. 'The missing woman's neighbour across the hall claims the victim was being stalked by a former boyfriend, but she only knows the guy as *l'Americano*.'

'No clues as to his identity?'

'We're checking CCTV outside the convenience store opposite the block of apartments in the hope of getting the registration number of his vehicle. The neighbour says she's seen it a few times recently and it should be recognisable seeing as it's one of those big 4x4s. I've got people checking the footage as we speak. The trouble is that there are hundreds, no, thousands, of Americans in Florence so finding him won't be easy.'

'Well, as and when you locate him, if you need a hand with interviewing him, just say the word.'

I went on to report back on my lack of success in getting anything out of Charles Vincent or Duggie Ogilvie and then I queried whether they had had any luck tracing the angry author on Twitter who had been harassing Taylor. It came as no surprise to hear that they didn't appear to be getting anywhere fast. I sympathised. Getting information out of the big social media companies could be like getting blood out of a stone.

Innocenti asked me how my evening with the two ladies had gone and I told them what had happened – minus where things might have led if I hadn't had a seriously flatulent dog. When I broke the news that Selena had gone for a dinner date with her co-star and reminded them that he was still married, they both looked up with renewed interest. Innocenti reached for his faithful notebook once again and explained why this news might be important.

'We got the full files through from the Los Angeles police this morning and something in Scott Norris's file jumped out at us. His wife, Jacqueline, is a former Olympic athlete. Guess in what event.' Without giving me a chance to answer, he continued with considerable satisfaction, 'That's right: archery.'

'Well, well, that *is* a coincidence, but presumably she's still on the other side of the Atlantic.' I've never liked coincidences. All right, they *can* happen, but in my experience nine times out of ten they aren't what they seem.

'We're waiting to hear. We sent the LAPD a message before coming to pick you up. Hopefully we'll hear back later today. Most importantly, we now have a possible motive. Maybe she's learnt of her husband's interest in Selena Gardner, and she's come over to kill him.'

'That seems a bit extreme.' I could hardly believe what I was hearing.

'I've known worse.' Virgilio shrugged.

'You're saying you think she might have come over to kill her husband and she killed Lopez by mistake? And then she tried again yesterday and hit Emmy instead of her husband? Wow, if that's the case, she's clumsier than Dizzy.' I found myself comparing this murderous scenario to the reaction of Signor Dante's wife to news of *his* infidelity. There was a considerable difference between a plateful of pasta in the face and an arrow in the back.

'Anything's possible.'

Virgilio wasn't worrying about speed limits, and we got to the coast in little over an hour. The villa where Tonio Fortunato was allegedly staying was in an enviable position. Although it was on the main coast road, squeezed between the railway line and the sea, it was hidden away from sight by thick hedges and protected from intruders by a serious metal fence. The property was high on a cliff in remarkably unspoilt surroundings, well above the tourist beaches below, and the brilliant azure sea stretched off to the north and south for miles and miles. Lush vegetation and a few white sails offshore added to the picturesque view. It was certainly very different from one of His Majesty's prisons and I could see the attraction to a recently released convict. We pulled up in front of the two-metre-tall steel gates and exchanged glances. Virgilio voiced what we were all thinking.

'Signor Fortunato would appear to be living up to his name. Definitely very fortunate indeed to be living here.'

I'd been thinking back to the Fortunato case, and it hadn't escaped my mind that he and his gang had created a business worth millions and only a fraction of his presumed profits had been recovered. I caught Virgilio's eye. 'Or maybe the owner of the villa is Fortunato himself. It wouldn't surprise me. He had a taste for the high life – in fact it was his taste for fast cars, beautiful blondes and haute cuisine that drew my attention to him in the first place. For somebody who described himself as a simple accountant, he appeared to be living seriously above his means.'

'Let's see if he's in. Innocenti, the bell...'

Sergeant Innocenti got out of the car and went across to a steel panel set into one of the stone gateposts. He pressed the button and waited. After ten seconds or so, a metallic voice came from the speaker.

'Yes, who is it?' It sounded like a young woman. Her accent struck me as southern Italian, but I wasn't too good at locating Italians by their accents yet.

'Police.'

'Police?'

'That's right. We're from the Florence Murder Squad. We need to ask you some questions. Open the gate, please.'

'Murder...?'

A yellow light on top of the gatepost started flashing and the gates swung slowly open to reveal a stylish modern villa with a canary-yellow Ferrari parked outside. Sight of the flashy sports car struck a familiar chord and made me think it very likely that we were going to find our man here. Virgilio drove in and we got out of the car. As we did so, the gates behind us hummed shut and at the same time a shapely blonde in her late twenties or early thirties appeared at the front door. She was wearing a bikini that matched the colour of the Ferrari, but which was considerably less substantial and further strengthened my belief that Fortunato would be around here somewhere.

We went over to where she was standing and Virgilio produced his warrant card and flashed it in her face. 'My name's Inspector Pisano from the Florence *Squadra Mobile*. We're investigating a murder. Can we come in?'

'Yes, of course.'

She stepped back and led us into a huge living room with slide-fold glass doors that were open onto a sun terrace with a pool beyond. In the pool, a suntanned male figure was swimming slowly up and down. Virgilio pointed towards him.

'Is that Tonio Fortunato?'

She nodded. 'Yes, what do you want with him?'

'Just to ask him some questions.'

Virgilio walked out onto the terrace, and we all followed him down to the edge of the pool. As Fortunato surfaced near us after another length, the woman knelt down and attracted his attention in Italian.

'Tonio, it's the police. They want to speak to you.'

He stretched out his hands and steadied himself against the edge of the pool, shook his thick head of hair out of his eyes and peered up at us. As his gaze alighted on me, I saw his expression change to one of considerable surprise but, interestingly, not antagonism.

'Armstrong! What the bloody hell are you doing here?' His East End accent was as strong as ever. 'I thought I'd seen the last of you eight years ago.'

'You and me both, Tonio. Why don't you climb out of the pool so we can have a little chat?'

He swam over to the steps and climbed out. As he did so, I noticed that he had lost a good bit of weight since I had last seen him. Evidently prison rations must have been less appealing than his previous diet of foie gras and prime steak. He picked up a towel robe and slipped it on as he strolled back towards us. He pointed to a collection of wicker armchairs around a low table sheltered from the sun by a vine-covered trellis.

'Do sit down, gentlemen.' He glanced across at the blonde and switched to near perfect Italian. 'Dig a bottle of champagne out of the fridge, darling, would you? It's not every day that old friends are reunited.'

She looked puzzled but turned and went back into the house as ordered. I saw Innocenti's eyes following her as she went back up the steps, but I kept my attention on Fortunato. I sat down opposite him and introduced the others before launching into the reason we were here. For now, I made no mention of the fact that I had retired from the Met.

'We've come to talk to you because we're investigating a murder.'

He looked genuinely surprised.

'A murder...? Wait a minute; you don't think I'm involved in anything like that, do you?'

'That's what we're here to find out.' Virgilio took over the questioning in Italian. 'Can you tell me, please, where you were yesterday morning between eleven and twelve?'

'Yesterday... that was Friday, wasn't it? I was here with Rita – that's Rita, my wife. Why, where was I supposed to be?' He answered in Italian.

Virgilio ignored his question. 'And can you tell me where you were on Wednesday afternoon around four o'clock?'

'Wednesday, Rita and I were in Rome. We had lunch with a bunch of friends and were in the restaurant all afternoon until almost five.' He turned towards me and switched to English. 'What's going on, Armstrong? I'm no murderer; you know that.'

'Is there anybody apart from your wife who can confirm your whereabouts yesterday morning?' I was still trying to work out why I had no recollection of a wife. Was this a very recent thing maybe?

I saw him thinking hard. He certainly didn't look guilty, but I remembered how convincing he'd been in interviews back when I'd been trying to pin him with a charge of multiple offences under Section 11 of the Theft Act, 1968. Suddenly he looked up with an expression of relief on his face. 'Yesterday late morning, you said? The pool man was here. He'll be able to confirm that I was home then. I'll give you his number and I can give you the name of the restaurant in Rome as well. Check up, by all means, and you'll see I'm not your man. What's going on and why me? I've served my time and I'm a law-abiding citizen these days. I've changed; ask anybody.'

At that moment his wife reappeared with an ice bucket and glasses, and I couldn't help thinking that the presence of a Ferrari, a blonde and champagne indicated that he hadn't changed all that much. Still, the pool man and the restaurant would be easy enough to check with and, if they confirmed Fortunato's story, Tonio was in the clear as far as the Boboli Gardens were concerned – unless, of course, he'd got himself a hired killer to do his dirty work for him. Although I was as keen as Virgilio to solve the case, I felt relief that it was looking as though I hadn't been the target after all. I would have felt guilty if the arrow that had struck Emmy had been meant for me.

Fortunato picked the bottle of Bollinger out of the ice and, ignoring our protests, opened it and filled five glasses. Rita duly handed them out and then perched on her husband's lap and stretched an affectionate arm around his neck. As she did so, a ring with a whopping great diamond on it glittered in the sunlight alongside a gold wedding ring. I pointed towards them.

'I didn't realise you'd got married, Tonio. Congratulations. When did that happen?'

'Four years ago.' Seeing my expression, he added a bit of explanation. 'Rita and I've known each other for years and I thought it only fair to make an honest woman of her. Besides, when you're married and behave yourself, it's easier to get conjugal visits, and after three years in Belmarsh I was dying for a bit of conjugal bliss.' He took a big mouthful of champagne and laughed at his own joke before looking suddenly serious. 'But I *am* an honest man nowadays, and that's a promise. I've seen the error of my ways and I've gone straight. One thing's for sure: I don't want to go back in the nick.

'I'm delighted to hear it. Tell me, how can you afford all this?' I waved towards the pool and the villa. 'This sort of place doesn't come cheap.'

'I'm a lucky man, Inspector Armstrong. Rita's a very wealthy lady and she loves me.' He gave her an affectionate kiss on the cheek, and she then surprised all of us by what she said next – or rather, how she said it.

'I love him to bits, Mr Armstrong. He's a lovely, lovely man. And he means what he says: he's given up his previous life. He's as straight as a die nowadays. I guarantee it.' The surprise was caused by the fact that she delivered this endorsement in fluent English with an accent that was even more London than his. Just to emphasise her bilingual abilities, she turned to Virgilio and Innocenti and repeated what she had just said in perfect Italian. Her husband kissed her again and drained his glass of champagne.

'Like I say, gentleman, I'm a lucky man. Now, unless you have any more questions, if you aren't going to drink your champagne, I think I'll do it for you.'

21

SATURDAY EVENING

In the car on the way home I was working it out in my head, and it was all coming back to me now. At the time of his arrest eight years ago, the suspicion had been that Fortunato had either squirrelled away most of his ill-gotten gains in anonymous offshore accounts or had syphoned money off into somebody else's account. The trouble was that if he had put money aside, he'd done it so well that even the Fraud Squad's financial experts hadn't been able to locate a single penny. He had consistently denied that there were any outstanding monies lying around but, by the sound of it, the lady who was now his wife might well have been a secret beneficiary.

Proving it, however, would be far from easy. I vowed to pass the information of his wealth on to Paul at Scotland Yard, but I wouldn't be holding my breath waiting for results. To be honest, I rather hoped Tonio would get away with it. Maybe he really was a changed man nowadays, as he had said. There was no doubt about one thing: he wasn't the person who had killed Donny Lopez or shot at Emmy yesterday. The pool man and the Roman restaurant had both confirmed his alibis and that was that.

We were almost back at my place when Virgilio's phone rang. Since he was driving, we all listened to the conversation on the speakers. It was one of his people in Florence, who reported that US Immigration had just produced the tantalising information that Scott Norris's wife had flown from LA to Paris only five days earlier, arriving on Monday – two days before the murder of Donny Lopez. Virgilio's people were checking with the French authorities to find out if she had stayed in Paris, or if she might have travelled on to Italy.

The other bit of news was that Forensics had belatedly confirmed that the plaster casts of tyre tracks at the side of the road in the hills where Lopez had been murdered and the tracks found by the wall of the Boboli Gardens had almost certainly been made by the same big vehicle. This added further weight to the theory that both assaults had been the work of the same person, making it even less likely that Tonio Fortunato had had a hand in either. And the same went for Anna, which was a relief.

It was gone six by the time we got back to my house and the two detectives stopped off for a drink with me before heading back to Florence. I called Dizzy to check that there hadn't been any incidents during today's shooting and the answer was reassuring. All had gone well, and she told me that they would be filming inside the cloisters of an eleventh-century monastery next morning. The good news was that this was less than twenty minutes' drive from my house while the bad news was that it was tucked away deep in the hills to the south of Florence, and Innocenti, who knew the area, told me that there was dense woodland all around it. No doubt this sort of terrain could offer our murderer the opportunity for yet another attempt unless we were very careful. At the end of the conversation, I asked Virgilio if he might have some officers to spare to provide added security, but he shook his head ruefully.

'Afraid not. Apart from the fact that tomorrow's a Sunday, I'm using most of my people on this missing person case. The woman's been gone for two days now and every hour that passes the more likely it becomes that we'll end up looking not for an abductee but for a body. I'm afraid time is of the essence. Still, with you and your dog and the big security men, you should be safe enough. Those old monasteries were generally semi-fortified – whether to keep people out or monks inside is another matter. You'll be okay.'

While Oscar wandered about, re-marking his territory, the three of us sat under the loggia and discussed the case so far. In view of the matching tyre marks, it was looking more and more likely that the death of Lopez and the arrow in Emmy's arm had been the work of the same person and that this person had not been part of the film company, actors or crew. I did my best to sum up what we'd got so far.

'As far as I can see, we have half a dozen possible scenarios. First, there's some distant relative of a long-defunct Florentine family who somehow holds a grudge against the film company and wants the movie stopped. Second, there's the so far anonymous person on Twitter who accused Martin Taylor of plagiarism. Third, there's Scott Norris's Olympic archer wife with a grudge against her unfaithful husband. Fourth – and very unlikely to my eyes – is the possibility that the two attacks were botched attempts to kill *me* by somebody from my past and, fifth, some unknown loony with a grudge against Hollywood, historical movies or the glorification of Lorenzo the Magnificent, a man who died five hundred years ago.' I took a long mouthful of cold beer. 'And, of course, there's always the mystery man or woman that Elvis saw hanging around the trailer park, whatever he or she had in mind, but none of them really sound like grounds for committing murder.'

Virgilio grunted in agreement. 'Like you, at first I thought the murder of Lopez had to be the work of somebody involved with the movie but, assuming the attacks were by the same person, that's virtually impossible, seeing as all bar two of the main suspects were on set yesterday when the director was hit. There's still an outside chance that there was somebody on the inside and somebody on the outside, but we're no further towards identifying who those people might be or what motive could be driving them.'

At that moment, his phone started ringing. He listened closely and when the call ended, he passed on news of his other case. 'We've had a breakthrough in the abduction case. CCTV has identified a white Toyota pickup seen outside the woman's apartment on several occasions, just like the neighbour said. From the angle of the camera there's no image of the driver, but we did get clear sight of the plates and it's been traced to an American, currently renting an apartment only fifteen minutes or so from here. My officers have been round and the property's empty and there's no sign of the car. The man's a lecturer in one of the American universities in Florence and there are books and papers all over the place, all in English. My guys aren't too hot linguistically, so I have to go over there now to take a look. Feel like coming along, Dan?'

Considering that Virgilio had just spent the afternoon driving a couple of hundred kilometres to check up on a possible murderer with me in his sights, I felt the least I could do was to say yes. We finished our drinks and I piled Oscar into the back of my car and followed them back down the hill to the main road for the short drive to the American's apartment. This turned out to be one of a series of half a dozen flats in a barn conversion in a tiny hamlet in the middle of well-tended vineyards. When we got there, there was still no sign of either the car or its owner. Instead, there were two squad cars parked outside and a young female officer at the door who instantly recognised Virgilio and produced a smart salute.

Inside the American's ground-floor flat, the scene was pretty chaotic. The sergeant in charge of the investigation came in and assured us that this wasn't down to his officers but that they had found the place in this state. Tidiness certainly didn't appear to be the American's strong point. The kitchen was a mess of dirty dishes and from the look of them and the smell in there they'd been lying about for some days. The living room was fairly spartan, and the only unusual items were dumb-bells and weights. Presumably the man worked out.

There was one bedroom with a double bed whose sheets looked as if they hadn't been laundered for a considerable time, and another small room, which he had clearly been using as a study. There was a desk by the window, covered in papers and notes, and in the centre was an empty space, clearly recognisable by the absence of the layer of dust that covered most of the other horizontal surfaces in the flat. This was presumably where his computer had stood.

I pointed at the desk. 'Laptop's gone. Do we think the place has been burgled? That might account for the chaos.'

Virgilio shook his head. 'The guys outside say there were no signs of forced entry. Everything was locked and they had to break a window by the door to get into the house themselves. No, I think our American friend was just a very messy person.'

'Maybe he had other things on his mind – like abduction, for instance.'

After shifting a pile of unsavoury-looking dirty laundry, I sat down on the chair by the desk and started going through the papers. There wasn't much of interest except for the fact that unmarked essays and books lying around appeared to indicate that the American had been a teacher. Of course, this wasn't unexpected: a number of American universities had what they called a Florence Program based here in Italy and most of these specialised in Italian art, architecture and history, with some offering Italian language courses as well. Students typically came over for short courses or semesters and could gain credits that counted towards their final degree back in the States. I concentrated on looking for any clues as to where he might have gone.

One discovery I made in the top drawer was a US passport in the name of Victor Albert Nero, born in Georgetown, Delaware, thirty-seven years earlier. I held it up and waved it at the other two.

'Wherever he's gone, he hasn't left the country.' I took a closer look at the passport. The photo showed Nero as thickset around the throat and neck, with close-cropped dark hair and dark eyes. As with all passport photos, his face was expressionless.

Virgilio was investigating the contents of the sole wardrobe in the room, while Innocenti was sifting through the pages of a pile of girlie magazines beside the bed with commendable thoroughness. Virgilio glanced back at me over his shoulder and nodded. 'He doesn't seem to have too much stuff. There's nothing here that tells us much about him apart from the fact that he had terrible taste in clothes.'

The uniformed sergeant from outside appeared at the door of the study with a phone in his hand and proffered it towards Virgilio. 'I've managed to get through to the head of the faculty where Nero works. Do you want to talk to her, sir? She's American.'

Virgilio took the phone and handed it across to me. 'Would you mind, Dan? You know the drill.'

I took the phone and heard an American woman's voice at the other end asking in passable Italian what was going on. I replied in English.

'Good afternoon, my name's Armstrong. Sorry to bother you at the weekend. I'm calling on behalf of Inspector Pisano of the Florence Murder Squad.'

'Murder? Did you say murder? Who's been murdered?'

'We're investigating a case of abduction and possible murder of a woman. We're keen to speak to one of your lecturers who might be able to help us with our enquiries. His name is Victor Albert Nero.'

I heard an exasperated hiss of breath at the other end. 'Oh God, no, not him again.'

'Again?'

'Victor hasn't been one of our success stories, I'm afraid. I've worked here for just over four years now and he's the first staff member I've had to let go.'

'Can you tell me when that that happened and why?'

'He left the university's employment two weeks ago. As for why, where do I start? Over the past few months, he's been coming in later and later, and then he stopped turning up for his lectures at all. When he was here, he was behaving increasingly erratically – everybody noticed it. But that's just the tip of the iceberg. There are currently no fewer than three complaints against him that are being investigated by the board, all from young female students.'

'What sort of complaints?'

'Sexual harassment, innuendo, inappropriate touching... you get the picture.'

I certainly did. 'I'm with the police at his apartment near Montespertoli now, but there's no sign of him. Would you have another address for him?'

'Just one moment, please.' I waited while she checked her files, but the result came back negative. 'I'm sorry, but the only address I have is that one.'

'Would there be anybody there who might know more about him? Anybody he was friends with?'

'I honestly don't think so, but I'll ask around. He was very much a loner and he avoided people. Mind you, most people avoided him because he was a strange man.'

'In what way – apart from the inappropriate behaviour towards women?'

'The general consensus here was that he was not quite as mentally well balanced as he should have been. He was prone to outbursts of anger, and these have been getting more common over the past year or so. He actually put his fist through a wooden door on one occasion. He claimed it was accidental, but people around him said it was done on purpose and out of frustration.'

'Was he a strong man?'

'Definitely. He was tall, probably six three or six four, and he was bulky with it. I think I have some photos somewhere of him at a drinks thing we did back in the spring to celebrate fifty years of the Florence Program. Can I give you a call if I locate them?' There was a moment's pause. 'To be honest, Mr Armstrong, he frightened me, and I'm sure I wasn't the only one.'

I assured her that any photos would be very welcome and gave her Virgilio's number. I felt like asking why she'd employed such an apparently unsuitable person, but she anticipated my question.

'Before you ask, I'm afraid I had no hand in employing him. He was sent to us from our alma mater back in the States, and I have a feeling they deliberately sent him here to get rid of him. Suspiciously, when I told them I'd been forced to let him go, I got the impression they weren't surprised.'

I thanked her and handed the phone back to the uniformed sergeant, who listened in while I recounted in Italian what I'd just been told. As I did so, I saw the three men exchange glances. This wasn't sounding good. A strong, tall man with an unstable background didn't bode well for the safety of the missing woman. I returned to sifting through the drawers and files but without finding anything of interest. By the time we'd finished, we were no wiser as to where he might have gone.

Back outside, Virgilio sent officers to question the occupants of the other flats and nearby houses to see if by any chance they might have information about Nero's whereabouts. He ordered two officers to conceal themselves near the property in case the man came back and then turned to me with a helpless shrug.

'I'll put out a general alert for Nero. Hopefully the lady you've just spoken to will be able to let us have a decent photo but, if not, we can copy his face from his passport photo, and I'll see that it gets circulated along with a description of his car. I just hope we'll be able to trace him before he harms the woman.' His tone became more ominous. 'If he hasn't already done so.'

'And I'll do my best to ensure that the film company's trip to the old abbey goes off without incident.'

'How much longer till they head off back to the States?'

'Just tomorrow and Monday and then that's that.' I caught Virgilio's eye. 'I'll heave a sigh of relief when they pack up and leave. If only we were any closer to cracking the Donny Lopez murder first.'

'You and me both. The American embassy are getting very uptight and they're leaning on the minister in Rome who leans on the *questore* up here and no prizes for guessing who he leans on.' Virgilio gave a little sigh of frustration. 'Still, maybe we'll hear from Twitter that they've come up with an ID for the guy trolling the writer or we might get some news about Scott Norris's archer wife.'

'And if we don't?'

'Then we're back to square one.'

I felt as frustrated as he sounded. Throughout my whole career I had hated loose ends and unsolved cases. Everybody in my chosen profession had told me that some cases inevitably would never be solved but that didn't make them any easier to stomach. I spent the evening turning the events of the past few days over and over in my head, desperately searching for something I might have overlooked, but to no avail.

22

SUNDAY MORNING

Next morning I got up early, donned my striped costume and set off in the car with Oscar for the *Abbazia di San Bernardo*. This old monastery lay at the end of a seriously rutted track in a wooded valley not far from Montaione, the town to which Anna had taken Selena and me the other day, and it certainly was way out in the sticks as Innocenti had said. Like most Cistercian monasteries, the building was situated by a river, which would once have watered the fields where the community of monks had lived an austere life devoted to hard manual labour and strict religious observance. A check on Google the previous night had told me that it had been founded seven hundred years earlier but had been deserted since before the Second World War. The roof had collapsed in places, and it was now in a forlorn state. The cluster of modern trucks and vans unloading shiny twenty-first-century equipment looked singularly out of place in these tranquil, historic surroundings.

Under other circumstances, I would have thoroughly enjoyed visiting a place like this, but not this morning. Although today's shoot was classified as principally being made up of 'interior' scenes, the fact was that the gaping window openings and empty doorways, whose doors had long since been carried off by local scavengers, provided an open invitation to our homicidal archer to try again. Not having police here to check the surroundings was a serious handicap, although in order to do an effective job it would have taken dozens of officers to patrol the area and even then, it wouldn't have been too hard for a dedicated assailant to get close enough to pick his or her target. Together with Big Jim and his colleague who I had mentally christened Slightly Smaller Chuck – not that anybody would have dreamt of calling this bulky man-mountain anything of the sort – I did a tour of the surrounding fields and woods that only confirmed my worst fears. The area offered numerous places to hide and almost invited an attack. It occurred to me as we walked around the outside of the building that if the assailant really was out to get *me*, out here in the scrub in my yellow and red stripes I was a sitting duck. Although I still felt confident that I wasn't the target, it was an uncomfortable feeling all the same.

Unable to do anything about the exterior, I did a careful reconnaissance of the inside of the dilapidated buildings, deliberately noting the most and least exposed areas. When I had got a good idea of the layout, I walked Emmy around with me and together we agreed on the safest places for him to film, although 'safe' was a very relative word out here. Fortunately he had already decided that most of the scenes would take place inside the cloisters. These, the inner sanctum of any monastery, were completely closed off from outside but that still meant that people going to and fro would have to run the gauntlet of the open windows and doorways.

The food van had parked close alongside the old barn – also minus its roof – and I asked for the tables to be set up inside the thick stone walls of that building so as to offer as much protection as possible. I helped myself to a coffee – plus the inevitable packet of biscuits for my ever-hungry companion – and murmured a silent prayer that the archer would have given up and gone.

But I wasn't holding my breath.

The producer and stars arrived shortly after nine and I made sure they were hurried through the ruins of the church to the relative safety of the cloisters. Big Jim stood guard at the front door while Chuck positioned himself at the rear of the building. As filming started, I stood in a corner of the cloisters and admired the simple beauty of the ancient but unadorned stone pillars and the wonderful way the flagstones on the floors had been worn smooth by the passage of sandals over the centuries. The centre of the cloisters, which had no doubt once been a beautifully tended garden, was now almost submerged beneath the tangled remains of a centuries-old rambling rose. It was a mass of little pink flowers and charming in a rather forlorn way in these tumbledown surroundings. Apart from checking out the surroundings, I tried to think myself into the head of a possible assailant.

Where would he go to shoot his arrows? I still found myself thinking of the archer as a man, although the latest information about Scott's wife being in Europe made that less likely. I was hampered by not knowing whether the archer was only interested in hitting any random member of the cast and crew or whether he or she had a specific person in mind. If the targets were picked at random, the archer could afford to take up position almost anywhere within the surrounding trees, which would mean a shot of around sixty or seventy metres to the monastery. From what Signor Rufina had told me about the accuracy of bows and arrows in experienced hands, that would be a feasible distance for an expert. If the killer wanted to be able to pick out one person in particular, it would probably be necessary to get closer. Surveying all of the surrounding woods was impossible, so I decided to concentrate on places closer to the walls where it would be possible for someone to lie in wait.

Leaving the actors and crew to their work under the watchful eyes of the two big security guards, Oscar and I went out and started to make a broad sweep around the monastery, staying less than fifty metres or so from the walls. The fields that would once have been tended by the monks were now overgrown, and clumps of brambles made them difficult to navigate. I followed winding tracks made by animals or hunters and was soon caught in a particularly vicious thicket and realised I was at risk of laddering my tights. I was just bending down, surveying the damage and trying to unpick myself, when I heard the unmistakable twang of a bowstring some way ahead of me. I straightened up just as another thwack told me the archer had shot a second arrow and this time I distinctly saw a movement about a hundred yards ahead of me. Reacting instinctively – and probably stupidly given that I was unarmed – I shouted at the top of my voice at him.

'Hey, you! What're you doing?'

It only occurred to me afterwards that I was shouting in English, but the effect was immediate. The figure, partly hidden behind a tall clump of yellow-flowered broom, turned away and started to make a run for it, the bow and a quiver of arrows clearly visible. Whether this was a man or a tall woman was impossible to tell as he or she was well concealed beneath a dark-green hoodie that blended into the background and I couldn't see their face. I wasted precious seconds ripping my way out of the brambles and destroying my red tights in the process before setting off in pursuit. I run regularly and I consider myself pretty fit for a fifty-six-year-old, but in these surroundings I didn't stand a chance.

The archer obviously knew the way and had followed a path that led towards the safety of the trees. As for me, it took me several minutes to cover the intervening distance through the chaos of scrub and brambles until I reached the spot where I'd first seen the archer and by that time, he or she had disappeared from sight.

With Oscar running joyfully ahead of me, no doubt convinced that this was some sort of game, I ran along the path until I reached the edge of the woods. Here the path split and there was no sign of the archer. I stopped and listened intently but couldn't hear a sound. Either they'd gone into hiding or had already made it far enough up the hill to be out of my hearing. As I stood there, my thoughts returned to the film crew inside the monastery. Had one or both of the arrows struck a human target and, if so, who? Mouthing a silent prayer that it hadn't been Anna, I tossed a mental coin and set off up the slightly wider of the two paths. I had climbed fifty yards or so when this path split in two yet again. I paused to consider my options and, as I did so, it occurred to me that I might be running into an ambush if I continued – even assuming I managed to choose the right path. My gaudy costume would make me a sitting target and the prospect of an arrow in the chest didn't appeal at all, so I listened intently once more but all I heard was my dog panting – or that might have been me – and a distant woodpecker hammering at the bark of a tree. Reluctantly, I opted for discretion, turned around, and made my way back to the monastery, fervently hoping that neither of the two arrows had hit anybody in there.

On my way back, I pulled out my phone and called Virgilio, but it went to voicemail. I left a brief message about what had happened and tried Innocenti, but with the same result. Hopefully one of them would get back to me as soon as possible.

I returned to find a scene of stunned silence and barely concealed terror. It looked as though everybody had clustered into the old barn for protection, several now grasping what looked like glasses of Scotch or grappa to fortify them, and in the midst of them was Scott Norris, slumped back on a chair, the yellow lines on his striped tunic now a uniform red, swamped with blood. Beside him, Selena was standing helplessly, looking as white as a sheet. I pushed my way through the crowd to him and took a closer look. The blood had come from his neck, and somebody had wrapped a towel around the wound to staunch the flow. Scott was holding his right hand tightly pressed against the towel and he was clearly in shock. I reached over and gently removed his hand from the towel and pulled it away from his throat, dreading what I might find.

'Is it bad?' His voice was strained, but he was still sounding rational.

The towel came away and I felt a surge of relief. Yes, there was a nasty horizontal slice across his neck, but his main artery and windpipe were intact and although he had lost a lot of blood, it wasn't spurting out. I replaced the cloth gently and gave him the good news.

'It's okay, Scott, I'm sure you're going to be okay. You've been very lucky. Half an inch to the right and it might have killed you. As it is, you'll have an impressive battle scar that you can display to your fans or, if you prefer, just put on a roll neck and hide it, but I'm sure you're going to be fine.'

Relief flooded across his face, and I gave him a reassuring pat on the shoulder before straightening up and turning towards the expectant crowd. 'I'm sure he's going to be okay, guys.' There was an audible sigh of relief. 'Now, has anybody called the ambulance?'

'Yes, I did about ten minutes ago.' I saw Anna's face in the crowd and gave her a wave.

'That's great. Thanks. What about the police?'

'Yes, I dialled 112 and they say they're sending people.'

I caught sight of Dizzy standing by the door alongside Gabriel Lyons. 'Dizzy, could you get the first-aid kit? I think I'd better fix Scott up with a better dressing until the paramedics get here.'

I saw Dizzy scoot off and I crouched back down alongside Scott again. He was looking understandably weary as a result of the shock and the loss of blood, and I thought it best to keep him alert.

'How did it happen, Scott?'

He groaned and looked up at me. 'It was my own fault. I was walking back along the corridor and I stopped to tie my shoelace. It didn't occur to me that I was right beside a big opening on the wall, and I must have been a sitting target.' Dizzy came rushing back with the first-aid kit, miraculously without tripping over anything on the way, and while I replaced the sodden towel with a clean dressing, Scott looked up at me in mystification. 'Who could it have been, Dan? Who would want to kill *me*?'

The fact was that I had a horrible feeling I did know who had been trying to kill him and that this was none other than his wife. I was still debating whether to break this news to him when my phone started ringing and I saw it was Virgilio. I decided to get away from everybody before taking the call, so I told Scott I'd be right back and headed outside.

'Hi, Virgilio, thanks for the call back.' I told him what had happened and how, frustratingly, I'd managed to let the would-be killer get away. He was quick to offer reassurance.

'You did the right thing, Dan. The murderer has shown he's not afraid to kill. God knows what would have happened to you if you'd caught up with him.'

'Or her. Don't forget who the victim was.'

'Yes, indeed. Have you told Scott yet?'

'No, I thought it might be better to wait until we hear back from the French police. No point in sowing marital disharmony until we have the proof.'

'Good point. Innocenti and I are on our way there right now. We should be with you in fifteen minutes or so.'

'Great. Any developments with your missing woman?'

'Yes... some new information, but I'm not quite sure what it means.'

Before I could ask him to elaborate, I saw an ambulance come bumping up the track. I rang off and showed the two paramedics the way to the victim. Once Scott was in their capable hands, I went out and sat down for a rest on a huge, sculpted stone that had probably fallen from one of the collapsed arches. My worried-looking dog slumped down at my feet as I let my eyes range over the ruins of the monastery, whose peace had been so rudely shattered this morning. I reflected that while we often think of the Middle Ages as a violent time, the twenty-first century can be violent as well. I'd only been there a minute or two when I felt a hand on my shoulder. Looking up, I saw it was Anna.

'Here, you look as if you could do with this.' She pushed a paper cup of strong black coffee into my hand. 'Go on. Drink up.'

I gave her a smile and did as instructed, discovering that somebody had added a generous shot of grappa to the coffee. I felt it burn as it went down, and it was most welcome. I shifted sideways to make room for her to sit beside me. I could feel her warmth through the sleeve of my tunic, and it felt good. In an attempt to lighten the mood, I pointed at my shredded tights and scratched legs. 'Wardrobe are going to hate me for ruining their precious red tights.'

She smiled back at me. 'I noticed. That's the other reason I came looking for you.' Before I could protest, she slid down onto her knees and revealed that I wasn't the only person to have raided the first-aid kit. Shrugging off the amorous advances of my dog, who was delighted to find her down at his level for a change, she produced a pair of scissors and set about removing the ragged tights. The feel of her fingers on my skin was stimulating and I'm sure there was a silly smile on my face by the time she had finished dabbing all the cuts with antiseptic and wiping them clean. A couple of them were big enough to require sticking plasters, but otherwise my legs looked a lot better after her ministrations. It would appear that she had noticed. As she got up and sat back down alongside me, she pointed downwards.

'And you were worried about showing off your legs. I think they look fine.'

This was the first time in my life that anybody had complimented me on my legs, so I wasn't too sure how to react, but then I found myself spontaneously leaning across to kiss her softly on the cheek. 'Thank you. That was very kind of you.'

She gave my forearm a little squeeze in return, but any further intimacy was interrupted by the familiar sound of police sirens approaching fast. I gave her an apologetic smile and jumped to my feet. 'I'd better go. And thanks again.'

Virgilio and Innocenti arrived right behind a squad car with two uniformed officers in it. They all came running and I was able to give them the good news that it looked as though Scott was going to be okay. While Innocenti and the uniformed officers went in to survey the scene of the crime, I led Virgilio outside and pointed out where the archer had been hiding and had made their escape. As we walked about, I described in as much detail as possible what had happened and pointed out the path the archer had used to make his – or more probably her – getaway.

'I've no way of knowing whether the attacker was a man or a woman as all I saw was their back. He or she was quite tall and their head was covered by a hood so it's quite possible *he* might have been a *she*. Any idea when you hope to hear from the French police about Scott Norris's Olympic archer wife?'

'I've been promised a call this morning to confirm if she's still in France. We've checked and she's apparently a tall, fit woman so she might well be the person you chased. However, if she is still in France, I think I have another candidate for our archer.' He stopped as we reached an old dry-stone wall and leant against it, turning towards me. 'But there's something else, Dan.' He was sounding serious. 'You asked if there had been any developments on the other case, the missing woman. Well, there *has* been a development. The dean of the American university sent me over a couple of photos of Nero at their spring party and we've circulated a close-up one of him to all stations. The thing is... there was a second photo that's thrown up something interesting.'

'Really, what?'

He pulled out his phone, scrolled through and passed it across to me. 'See for yourself.'

I turned my back to the sun so that I could take a good look at the photo. There were five people in the photo, all smartly dressed. Nero was clearly recognisable from his passport photo, towering above everybody else, looking uncomfortable in an over-tight tux, but he wasn't the most interesting person in the picture. Alongside him was a familiar figure wearing a very smart evening gown. I zoomed in for a closer look but there could be no doubt about it.

The woman was Anna.

Virgilio's voice interrupted all the confused thoughts rushing through my head. 'Now, it may just be sheer chance. After all, they're both lecturers – apparently his subject was history as well – and it's very likely the American university invited academics from other institutions to their party. But something else has cropped up that makes this all very murky indeed. You know that list of names of archery competitors that you got from the picture framer? I was going through it earlier and one name suddenly leapt out at me: V. A. Nero.'

'Wow!' I suddenly felt glad I had the stone wall to lean on. My first reaction was that I must be losing my touch. Once upon a time I, too, would have made that connection but months away from Scotland Yard and my advancing years must have taken their toll. 'Full marks for spotting it. I feel suitably shamed.'

'Don't beat yourself up, Dan. There were over a hundred names on that list and when you saw it you had no idea who Nero was. You could hardly be expected to remember all the names on the list.'

'Let's get this clear: this means that it could be that Victor Albert Nero is not only the prime suspect in an abduction case, but he could also maybe be the phantom archer, responsible for murdering Lopez and injuring the others?' I looked at him in bewilderment. 'Is that what we're saying?'

'That's what it looks like. God knows how or why, but it's too much of a coincidence to ignore.'

As he was speaking, the obvious corollary of this hypothesis had occurred to me. 'All along we've been saying that these arrows might be the work of more than one person – one on the outside and one on the inside. Given that these two know each other, do we think Anna might be the person on the inside?' I must have sounded completely gobsmacked as my dog roused himself from sniffing an alluring heap of rabbit droppings and wandered over to give me an encouraging nudge with his – fortunately unsullied – nose. I scratched his ears reflectively while Virgilio replied.

'I honestly don't know, Dan, but it *is* suspicious. Now listen: this photo proves nothing. They're just standing next to each other with other people around them. Even if they are friends, the main problem we have is to establish motive. What possible motive might Victor Nero have that could have caused him to kill Lopez and wound the others? And if they really were working hand in hand, what on earth could have turned Anna Galardo into a killer, or at least an accessory to a murder?'

'Indeed. And if they really are in this together, then where does the abducted woman come in? Was she somehow involved, or did she maybe see or hear something she shouldn't have? Did they cart her off and kill her to keep her quiet?' All the time my subconscious was screaming *Anna?* at me in disbelief. 'But I just can't see Anna as a murderer or even an accomplice to murder, can you?'

'In all honesty no, but stranger things have happened.'

He was, of course, right. If my thirty years in the murder squad had taught me anything, it was that looks can be deceptive and not everything is always as it seems. But Anna...?

I took a few deep breaths. 'So how do you want to play it? Do you want to interview her on your own or with me or what? Alternatively, maybe it's better not to give anything away for now, but just to keep a close eye on her. What do you think?'

'The latter, I think. We don't mention the photo and the possible connection to Nero, but we definitely keep a closer eye on her.'

I was thinking hard. 'Would it be possible for me to take another look at Nero's apartment? When we were there before, we were looking for a connection to the missing woman. If there's the chance that he could be involved with the arrows and Lopez's death, I'd like to go through his stuff again, just in case I spot something I missed first time round.'

'Of course. I'll call the officers guarding the house and tell them you're coming.'

'There's just one thing – maybe I should stay here to provide support and protection to the film company? Although I've been precious little help so far.'

'You go. Don't worry, Innocenti and I will be here with the other officers for a couple of hours at least, and soon Forensics will be here as well, so you aren't needed. Besides, I think we can take it as definite that the attacker – whoever he or she was – is long gone by now.'

23

SUNDAY MORNING

All the way over to Nero's apartment I couldn't shift thoughts of Anna from my head. Could she really be linked with the murder and the attempted murders and even maybe the disappearance of the missing woman? Less than half an hour earlier I had kissed her fondly and I was in no doubt that my feelings for this intelligent, caring and attractive woman had been developing fast. The photo had come as a punch in the guts, and now I didn't know what to think.

I parked just down the road from Nero's place and walked up the lane towards it with Oscar. When I neared the apartment block, one of the uniformed officers emerged from a nearby garden and came over to let me in. I couldn't miss the grin on his face as he checked out my costume – and my knobbly knees – but I was getting used to this by now and, besides, I had more important things on my mind. The policeman was carrying one of those vicious little Glock machine guns that give me the creeps. The thought that the pressure of a single finger on the trigger of something like this could kill a roomful of people in a matter of seconds has always struck me as terrifying. I've never been a fan of guns, although I've done several weapons courses over the years. Mind you, with a murderer on the loose, I didn't blame the officer. Better to be prepared.

I started in the kitchen, intending to work my way through each of the rooms one by one, and my first discovery came almost immediately. Earlier on, one of the police officers searching the house had emptied the contents of the dustbin onto a plastic sheet on the kitchen table and had spread the rubbish out, sifting through it, searching for clues. I did the same and as I did so I suddenly found myself confronted by a handful of feathers, no doubt dismissed by the previous search team as left over from a chicken that Nero had roasted. What leapt out at me as I set eyes on them was the way that somebody had quite clearly sliced pieces of the feathers away – a strange thing for a cook to do but exactly what somebody making flights for arrows would do.

If this wasn't enough, I received further confirmation of what Nero had been doing when I found an empty tube of glue stuffed inside the rotting carcass of the unfortunate chicken a bit further along the table. Together with it were several dozen gaudy orange plastic flights, neatly chopped from arrows to make way for the new feathered vanes. There could be no doubt about it: Nero was our archer. The next question was why?

I checked through the rest of the kitchen waste and then went into the lounge. From there I carried on into the bedroom, methodically checking everything I came to until I reached the study, and it was almost at the end of my search that I made the breakthrough. I was standing there, thinking about calling Virgilio to tell him about the feathers, when my eye spotted an anomaly.

There were barely a couple of dozen books on the single book-shelf and now, for the very first time, I realised that half a dozen of them looked like duplicates, the red spines of the paperbacks carbon copies of each other. I went across and pulled them off the shelf. Sure enough, all six were pristine copies of the same book, written in English. The title of the books was *In Search of Power* and the author's name printed across the bottom of the cover was V. A. Nero.

I perched on the corner of the desk and leafed through a copy. It didn't take me long to realise that the content of the book and the plot of the movie were remarkably similar – definitely close enough to convince a judge that wholesale plagiary had been committed. The parallels were unmissable.

It was a dual timeline book, part thriller, part historical novel, set in London rather than LA, but with some chapters set in Florence at the time of the Renaissance. This historical part featured Lorenzo the Magnificent and highlighted none other than the Pazzi conspiracy. It was now clear to me why Martin Taylor had avoided any mention of that family in his screenplay: that would have made it too obvious that he'd copied V. A. Nero's ideas. And then, to dispel any doubt I might still be harbouring about this man being our murderer, a date on a page struck a familiar chord. The Pazzi conspiracy had taken place on 26 April 1478. When Americans write dates, they always put the month first, so the Twitter handle of the mystery man who had accused Taylor of plagiary, which I seemed to remember as @author4261478, was actually a numerical representation of that infamous date.

It was now clear that Nero was the killer bowman and he had almost certainly been aiming at Martin Taylor all along. Poor Donny Lopez had been unlucky enough to be in the wrong place at the wrong time and had been killed in a simple case of mistaken identity. Emmy and Scott had been hit because, at a distance and wearing the same costumes, the murderer had either missed his intended target or had mistaken them for Taylor and the food-truck blackboard had taken the hit in place of Taylor because of the slightest of touches with the wire fence. Where the missing woman came into it remained a mystery for now, but Nero's guilt in the arrow case appeared confirmed. I picked up my phone and called Virgilio.

'Are you still at the monastery? Is everybody still there?'

'Yes, the director tells me they're going to finish filming a few more scenes without Norris this afternoon and then that'll be it. Tomorrow they'll do one last interior scene and then pack up and most of the cast and crew will leave for the USA.'

'Don't let Martin Taylor, the writer, out of your sight.' I went on to tell Virgilio what I'd discovered, after which I picked up a copy of one of the books, hurried out of the flat and back to my car. The interview with Taylor was something I wouldn't have missed for the world.

On the way there my phone rang, and I saw that it was Virgilio again.

'*Ciao*, Dan. Guess what: the French police have just been in touch to report that not only is Scott Norris's wife still in Paris, but she's staying at the Ritz no less, sharing a very expensive suite with a gentleman friend of hers. It would appear that she has the same relaxed attitude towards her wedding vows as her husband.'

'So much for the jealous wife picking up her bow and arrow and coming down here to get revenge. Well, at least we now know who the real perpetrator is.'

* * *

The interview with Martin Taylor took place in what looked as if it had been the monastery's stables or maybe a cowshed. Now all that was left of its previous occupants were rusty metal rings in the walls, worm-eaten posts protruding from the earthen floor and a stone trough against the far wall, almost submerged beneath a blanket of spiders' webs. A couple of officers set up a trestle table and chairs and Virgilio and I sat down on one side while Taylor sat opposite us, an apprehensive expression on his face. His apprehension turned to alarm as I pushed the paperback across the table to him. The blood drained from his cheeks, and he looked for a moment as if he was going to be sick.

'Ever seen this before, Mr Taylor?'

He took the book as if it were about to bite him and leafed through the pages. He made a pathetic attempt to deny any knowledge of it before finally conceding. He slumped forward onto the table, his head in his hands, and from the way his shoulders were shaking it looked as though he was weeping. Normally in an interview I would tend to give the interviewees time to pull themselves together before proceeding, but I could feel a wave of anger rising up inside me and I was in no mood for sparing his feelings.

'Mr Taylor, do you realise that, because of you, one person is dead and two others are very lucky just to have been injured? Do you?'

Virgilio must have heard the rising anger in my voice, so he took over. 'Why didn't you tell us? If we'd known that somebody was after you, we could have offered you protection, and the chances are that nobody would have got hurt. By using all the resources of the police we would probably have been able to identify him in time and could have arrested him before he killed anybody. Do you realise that all of this could have been averted? What have you to say for yourself?'

We had to wait a full minute for a reply.

'I've never seen this book before in my life.' Taylor looked up from the table and stared across at us with watery eyes. 'That's the truth.' He glanced down at the book. 'It looks as though he self-published it. I'm not surprised. Montague told me it was appallingly badly written. He said no self-respecting publisher would have touched it with a bargepole.'

'Montague?'

'My agent in London.'

'Your agent?' Virgilio sounded unclear although I knew what Taylor meant.

Taylor explained for Virgilio's benefit. 'The literary agent who handles all my books and screenplays.'

'He showed you the manuscript?'

Taylor shook his head. 'No, he just told me about it. We were having dinner together one day last year and I told him I was struggling for ideas. He told me about this mess of a manuscript he'd been sent by some random American. He said it was so full of typos and so confusing it was almost illegible, but that he rather liked the basic premise. It probably didn't take him more than two or three minutes to run though the bare bones of the story and it struck a chord with me as well. He didn't tell me the author's name or the title of the book although, thinking about it, when he read my version some months later, he was the one who came up with the title *Lust for Power*.' He was looking seriously crestfallen by now. 'In retrospect that's a bit too close for comfort, isn't it?'

I took over again. 'It also sounds pretty damn unprofessional on the part of your agent. Why didn't you tell us all this earlier? You must have realised there was a problem when you started getting attacked on Twitter by somebody whose handle was the date of the Pazzi conspiracy. Little wonder you remembered it so well.'

'I know I should have come clean, but it's my whole reputation that's on the line. I knew that if it came out that the screenplay wasn't all my own work, the film company's lawyers would have had a field day with me. You know what they're like over in the States. They could bankrupt me.'

'I hope they do. I hope they take you for every penny you have.' I fixed him with a contemptuous stare. 'Now I suggest you go and have a talk to Gabriel Lyons or, on second thoughts, you could try apologising to Emmy and Scott first. It's a pity you can't apologise to Donny Lopez, isn't it?'

He left the building a broken man, but neither of us had a shred of sympathy for him. His duplicity and his pride had been his downfall, but that didn't help poor Donny Lopez.

'So now we know for sure who our murderer is. Nero's our man without a shadow of a doubt and what we need to do is to find him as quickly as we can.' Virgilio turned towards me and caught my eye. 'I'm afraid the next person I need to interview is Anna Galardo. If you don't want to take part, I quite understand. It'll be in Italian so I can get Innocenti to come in and take your place.'

'No, I need to hear this. Get Innocenti in by all means. I'll sit over to one side, and you do the talking.' But I wasn't looking forward to it.

Anna was summoned and she arrived looking curious but relaxed. Virgilio didn't waste time. He passed his phone across the table to her, the photo of the university party on the screen. We all studied her reaction closely as she picked it up and looked at it for a few moments. I was relieved to see little more than casual interest on her face, along with increased curiosity. She looked up again.

'I've seen this photo before. It was taken at an evening drinks do at one of the American universities in Florence. What's so special about it?'

'Can you tell me the names of the people in the photo with you, please?'

'The couple alongside me are John and Marina Greendale: he teaches Roman and Etruscan history and his wife is head of the

Italian department at our university. Beyond them, I think the guy with the long hair teaches English at the British Institute and the big guy on the other side of me is a history lecturer at the American university who were hosting the reception – or at least he was until I heard that he got himself fired a few weeks ago. I'm not really surprised. He was a weird sort of guy.' She sounded perfectly normal when talking about Nero and my spirits began to rise. Hopefully my instincts that she had nothing to do with murder were correct.

'And his name?' Virgilio had adopted a friendly, encouraging tone, but I knew that didn't mean anything. I'd heard him use that same tactic on guilty suspects before and it often worked.

She had to stop and think for a few seconds. 'Nero, Vic Nero.'

'Can you tell me why he was fired?'

'I heard it from a friend who teaches over there at his university so I don't know the full details, but she told me they'd all seen it coming for weeks, months. Apparently he'd been becoming more and more uninterested – not marking assignments, coming in late, that sort of thing. She said he had always had a short fuse, but it got worse and there was talk of him kicking or punching a hole in a wall or something like that. If you need to know more, I can give you the number of my friend or even her boss, the dean. I've met her a few times as well. She's a nice lady and she's bound to know everything that goes on there.'

'Thank you, but we've already spoken to her. It was she who supplied the photo.'

'So does this mean you're interested in Nero?' Anna suddenly stopped dead and slapped the tabletop, her eyes wide open in disbelief. 'The archery! Oh, good Lord, don't tell me he's the murderer. I don't believe it.' If it was an act, it was masterfully performed. My spirits rose as I felt sure this was further confirmation that Anna wasn't involved.

'You knew about his interest in archery?'

'That was all he talked about that evening. Clearly, it was his thing. He was boasting about how he entered competitions and won prizes and all sorts. He spent ages telling us about it; that and his house in the country.'

'What about his house?'

Anna paused for thought. 'I think he said he bought it back in the winter and he spent every weekend out there working on it, trying to make it habitable.'

'His house or his apartment?'

'House, I'm pretty sure it was an old tumbledown house.'

Virgilio turned his head and shot me a glance. Nero's apartment didn't fit this description and I felt as puzzled as he looked. Although I'd said I wouldn't speak, I decided to join in.

'It isn't habitable, then?'

'God, no. He showed us some photos. He was ever so proud of it, but it was little more than a ruin. He said it didn't even have a roof until a few months ago.'

'So he doesn't live there?'

'I doubt it. It looked like a building site. I seem to remember that Barbara – that's my friend who works... worked with him – said he was renting somewhere out in the country.'

So Nero had bought a house. Could it be that this was where he had disappeared to and where he was maybe holding the missing woman? I felt an upsurge of optimism. Maybe we finally had a lead we could follow. 'Whereabouts is the house that he bought? Did he tell you?'

She shook her head and the two detectives and I gave a collective sigh of disappointment. 'I'm sorry, he didn't say, except that it was in the back of beyond. No, wait, he did say it wasn't far from San Gimignano, but that covers a lot of territory. But like I said, I can give you Barbara's phone number. She'll know more.'

Another question came to me. 'Did Barbara say why he started losing interest, coming in late for work and so on?'

'I believe she said there was talk of some woman, something about him being besotted by some poor woman who didn't want anything to do with him.'

'Why do you say "poor" woman?'

'Because I can't really imagine any woman falling for him. I spent half an hour in his company that night and I was only too glad to get away. He was a big clumsy hulk with the social skills of a gorilla.' She shot me a little smile. 'I had to fend him off – really, he started groping me right there in the middle of the party. Afterwards, Barbara told me just about every woman on their staff got propositioned or worse by him sooner or later, and as for the young girl students... From what she said, I believe the reason he finally got the sack was because of complaints lodged by his female students.'

'Can you give us your friend's number, please, and we'll call her?' After taking down the number, Virgilio picked up the interview again. 'And you can't remember any more about where this house of his might be? Can you think of anything else that might help us?'

'I'm sorry, but that's all I remember. To be honest, I switched off after a bit and was just trying to think of a polite way of getting away. Like I said, he was a creepy sort of guy. But I'm sure Barbara will be able to tell you more.'

'Thank you, we'll call her right away. And thank you for giving us this information. It'll be very useful.'

'Do you have any more questions or is that it?'

Virgilio and I exchanged glances and I read the same expression of satisfaction and relief on his face as I was feeling. From what we had just seen and heard, it seemed pretty clear that Anna wasn't involved with Nero. He gave her a smile.

'I think that's all for now. Thank you.'

She stood up and I stood up as well. 'I'll come out with you, Anna. I could do with a drink.'

We went over to the refreshment truck and I ordered an espresso for her and a beer for me. As we sipped our drinks, I told her how I'd found the feathers and the sliced-off plastic arrow vanes as well as the paperbacks that pointed the finger firmly at Nero. It was clear that he was Donny Lopez's killer and I told her that Martin Taylor was now in serious trouble and, to my mind, he deserved every bit of what was coming to him. I looked at my watch and was surprised to see that it was almost one o'clock. I had a sudden thought: Virgilio and I were supposed to be playing tennis at two but that wasn't going to be happening after all this. Anna and I stood and chatted for a few minutes before I felt I should go back to Virgilio to tell him we should cancel the tennis and decide what the next steps should be.

However, just before leaving, I said something extremely stupid.

'You can't imagine how pleased I was to hear that you had nothing to do with Donny Lopez's death and these other murder attempts. Seeing you in that photo with Nero was scary.'

Anna straightened up and stared at me in amazement, the smile on her face now long gone. 'You thought *I* might be involved in murder? Me a murderer?' Her voice rose in indignation, and I did my best to dig myself out of the hole into which my thought-less remark had just plunged me.

'No, of course not. Not a murderer but maybe somehow connected with what was going on...' I struggled to find the right words. 'It was just that we had to be sure...' An image of my ex-wife with an expression on her face of disbelief at my crass stupidity suddenly appeared before my eyes. What was it Anna had just said about the 'social skills of a gorilla'? No self-respecting gorilla would have made the mistake I'd just made. I even spotted a look of what might have been incredulity on my dog's face. I was still desperately searching for the right words when Anna took two steps back.

'You had to be sure that I wasn't prepared to commit murder? What kind of monster do you think I am?' She crushed her paper cup in her hand and walked over to the black rubbish sack by the refreshment van and threw it in. Without looking back, she then just kept on walking, disappearing through the empty gateway into the monastery. I stood there helplessly, debating whether I should follow her or whether that would just add more fuel to the flames. My thoughts were interrupted by a familiar voice from behind me.

'Dan, old love, women aren't exactly my forte, but even *I* know you've just dropped yourself into deep doo-doo.' It was Duggie Ogilvie and there was a sympathetic smile on his face. 'But you'll find your way out of it, I'm sure.'

'I wish I shared your optimism, Duggie.'

'You'll be fine; just you wait and see. I've just heard the news. Isn't it wonderful that you've found who's been behind these horrid arrows? I'm so relieved it wasn't one of us. We're all weird in our own ways but I'm glad none of us was prepared to stoop to murder.' He gave me an avuncular pat on the elbow. '*Amor vincit omnia*; remember that. You don't need the Romans to tell you that love will overcome.'

24

SUNDAY AFTERNOON

Back in the stables, Virgilio and Innocenti had been busy. They had managed to get in contact with Anna's friend, Barbara, who had added a few more bits of information about Victor Nero, but nothing precise as to the location of his house in the country. Miraculously, seeing as it was a Sunday, Innocenti then managed to contact the mayor of San Gimignano, who passed them on to the lady in charge of the department where records of all property transactions were kept. She graciously promised to go into the office, even though it was lunchtime on her day off, to check on where the house bought by Nero might be. In the meantime, Virgilio had been in touch with both the *questura* in Florence and the local *Carabinieri* and a taskforce was already being assembled, ready to descend upon the suspect as soon as the property was located.

Since arriving in Tuscany and with Virgilio's help I had just about got my head around the plethora of different – and often competing – law enforcement bodies that there were in Italy. There was the *Polizia* to which Virgilio and his murder squad belonged and which bore the closest resemblance to the UK police force, dealing with most things from theft to serial killers. Then there were the *Carabinieri* who were in fact a branch of the military and who lived in barracks and tended to pop up all over the place, predominantly in the countryside, at airports, or guarding government buildings. As well as these, there were other branches such as the *Guardia di Finanza* who specialised in tax evasion and other financial misdemeanours, *Polizia Stradale* who controlled the road network and, on a local level, towns had *Polizia Municipale*.

One thing was for sure: today's taskforce would be armed to the teeth, and this worried me. With an armed murderer to confront, guns were a sensible precaution, but the trouble was that we had to work on the basis that the missing woman might hopefully still be alive and was being held hostage inside Nero's house. To find her alive, only for her then to be killed in a firefight, didn't bear thinking about. When the time came, we were going to have to think very carefully about how to go about it but, for now, the first thing was to find the house, and Virgilio was still wondering about that.

'Of course, we may find that he bought a property that's outside the confines of San Gimignano.' He sipped another strong espresso and leant back against the wall of the stables. 'Anna just said it wasn't far from San Gimignano. For all we know it might be in another *comune*.'

'Is there nobody else we could ask? What about the missing woman?' The sun was fully out now. The air had warmed up and Innocenti and I were drinking cold mineral water while the food-truck man had kindly produced a bowl of water for Oscar, who was making a right old mess slurping it up at my feet. 'You said her family are all down south, but what about her friends or work colleagues up here? Might she have told one of them about the weirdo who was stalking her? You never know; maybe he told her he had a house in the country or even took her there. Where did, does she work?'

'She works for a textile company in Prato.'

'Doing what?'

'Secretary to the boss.'

A little bell started ringing inside my head. Surely it couldn't be? 'And the name of the company?'

Innocenti flipped the pages of his notebook. 'OD Textiles.'

I could hardly believe my ears. 'So that means that her name is Giuseppina Napolitano.'

Both detectives stared at me as if I'd just stepped out of a flying saucer.

'And her boss is Osvaldo Dante.' Their eyes opened even wider. 'In which case I can reveal something that I imagine nobody's told you: she and her boss have been having an affair. I even have photos to prove it.' There was no time to lose so I brushed away their questions. 'I'll explain later. What this means is that if anybody knew her well, it was Signor Dante. Have you got his number? Give him a call. His wife may well have filed for divorce already, so it probably won't come as a total surprise to him that this is public knowledge, but this is a possible murder investigation. His feelings are the least of it.'

Innocenti called his colleagues at the *questura* for Dante's number and a matter of seconds later, Virgilio was on the phone to him. He put it on speaker, so we all listened in.

'Signor Dante, Osvaldo Dante? This is *Commissario* Pisano of the *squadra mobile* in Florence. I need to talk to you.'

'Yes, of course.' Dante sounded flustered but a call from the murder squad can do that to people. 'One moment, please.' We could hear plates and glasses clinking in the background so presumably he was having lunch and was now heading away from the table. A few seconds later the background noise diminished, and he spoke again. 'Yes, *commissario*, how can I help?'

Virgilio didn't waste time. 'Listen, Signor Dante, we know you've been having an affair with your secretary, Giuseppina Napolitano. What you do with your life's not my business, but what *is* my business is the very real danger that she now finds herself in. As you know, she was abducted three days ago. We now know the name of the man who abducted her, and we believe he may be holding her at a house in the country somewhere around San Gimignano. Did she ever tell you anything that might help us locate it?'

'Oh, God...' For a moment it sounded as though Dante was about to start sobbing but Virgilio was in no mood for histrionics.

'Think carefully, Signor Dante, your lady friend's life could depend on what you can tell us. Did she mention another man?'

There was a pregnant pause before Dante started talking. 'Yes, she did mention a man who was stalking her.' He sounded deflated but resigned. 'An American, she said. I know I should have told you before, but I've been caught up trying to save my marriage.'

I felt my hackles rise. So he'd chosen to throw his mistress to the wolves by withholding potentially important information. I very nearly butted in to tell him what I thought of him, but years of training meant that I restrained myself, as did Virgilio.

'Tell us more about the American.' He was using his calm, soothing voice but I knew him well enough to sense the anger beneath the surface.

There was another long silence before Dante replied. 'I don't really know much. She told me she met the man at a friend's party in Florence. He wouldn't leave her alone and he even followed her home. She told me he was a huge man, and she was really scared.'

'Think hard, Signor Dante: did she ever talk about him having a house in the country?'

'Now I come to think of it, I seem to remember she said he tried to get her to go with him to see his house near Certaldo. Yes, I'm certain she said Certaldo. She refused to go off into the countryside with him, but he was very insistent and, like I said, she told me he made her feel afraid. I told her to go to the police, but she said she could handle him herself.'

That appeared to be all Dante knew and Virgilio soon ended the call. Innocenti already had his phone in his hand. 'I'm on it, boss. Give me a few minutes to contact Certaldo.'

I had visited Certaldo once. It was a little town with a nondescript modern part and a delightful medieval old quarter on the hill above it. It wasn't far from San Gimignano, but it was big enough to have its own town hall. Hopefully Innocenti would be able to persuade or bully the town authorities into checking their records straight away. From where we were now to Certaldo was probably fifteen or twenty minutes so, as time was of the essence, I made a suggestion.

'If you guys don't need me here, I think I might drive over to Certaldo. I'll grab a sandwich when I get there and I'll be waiting when you hear back about the location of Nero's house.'

Virgilio nodded approvingly. 'Good idea. I'll tell my people and the *Carabinieri* to do the same. It'll take them half an hour or more to get there from Florence, so it makes sense to have them already in the area as soon as possible – assuming Dante's right and we get the information back from the *comune* in Certaldo. Text me when you get there and Innocenti and I'll come over and join you. We've pretty much finished here now.' He caught my eye. 'By the way, did I see Anna Galardo stomping off with steam coming out of her ears a few minutes ago?'

I nodded ruefully. 'Afraid so. You see, in case you didn't already know, I'm a moron.' I gave him a brief summary of what I'd said and how Anna had reacted and he, like Duggie Ogilvie, gave me an encouraging pat on the arm.

'You'll sort it out. Don't worry. I can see you like her and, for what it's worth, I can see she likes you.'

'I'm afraid that might be the wrong tense. I have a feeling she maybe used to like me, but I fear that might no longer be the case.'

I went in search of Gabriel Lyons to check that he had no objection to my going off to Certaldo and I found him in a huddle with Emmy, with Dizzy taking notes. I stopped when I saw that they were having a meeting, but the producer waved me forward.

'Dan, come over here.' This was a first. I don't think he'd ever referred to me by my name before and certainly not by my first name. 'I gather congratulations are in order. You can't imagine how relieved we were that you've identified the killer.'

'I didn't do much apart from laddering my tights.' I saw all three sets of eyes check out my scratched knees and a little smile flit across Dizzy's face.

'Nice pair of legs, Dan.'

'Don't be modest – not about your legs – Anna told us you were the person who worked out who the killer was.' Gabriel Lyons was looking and sounding a different man. 'We're safe again, so thanks a lot to you and to the cops.'

'Just doing my job. What're you going to do? Are you still planning on winding things up today or tomorrow, or will you stay on once we've apprehended the perpetrator?' I could have added 'as long as we *do* get him' but I didn't want to shake the producer out of his relaxed state.

'We've just been discussing that now and we've decided we'll finish up here this afternoon and do one last interior shoot back in Florence tomorrow and then that's it. The paramedics told us that

Scott's cut will need stitches, but he should be good to go by tomorrow so for today we can shoot around him.'

'That's excellent news. Do you want me to come along tomorrow, or shall I hand in my account today and save you a bit of cash?'

'Give Dizzy your account today by all means but include tomorrow. You're part of the team now and we want you with us right to the end.' I'd never seen him so magnanimous.

'What's going to happen to Martin Taylor?'

His expression soured. 'I'll leave that up to our legal team to figure out. By the sound of it, Taylor's responsible for everything that's happened. All right, he had no way of knowing a crazy lunatic would start killing people, but he's screwed up big time and produced some serious legal headaches for us and for himself. I've just fired him and told him to get the hell out of my sight.'

'You don't need him for tomorrow's final scenes?'

Emmy provided the answer. 'No, tomorrow's a ceremonial ball with lots of glitz and glamour, but very little dialogue. We'll be going back to the villa we were at the other day. They have a ballroom we can use, and Dizzy's found us a genuine Renaissance lookalike band. It promises to be spectacular.' He gave me a grin. 'Bring your dancing shoes.'

Mention of shoes reminded me that the first thing I needed to do now was to change out of my Renaissance costume before heading off to Certaldo. Striped pantaloons and sticking plasters are not a very fetching look.

25

SUNDAY AFTERNOON

The call from Virgilio came through forty minutes later. I was sitting outside a café in the modern part of Certaldo, just finishing a rather nice focaccia sandwich filled with grilled aubergine and goat's cheese. It was still a warm day, although light clouds high up were starting to blot out the sun. Maybe we were finally going to see the arrival of something a bit more autumnal.

The phone call was heartening.

'Certaldo it is. The address is Via dei Cipressi forty-eight, and the mayor said it's out in the back of beyond. Innocenti and I should be there in about fifteen minutes. We'll rendezvous with the taskforce first and then head on up to the house.'

'What would you like me to do?'

'Nothing silly, Dan. Remember, this guy has a lethal weapon and all you've got is a dog.'

Mention of Oscar gave me an idea. 'How about if I go up there, leave the car some way from the house, and then become just some guy taking his dog for a walk? I could take a good look at the place and see if there's any trace of Nero before you arrive with the cavalry.'

'Won't he recognise you?'

'He's only ever seen me in Renaissance costume, and I've changed into shorts and a T-shirt now. I'll put on a baseball cap and sunglasses and there's no way he'll recognise me.'

'Well, in that case, yes, go and do that. It'll be very useful. We'll stay out of sight until we hear from you. If you can give us a detailed description of the location and whether you think he or the woman are in there, that'll be great. But, Dan, just take care, okay?'

The barman was able to direct me to Via dei Cipressi, which turned out to be an unclassified road that very quickly deteriorated into a dusty, bumpy track that wound its way upwards, first through olive groves and vineyards and then into an uncultivated area of scrub. All around were massive clumps of bamboo, oleander and broom, and the landscape was dotted with umbrella pines and occasional cypress trees. Further over in the valley was thicker woodland, no doubt crawling with hopeful mushroom hunters at this time of year.

I counted off the numbers on the houses I passed: odd numbers on my left and even numbers on my right. After reaching number thirty-six pretty quickly, I saw that buildings started to become a lot less frequent and numbers on some of the scruffy barns and cottages were either missing or indecipherable. I carried on bumping slowly up the hill until I reached a rather nice stone *casa colonica* – a big old farmhouse – that looked as if it had had a major makeover quite recently. More importantly, the metal gates bore a clear and unmistakable number fifty. I had passed Nero's place.

I drove on a hundred metres or so until I found a spot where I could park the car and I climbed out to release Oscar. As I did so I thought back. The last property I'd passed on my right before the renovated house had probably been a hundred metres or so back down the hill. As far as I could remember, it had been a little stone cottage, set back from the track at least fifty metres. Presumably this had been number forty-eight but, just to be on the safe side before calling in an armed assault, I walked back down the track, past the renovated house where a huge German Shepherd came out and had a barking match with Oscar. I went over and grabbed my excited dog by the collar and dragged him away. We carried on down the hill and he and I stayed on the track. On both sides now was rough terrain with low thorny scrub, brambles, and quite probably snakes in there as well. I'm not a reptile fan and I certainly didn't want to expose my dog to a bite from a venomous viper. I had no idea whether there were poisonous snakes in this area, but I had no intention of finding out.

When I came to Nero's house I studied it carefully, but casually, in case he might be watching me. As if reading my mind, Oscar stopped at a particularly interesting cypress tree and cocked his leg against it, allowing me to pause as though waiting for him and cast a number of glances in the direction of the house while he relieved himself. I hoped I wasn't giving anything more than the impression that I was just some random man taking his dog for a walk. The property looked like a simple workman's cottage and the pile of rubble and junk outside the front door showed that renovation work had been taking place there. There was no sign of life and, in particular, there was no sign of a white Toyota pickup. When I got down to the next house and checked that its number – almost hidden beneath the leaves of a centuries-old fig tree – was forty-six, I pulled out my phone and called Virgilio.

'*Ciao*, Dan. We're all here and ready. What's the situation?'

I gave him a brief description of the location and clear details of which house belonged to Nero. When I gave him the news that there was no sign of anybody there or of the car, he made a decision.

'Right. We'll move in. You keep well out of the way in case it deteriorates into a firefight. Here's hoping the woman's there and Nero isn't.'

'Good luck.'

Just along from where I was standing, a narrow path led off to one side and I followed it in order to keep out of the way of the police operation, but also so as to circle around and take up a position on the far side of Nero's house from the road in case he was there and tried to make a break for it when he saw the police arrive. The path joined a slightly broader track on which I saw fresh tyre prints. Could it be that Nero had another way of accessing his house? If so, might that mean he was already inside? I pulled out my phone and gave a quick warning to Virgilio and then hurried along the track. I was just passing the rear of the house when a cloud of dust on the main track indicated the arrival of the taskforce, and I stood and looked on from the shelter of a clump of pine trees.

There were five vehicles in total. At the front of the column was a blue *Carabinieri* Land Rover that swung onto the short drive to Nero's house and skidded to a halt outside the front door. Behind it, two minibuses disgorged a dozen or so *Carabinieri* and police officers, all armed to the teeth and wearing bulletproof vests. Behind them came Virgilio's Alfa and another police car. As the officers began to surround the house, the *Carabinieri* produced a hefty ram from the back of the Land Rover and made short work of smashing the front door open. Weapons at the ready, they poured inside, and I waited for the sound of gunfire, but as the seconds ticked by and I heard nothing, it began to look increasingly as if Nero wasn't there after all. Was Giuseppina Napolitano still alive and had they located her?

My thoughts were interrupted by a sound just along the track ahead of me and I turned in time to glimpse a big figure in a dark green hoodie appear from the direction of the house, run across the track, and disappear down another path into thick woods. Unmistakably there was a full-size bow in his hands. I pulled out my phone and called Virgilio as I gave chase.

'I've just seen him. He's over here on the opposite side of the house to the main track. He's run into the trees.'

'We'll be right there.'

I stuffed my phone back into my pocket and concentrated on making sure I took the same path as Nero had taken. I had no intention of letting him get away from me twice in one day. The path sloped slightly downwards, and I found myself running so fast I was jumping over tree roots and skidding on corners. It was one of these skids that probably saved my life. I came around a corner and almost fell, wrenching my ankle in the process. As I did so, an arrow whizzed past my ear and thudded into a tree beside me. I looked up and about thirty metres ahead of me I saw Nero. He had turned and was standing in the middle of the path, reaching for another arrow. Before he could reload, I hurled myself sideways into the bushes and scrambled away from the path on hands and knees until I could take refuge behind the reassuringly solid trunk of an oak. I looked around wildly and, to my great relief, I saw Oscar right behind me, tail wagging furiously as he was having great fun. I grabbed him by the collar and crouched down, doing my best to breathe as silently as possible while I pricked my ears and listened carefully.

Everything was silent for several seconds before voices and a whistle indicated the imminent arrival of the police from behind me. At the same time, I distinctly heard a twig snap and running footsteps retreating into the distance ahead of me. I jumped to my feet and set off down the path after Nero, now hampered by a very sore ankle. Oscar, with no such handicap, ran joyously ahead of me, tail wagging. About fifty metres further on the trees thinned and I saw daylight ahead. I slowed down and emerged cautiously from the shade of the forest and was confronted by a spine-chilling sight.

There, barely ten metres ahead of me, was the unmistakable shape of the big American and halfway between me and him was my happy dog, tail still wagging. Nero had another arrow at the ready and it was pointing squarely at Oscar.

'Turn around and go. Now!' The American accent was unmistakable. 'You got three seconds or I kill your dog. One... two...'

'All right, all right, I'll go. Just don't hurt the dog.'

Two things then happened simultaneously. I opened my mouth to call Oscar and, at that exact moment, a volley of shots rang out. Nero swivelled his shoulders and pointed the arrow directly at me as we heard Virgilio's voice, shouting from the trees behind me.

'Put the bow down, Nero. It's all over. If we shoot again, it won't be in the air next time.' He was speaking in English and, in spite of the circumstances, I was impressed at how fluent he was sounding.

'I'll kill this guy if you come any nearer. I mean it. Back off or I'll fire.'

I was close enough to see the sweat on the big man's brow and to hear his rasping breath. I was also close enough to see the point of the arrow shining in the hazy sunlight. It was aimed directly at me, and I felt a cold sensation in the pit of my stomach. He was so close that I knew I stood no chance of avoiding it if he chose to release it. Slowly and carefully, I raised my hands in the air and addressed him directly.

'Killing me won't do you any good. There are a dozen police marksmen here and they have you in their sights.' As I spoke I saw two little red dots appear on the front of Nero's chest. The police had him in their sights all right. The trouble was that if they shot him he would inevitably release the arrow and there was every likelihood that it would hit me. I had no illusions as to my chances if that happened. Seeing him looking wildly in all directions, a manic expression of desperation on his face, I decided to try a different approach. 'I've read your book and I think it's really good.'

His focus returned to me. 'What do *you* know?' There was both anger and contempt in his eyes. His voice rose in pitch, and I realised my mistake. I had awoken the beast. 'You're all bastards! You stole my book! You stole it!'

I stood stock-still, eyes locked on the point of the arrow that was now jerking in his hands as he became ever more agitated. The tension in the air was palpable and there wasn't a sound anywhere, not even birdsong. Oscar, still positioned between me and Nero, must have felt it as well as he suddenly raised his nose to the heavens and let out a primeval wolf howl. As he did so, Nero's eyes left me for a second and focused on the dog. Simultaneously I threw myself sideways and rolled over and over, vaguely conscious of a crackle of shots from behind me.

I came to rest against a tree stump and lay still for a second or two, checking I was still alive and uninjured, before a cold wet nose prodded me in the ear and I looked up into the hairy face of my dog, his tail wagging uncertainly. I raised myself on my elbows until I could look back into the clearing behind Oscar and spotted the body of the big American. He was sprawled on his back, the bow still in his hand, immobile. Goodness only knew where the arrow had finished up, but the main thing from my point of view was that it hadn't ended up sticking in me.

'Dan, you okay?' It was Innocenti, still holding his pistol. Behind him armed police officers were pouring out of the trees.

I sat up and did a double-check. Somewhat to my surprise, I realised that I was okay apart from a few more cuts and scratches to my bare legs, and I looked up at him. 'I'm fine. What about Nero?'

Slipping his gun back in its holster under his armpit, he reached down and offered to help me to my feet.

'Dead.'

Before getting up, I grabbed Oscar and gave him a hug. 'I don't know what I'd do without you, dog.'

He responded by trying to kiss me, but I recoiled in time. Affection's a wonderful thing but being kissed by a Labrador isn't as romantic as it sounds. I took Innocenti's hand and let him haul me to my feet just as Virgilio came over and wagged a finger at me. 'Dan, what did I tell you about not doing anything stupid?'

'You sound like my ex-wife.' I gave him a little grin, but I could feel myself bathed in cold sweat.

His face cracked into a smile. 'Anyway, I'm relieved you're okay and thanks for following Nero. I'm afraid he's stone dead. He won't be firing any more arrows at anybody.'

'What about the woman? Giuseppina Napolitano? Did you find her? Is she...?'

'She's alive. She's in a poor state – he had her chained to a wall – but she's alive and she'll recover – at least physically.' He glanced at his watch. 'Just as well we cancelled our tennis match, isn't it?'

'That reminds me, I've invited you and Lina to my place for a barbecue tonight. Are you still up for it?'

'I'm always up for food, but maybe best if we put it off for a day or two. Now that we've finally settled this matter, there's going to be a mountain of red tape to sort out, not least as the perpetrator's been shot dead and he was American. The embassy's already up in arms about the death of Lopez so I imagine I'll have the *questore* on my back as a result of this. Besides, didn't you say you were going to invite Anna along this evening as well? From the way she stormed off earlier, I'm not sure she's likely to take you up on your invitation.'

'I'm afraid you're right. I'll message her, saying dinner's off. That way she and I'll both have time to sleep on it. Maybe she'll like me more in the cold light of dawn tomorrow.'

'I'm sure she will.'

I didn't answer. I didn't share his optimism.

26

MONDAY

Dawn the next day was grey and damp, but certainly not cold. I hadn't slept well, my brain churning over the events of the previous day. Prime among these, of course, was my near-death experience. I'd only once before had a weapon pointed at me in anger at close range, and it's not a sensation I would recommend to anybody. Another memory that had been swirling around in my head had been the sight of Giuseppina Napolitano, wrapped in a blanket, supported by two paramedics, as they carried her off to the hospital. She had emerged from Dante's house pale and drawn, her hair a straggly mess; a far cry from the alluring siren I had seen with Signor Dante less than two weeks earlier. One thing was for sure: when she heard how her former paramour, Osvaldo Dante, had concealed evidence that might have led to her release, I didn't see that relationship progressing any further.

The other image that had kept me awake had been that of Anna's face when I had made that stupid comment. There had been surprise and outrage etched in her features, but I felt sure there had been sadness, or at least disappointment, there as well. Did this mean she might have been getting close to me, only for me to ruin things with my crass remark? As I contemplated having lost her I realised ever more clearly that I'd been developing real feelings for her in the short time I'd known her. And now I'd thrown that all away.

Just to add to my woes, I woke up to find my right ankle swollen and walking uncomfortable. I dug out a squashed tube of cream – long past its expiry date – from my tennis bag and plastered it on, and by the time I came back from a shorter than usual early morning walk with Oscar, the ankle had improved enough for me to be able to walk, not normally, but reasonably.

I dressed in ordinary clothes and packed up the remnants of my torn costume ready to return it to Dizzy. As I looked at the bright red and yellow stripes, I couldn't help reflecting on how senseless this whole episode had been. One writer copied from another writer, and the result had been two deaths and two other people wounded who could so easily have died as well. And all for what? For hurt pride and, as ever, money. Now that Victor Nero was dead, I had no doubt that the film company would quietly drop any mention of their movie being based on stolen ideas and they would go on to make millions on the strength of great actors, a talented director and the Pazzi conspiracy by another name.

I drove down to Florence and out on the road to Fiesole again. When I reached the gateway to the villa I spotted Big Jim standing guard with his clipboard in his hand. He greeted me not only with a smile but with a pumping handshake through the open window that almost removed my arm from its socket.

'Hey, Dan, good to see you're okay! That's great, man. The police called last night and told us all about it. Is it true you were almost killed with an arrow, but your dog saved you?'

I found myself smiling. It sounded as if the rumour grapevine had already been working overtime. No doubt by lunchtime the story would be that Oscar had fired a gun at Nero himself. I assured Jim that I was fine, and that Oscar would be signing auto-graphs later on. This scene was repeated with subtle variations time and time again as I bumped into familiar faces inside the villa until I spotted Dizzy and went over to give her back my costume. To my surprise she threw her arms around my neck and kissed me on the cheeks not once, not twice, but about half a dozen times.

'Dan, you hero, you. You're so brave.'

I unwrapped her arms from around me and gave her a little smile. 'I don't know who you've been talking to, but the hero was Oscar. I just stood there and tried not to get killed.'

She dropped to her knees and enveloped my happy Labrador in a warm hug. 'Who's a good dog, Oscar! Well, I, for one, am very glad you didn't get killed, Dan. What an awful experience it must have been!'

I tried to hand her back the remains of my costume, but she waved the clothes away. 'Don't even think about it. I was going to ask if you'd like to keep your costume – you know, as a souvenir. Wardrobe have found you a new pair of red tights so you can join in today's ballroom scene. Emmy said it's only right you should be in at the end.'

'I'm afraid I have a sore ankle, so I won't be able to dance.' This would at least remove the need for the post-production technical experts to edit me out of their movie. I've never been renowned for my dancing skills – ask my ex-wife.

'Don't worry. I'm sure Emmy will find a suitable part for a wounded hero.'

I took the pack of red tights from her. 'I'm afraid this wounded hero will need somewhere to get changed.'

She pointed to a door a little way along the marble-paved corridor. 'Just down there. I'll talk to Oscar while you're changing.'

The cloakroom was about the same size as my bedroom, and more elegant than any bathroom I'd ever seen in my life. Alarmingly, it also contained no fewer than seven mirrors – I counted them as I studied my reflections. With my greying temples and my ever-increasing collection of wrinkles, not to mention a pair of red tights halfway up my legs, I hardly projected a hunky male image. I began to see why Anna might do well to steer clear of an old fool like me. Still, the show, as they say, had to go on, so I duly dressed in my Renaissance gear for one last time and went out to stow my normal clothes in the car. When I got back it was to find Dizzy and Oscar entwined in a passionate embrace on a Louis XVI sofa that, if it was authentic, was probably worth a whole lot more than my car. This reminded me of something I'd been meaning to say to her.

'Dizzy, tell me to mind my own business, by all means, but I was wondering if maybe you and Charles had a thing going on. Did I read the signs right?'

To my surprise she giggled. 'Me and Charles? No way. Now, if you were to say me and Loredana, you might be onto something.' The giggle turned into a full-blooded laugh. 'And here I was thinking you were some kind of super-sleuth.'

I did my best to process this new information. 'Clearly I still have a lot to learn. Anyway, I'm glad for your sake, because I was going to warn you that Charles appears to be playing around.'

Her expression became more serious. 'Charles can be a nice guy, but he treats women like dirt. And the sad thing is that he doesn't realise he's doing it. But he doesn't always win. I've sort of become his shoulder to cry on. He told me he tried his luck with Selena and she called him "an overgrown kid" and sent him off to "grow up". I think his male pride took a hit there and he deserved it.'

Today's scenes were all scheduled to take place in the ballroom at the rear of the villa. I left Oscar with his new best friend and followed everybody else through the house to the spectacular ballroom. This was a massive room with a double-height ceiling hung with sparkling candelabras. A low stage had been set up at the far end on which there was an authentic-looking Renaissance band in costume, boasting instruments such as a harpsichord, several lutes and tambourines and a strange wiggly wind instrument that looked like a snake. I remembered reading that bagpipes had been popular back in the fifteenth century and I was relieved not to see a set of these on the stage. In my experience, bagpipe music needs the consumption of a lot of malt Scotch beforehand to make it palatable – although I'm sure many Scots would disagree with me.

I was fascinated to see that the room had been set up so that the central and right-hand sides were in keeping with the period while along the left-hand side were cameras, lights and all the paraphernalia of film-making, including Emmy's chair. I queued up by the entrance with all the other cast and crew in costume and spotted Anna, looking lovely as ever, deep in conversation with Dizzy and Emmy. I chatted to my friend Hank, the 'best boy', and found him delighted that the threat hanging over the production had finally been lifted, as were all the other people I met. It felt rather nice to be on familiar terms with these people from such a very different walk of life, and I wished them all well for the conclusion of the movie back in the USA.

I saw Donny Lopez's assistant, Loredana, looking amazing as usual, and thought back to how I had misread the signs that time I had seen Dizzy and Charles together. Presumably he had gone to Dizzy to pour his heart out after being rejected by Selena and she had lent a sympathetic – and disinterested – ear. Selena herself was looking every inch the superstar that she undeniably was, and I felt quite overcome when she made a beeline for me and threw her arms around me to kiss me on the cheeks and hug me tight.

'Dan, you did it! You saved us all.'

'To be honest, it was the police. I just happened to end up in the firing line.'

'That's not the way I heard it. Now, has Gabriel told you how he plans on rewarding you?'

'He's been paying me handsomely to do my job. I don't need more.'

She gave a dismissive wave of the hand. 'Of course you do. I've been talking to him and he's going to invite you over for the premiere. That'll probably be in January or February next year. The company will fly you over and put you up somewhere good. It's the least we can do. And while you're there I want to have you and Anna round to my place for dinner one night.' An afterthought occurred to her. 'And don't forget to bring a couple of copies of your new book with you. We'll see what we can do with it.'

'That's really kind of Mr Lyons and so very nice of you, but somehow I don't think Anna will feel like sitting down for dinner with me ever again.'

'Don't be silly, of course she will.' She gave me a mischievous grin. 'Trust me, I know what I'm talking about.'

I wasn't so sure, but I knew I had to go and see the producer. 'Thank you so much. I must go and thank Mr Lyons.' A thought occurred to me before I left Selena. 'Could I ask just one favour while I think of it? My colleague and friend at Scotland Yard is one of your greatest fans. I don't suppose I could have a photo of you and me together to send to him?' I delved into my pantaloons and handed my phone to Hank, who shot off half a dozen photos while one of the most beautiful women in the world alternately hugged and kissed me. I have to admit that it felt good, and I knew that Paul was going to be green with envy.

Before I could look for Gabriel Lyons to thank him, I was called to join a group of cheering men as Scott, aka Lorenzo the Magnificent, strode into the room. He looked suitably impressive and remarkably relaxed after his ordeal yesterday, although I noticed that he was now wearing a higher collar than in previous days, no doubt to conceal the dressing on his wound. I wondered if he had told his wife about his narrow escape from death, and whether she and her paramour in Paris had been too bothered by the news. I wondered how things were progressing between Scott and Selena and marvelled once again at the relaxed attitude some people had to their wedding vows.

After cheering three or four times until Emmy was satisfied, I headed off to look for the producer. I found him deep in conversation with the 'gaffer' but as soon as he saw me he came over and, to my amazement, gripped me in a bear hug.

'Dan, you did great! Terrific. So grateful.' He then went on to tell me what Selena had already told me about inviting me over to the premiere and I protested weakly and then accepted gratefully. Any further conversation was drowned out by the band starting up.

A professional choreographer had been engaged to organise the dancing, and I was glad that my sore ankle – which wasn't really giving me that much trouble now – meant that I had a convincing excuse for lurking at the back and just watching. As the remarkably tuneful music echoed through the ballroom, people were partnered, and instructions given. From what I could see and hear, the instructions were pretty intricate and the dances technically challenging, and I was doubly grateful not to be involved.

Interestingly, in one scene Charles instructed to strut across the room and grab a dancing partner from the crowd of onlookers. This was interesting because the lady he was told to choose was Anna. As the couple swept around the dance floor, I felt what could only be described as a twinge – well, more than a twinge really – of jealousy.

As I was not needed for a while, and to save myself the torture of watching Anna in the arms of a handsome and allegedly horny young actor, I went out to see how Oscar was finding life in Dizzy's caravan. Unsurprisingly, he was loving it. This time I found him sprawled across Dizzy's lap while she somehow managed to carry on working with her laptop balanced precariously on the Labrador. Opposite them was Duggie Ogilvie with a glass of Scotch in his hand. The clock on the wall told me it was one minute past twelve, so he was starting early – if, indeed, he had ever stopped. All three looked up as I came in, but none of them got up: Oscar because he was far too comfortable, Dizzy because she had sixty pounds of canine bone and muscle draped all over her, and Duggie because he was far more interested in his drink. He did, however, engage me in conversation.

'Hi Dan, how's it going in the ballroom?'

'It's all going well, as far as I can see. How come you're not there?'

'That's because I'm the bad guy. I've just been caught after betraying Lorenzo to his enemies and I'm currently hanging from a hook in the dungeons beneath the Signoria Palace, minus a few of my dangly bits.'

'Sounds uncomfortable.'

He grinned, stretched, and took another sip of Scotch. 'I've known worse.'

Dizzy took a break from typing. 'Did you have your big scene yet, Dan?'

'My big scene? What big scene?'

'Emmy slipped it in specially for you. You'd better get back in there because you're going to be called.'

I was called about ten minutes later. Back in the ballroom the music was still playing, but the volume had subsided considerably, and I realised for the first time that it must have been amplified before. Emmy called me forward, and I felt more than a little self-conscious as he pulled me out onto the empty dance floor. To be on the safe side, I allowed my limp to get noticeably worse in case he was thinking of getting me to dance.

'Right, Dan, this is a close-up scene. Don't worry, you don't have to dance. Charles's character's just about to discover that his latest conquest belongs to another man. All I want you to do is to stand over there by that statue of Apollo, as if you're hiding behind it with the woman in question. Just wrap your arms around the woman and kiss her. I'll tell you when to start and when to stop. Don't worry, you don't have to say anything or do anything. Just stand there and kiss her, okay?'

He gave me a gentle push and I limped theatrically across to the statue, acutely conscious of dozens of eyes watching me. When I got to the statue, it was to discover that the woman standing there was none other than Anna, her cheeks flushed, looking as embarrassed as I was. I glanced back at Emmy and saw him grinning mischievously. Clearly, this was a stitch-up.

'Hello, Dan.' Anna's tone wasn't cold, but it wasn't overly affectionate either.

'*Ciao*, Anna.' I looked around wildly. 'Look, we don't need to do this. I'm sure if I ask Emmy he'll find somebody else to kiss you.' But the director had already turned away.

Pre-empting any further discussion, Emmy's voice came booming across from his loudhailer. 'Okay, everybody good to go? Dan, Anna, you know what you gotta do. And... action.'

I turned desperately back towards Anna as she reached out and put her arms around my neck, pulling me towards her. 'We can't disappoint Emmy.' And she kissed me softly on the lips. Two seconds later, while my head and heart were still swirling with emotion, I heard the director's voice again.

'Cut, cut, cut. I said kiss her, Dan, not rub noses. Just kiss her good and proper, will you? I need to see some real passion. Now, all ready again? Okay... and, action.'

I leant down and kissed Anna again, this time with a lot more warmth, and I distinctly felt her melt against me. She kissed me back and I loved every second of it. I was vaguely conscious of a metallic voice somewhere behind me shouting 'Cut' a few seconds later, but neither of us wanted the kiss to end. Finally we separated, and I looked her in the eyes at close range.

'That was nice.' I didn't know what else to say. I felt totally clueless.

She smiled at me. 'That was *very* nice. I'm so glad you didn't get hurt yesterday.'

'Me, too, but I know I hurt you, and I'm really sorry, Anna. I'm an idiot.'

She gave me another tiny, gentle kiss on the lips and smiled again, a warm, loving smile. 'I know, but you're my idiot.'

ACKNOWLEDGMENTS

Warmest thanks to my editor, Emily Ruston, and to everybody at Boldwood, my wonderful publishers. Thanks also to Sue Smith and Emily Reader for copyediting and proofreading the book, and to Simon Mattacks, whose narration of the audio version manages to sound exactly as I imagine Dan to sound and brings him to life. Finally a mention to Merlin the Labrador, the bestest dog in the whole world, in whose memory Oscar stands proud.

MORE FROM T.A. WILLIAMS

We hope you enjoyed reading *Murder In Florence*. If you did, please leave a review.

If you'd like to gift a copy, this book is also available as an ebook, hardback, large print, digital audio download and audiobook CD.

Sign up to T.A. Williams' mailing list for news, competitions and updates on future books.

https://bit.ly/TAWilliamsNews

Explore the rest of the Armstrong and Oscar Cozy Mystery series...

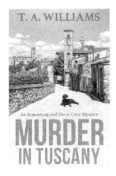  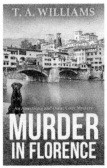

ABOUT THE AUTHOR

T. A. Williams is the author of over twenty bestselling romances for HQ and Canelo and is now turning his hand to cosy crime, set in his beloved Italy, for Boldwood. The series introduces us to to DCI Armstrong and his labrador Oscar. Trevor lives in Devon with his Italian wife.

Visit T. A. Williams' website:

http://www.tawilliamsbooks.com

Follow T. A. Williams' on social media:

twitter.com/TAWilliamsBooks

facebook.com/TrevorWilliamsBooks

Poison
& Pens

POISON & PENS IS THE HOME OF
COZY MYSTERIES SO POUR YOURSELF
A CUP OF TEA & GET SLEUTHING!

DISCOVER PAGE-TURNING NOVELS FROM
YOUR FAVOURITE AUTHORS &
MEET NEW FRIENDS

JOIN OUR
FACEBOOK GROUP

BIT.LYPOISONANDPENSFB

SIGN UP TO OUR
NEWSLETTER

BIT.LY/POISONANDPENSNEWS

Boldw∞d

Boldwood Books is an award-winning fiction
publishing company seeking out the best
stories from around the world.

Find out more at www.boldwoodbooks.com

Join our reader community for brilliant books,
competitions and offers!

Follow us
@BoldwoodBooks
@BookandTonic

Sign up to our weekly
deals newsletter

https://bit.ly/BoldwoodBNewsletter

Printed in Great Britain
by Amazon